D1310722

CHASE
HER
SHADOW

BOOKS BY D.K. HOOD

D.K. HOOD

CHASE HER SHADOW

bookouture

Published by Bookouture in 2022

An imprint of Storyfire Ltd.
Carmelite House
50 Victoria Embankment
London EC4Y 0DZ

www.bookouture.com

ISBN: 978-1-80314-900-4
eBook ISBN: 978-1-80314-899-1

I wrote this Halloween story for all my readers who now sleep with the lights on.

PROLOGUE

SUNDAY

Six days before Halloween

Cold, so cold, Willow Smith opened her eyes and peered into the night. A shaft of moonlight pierced the darkness filtering through the sheer white drapes fluttering and twirling in a ghostly dance. Uncomprehending, she blinked. The cold nights had set in already this year, and there was no way she'd left a window open. Shivering as an icy blast brushed her bare shoulders, she subconsciously ran her palm over the other side of the bed and a pang of loss gripped her hard enough to tear out her heart. He was gone. Oliver had been missing in action for years now, but she still missed him and had never given up hope. Halloween was the night her husband and his entire platoon had died in combat. No longer a time to trick-or-treat, the days before All Hallows now haunted her and each year it went by in unimaginable loneliness.

Sometimes, she'd swear she heard him moving around the house as if his ghost were telling her he was watching over her.

This year, to escape the heartache, she'd planned a vacation with friends and had packed her bags and was ready to leave at dawn. Confused by the open window, she shook her head, slipped from the bed, and walked across the room to close it. As she raised both hands to pull down the old sash-style frame, something in the garden moved. A shadow of a man wearing combat gear and a helmet with night-vision goggles drifted across the driveway, disappearing under the stoop. It resembled the last image she had of her husband. She gaped in disbelief and pressed one hand to her mouth. She wanted so much to call out his name—to make contact—but what if it weren't Oliver's ghost? All of his team looked alike when dressed for a mission and it could be any one of them. Heart thumping so hard she could hear a pulse in her ears, she slid down the window and, pressing her back to the wall, she tried to rationalize what she'd seen. Only the whistle of wind had come in the darkness, and not the crunch of footsteps on the gravel that always alerted her to a visitor—and yet she'd seen him.

Listening hard as the old house moved, groaning and shifting as it did with each change of season, she stared at the open bedroom door. If anyone was coming to hurt her, the stairs would creak underfoot. As the wind whistled around the house, brushing fall leaves across the roof, she gathered her courage and moved silently to the nightstand. She took the Glock from the drawer and slid one round into the chamber. Holding it at arm's length, she stood in the open door and peered down the dark stairs to the foyer. A tall shadow moved across the windows and she froze. Swallowing hard, she tightened her damp palm around the butt of the pistol. In the shadows, wearing her dark blue PJs, she'd be invisible to an intruder. As she took the first step, a long feral howl came from deep in the forest as if warning her that danger lurked close by.

Trembling, she moved slowly down the stairs, feeling for each step under her bare feet. As she moved through the foyer, she made out a figure on the stoop. She aimed the pistol at the front door and gaped in horror as the doorknob slowly turned. The door flew open and a shadow fell across the foyer. Panic gripped her by the throat and her hands trembled as she raised her voice. "I'm armed. Just turn around now and leave. I've called the sheriff."

No sound came from the front door, no shadows moved. Was her mind playing tricks on her? Perhaps she hadn't shut the door properly and the wind had blown it open—but she'd seen the knob turning, hadn't she? This close to Halloween, maybe her imagination was getting the best of her. Holding the Glock out in front of her, she closed the door and slid the bolt across. The next second, an ice-cold breeze flew up the hallway and wrapped around her legs. She froze mid-step as the familiar click of the backdoor closing echoed through the silence. Swinging the gun around, she crept toward the kitchen.

As she stepped inside, the phone in the kitchen rang. Startled, she cried out in fear and slumped against the wall. As the ringing continued, she inched inside the room, moving her weapon in all directions. Finding the kitchen empty and the back door closed, she dropped the weapon to her side. Heart pounding, she went to the phone. It was an old-style phone, olive green with a yellowing circular dial and curly cord. It had been there when they purchased the house and Oliver loved it. As she lifted the receiver, she stared at the kitchen clock just as the second hand swept past midnight. Fear and uncertainty crawled over her. She didn't want to answer the phone—it had been the same call, at this time, for the past three nights. Her fingers trembled as she pressed the cold receiver to her ear. "Yes."

"Hey, darling, I haven't got time to talk. Just calling to tell you I'll be seeing you real soon."

It was her husband's voice.

Shivers gripped Willow as she listened. Why didn't he ever continue the conversation? "Oliver?"

The line went dead.

"Oliver?"

Nothing.

Tears welling, Willow stared at the receiver for some moments before replacing it slowly. *Why are you doing this to me, Oliver?* The memory of the men in uniform who'd come to bring her the news of her husband's death and the ordeal of burying an empty coffin played through her mind. They'd told her Oliver had died in an explosion and nothing was left of him —yet she'd just spoken to him. Hadn't she? Or was someone playing a cruel joke on her?

Confused, she wiped her eyes and, swallowing over-whelming grief, checked the back door and then headed through the house. Creaks and groans chased after her and the howls from the forest seemed just outside. The house moved with each gust of wind, sending shivers down her spine as she hurried up the stairs. The moon was high, pouring its eerie light through the windows, but it offered no comfort and only raised goosebumps on her arms. When she walked into the bedroom, a hint of her husband's aftershave wafted toward her. Breathless with excitement, she ran into the bathroom hoping to find him there, but a dark empty room greeted her. Sobbing with disappointment, she turned away and gaped at the cup of hot chocolate sitting beside the bed beneath the lamp. Oliver always made her a cup when she couldn't sleep, but she didn't recall making one for herself tonight... or had she? She couldn't remember turning on the light either. Had she imagined the phone call too? Was she losing her mind or was she dreaming?

Confused, she slipped the Glock under the pillow and climbed into bed. After pinching herself, to make sure she was awake, she sipped the rich brew, glad of the warmth. The worries of the night seemed to slip away as she placed the cup back in its saucer and snuggled under the covers. As her eyelids became heavy, she heard footsteps brushing the carpet, but sleep had her in its grip. Somewhere in the fog surrounding her brain, she heard Oliver's voice calling her name. She tried to fight her way back, but the world and Oliver spiraled into darkness.

ONE

Five days before Halloween

Sheriff Jenna Alton crunched through the fall leaves to watch the horses frolic in the corral. It was a cool but beautiful morning and the blue sky stretched out across the multicolor lowlands on one side and up to the mountains and forests on the other. High above, eagles circled in the updrafts and just watching them made her happy. It was a privilege to see such majestic birds wild and free. In fact, life on her ranch was just about perfect. Living in Black Rock Falls and surrounded by nature had given her an inner peace she could never have imagined possible, even though she knew somewhere out there in the shadows a threat prowled—waiting and watching.

She'd come a long way since being undercover DEA Agent Avril Parker and taking down a drug cartel family, who'd vowed to kill her. Now living in the backwoods town of Black Rock Falls, Montana, with a name change, a new face, and Dave Kane—an ex-special forces sniper/ secret agent/profiler—as not only her deputy but husband, she believed life couldn't get any better. Yeah, the county was known as Serial Killer Central, and there'd been a series of books written about the criminals her team had removed from society, but she loved her work. Over the years as sheriff, she'd gathered a team around her to deal with just about any situation. Dr. Shane Wolfe used to be Kane's handler in special forces and was now the medical examiner for Black Rock Falls and surrounding counties. Deputy Jake Rowley she'd trained from a rookie and he was as solid as a rock. Deputy Zac Rio, a gold-badge-holding detective from LA with the hidden benefit of a retentive memory, could analyze crime scenes in an instant. The special member of the team was Duke, their neurotic bloodhound and tracker dog. During the course of her investigations, Jenna had made great friends with FBI Agents Ty Carter and Jo Wells and Carter's bomb-sniffer dog, Zorro, from the field office in Snakeskin Gully. When brutal killers came to town, Jenna's team sprang into action, and to date, only one killer had slipped through her net. Although, many believed the latter was a myth, as over a decade not one law enforcement agency had found a single clue to her identity, apart from Jenna. One day, the Midnight Stalker or Tarot Killer would slip into Black Rock Falls again, and next time they wouldn't slip through the net.

"You look a million miles away." Kane moved to her side, rested his forearms on the wooden fence, and placed one boot on the bottom railing. "Thinking about me again?" He grinned at her.

Laughing, Jenna leaned against him, glad of his warmth. "No, I can't get the Tarot Killer or Midnight Stalker, whatever name they've given her, out of my mind. She killed in my town and slipped through my fingers, and I can't let it go." She turned to look at him. "She intrigues me and I'm of two minds about her. From what we know, she's a mysterious woman who drifts from state to state killing psychopaths. She's a vigilante—a

Robin Hood character who many believe is a myth until investigators find a tarot card alongside murdered psychopathic killers."

"It's no longer our problem." Kane shrugged. "The FBI is investigating her across the state and working with local law enforcement, so unless she rolls back into town, our hands are tied. We don't have the jurisdiction to hunt her down." He looked at her. "Breakfast is almost ready. Are you feeling better now?"

Jenna nodded. "Yeah. I woke up feeling queasy, is all. I'm fine now. I just needed some fresh air."

"Queasy, huh?" Kane studied her face. "You do look a little pale. Are you well enough to eat?"

"Yeah." Jenna slipped her arm through his. "I'm starved."

When Duke barked wildly and ran toward the driveway, Jenna glanced at Kane. "Problem?"

"Nah, that's his happy bark." Kane led the way toward the house. "It must be someone we know to get through the security on the front gate."

To Jenna's surprise, Wolfe's ME's van appeared at the end of the driveway. It slipped in beside Kane's powerful black truck, affectionately known as the Beast. When Wolfe climbed out frowning, a knot tied in her stomach. For him to drop by to discuss a situation would be unusual, as he'd usually call, and he didn't wear the expression of someone coming for a social visit. She gave him a wave. "Hi, Shane, you're just in time for breakfast. What brings you around so early? Do we have a problem?"

"I have a suspicious death I need to discuss with y'all." Wolfe followed them up the porch steps. He removed his hat and ran a hand through his thick blond hair. "Coffee would be nice. The call came in before dawn and I headed up there with Rio." He dropped his hat on the hall table, shucked his coat, and dropped it over a peg in the mudroom.

As Kane tossed more strips of bacon into the pan, Jenna

poured the coffee and then sat at the kitchen table. She looked across the table at Wolfe. "What have you got for me?"

"An apparent suicide. A widow, thirty-eight years old, by the name of Willow Smith. I have a positive ID." Wolfe added the fixings to his cup. "I'm not convinced it's suicide. I'll need to complete an autopsy to confirm, but the circumstances and the scene don't add up. I'd like you to do a walkthrough of the scene. Seems she'd planned a trip and I have her luggage at my office. I bagged the cup and saucer on the bedside table. I've taken the trash, the bedsheets, laundry, and other items to process. She must have changed the bedding the night before. I found bed linen in the dryer. I left it there. After a wash and time in the dryer, I wouldn't find anything I could use. I don't figure I missed anything, but a second pair of eyes is an advantage, even though Rio was thorough. I'll give you the coordinates and the keys to the house. I'd go with you but I'm needed back at the office. I'll notify the next of kin for you and get the necessary paperwork signed for the examination."

Jenna sipped her coffee. "Sure. When did the call come in and what are the details?"

"A little after five." Wolfe turned the cup around on the table with the tips of his fingers and stared at it for a beat before raising his gaze to her. "The body was discovered by a friend, Marsha Walker. She came by early to collect Willow for a flight. They were heading for a Vegas vacation with a bunch of their friends." He grimaced. "I have the victim's and Mrs. Walker's prints for comparison if I find anything interesting. I need you to go over the house again to make sure I haven't missed anything."

"How did Mrs. Walker get inside the house?" Kane turned to look at Wolfe.

"She said she had a key. She would drop by to check on the place when Willow was away, but it wasn't usually necessary as Willow rarely locked the doors. There's nobody living near her and she had a weapon close at hand." Wolfe ran a hand down his face. "Mrs. Walker was hysterical when I arrived. It took some time to calm her. She mentioned Halloween was a bad time of the year for Willow, but she refused to believe she'd taken her own life. She'd spoken to her at nine last night and Willow was excited. They'd been planning a vacation for months."

Eating slowly, Jenna couldn't miss the concern etched in Wolfe's face. "What happened to her to make her anxious about Halloween?"

"Not her, exactly." Wolfe flicked a glance at Kane. "Willow's husband, Sergeant Oliver Smith, Marine corps, went MIA on Halloween in Afghanistan some years ago and she wanted to get away for the celebration."

"So, what makes you figure it's not suicide?" Kane slid food-laden plates to everyone.

"I can't prove anything." Wolfe lifted a strip of bacon from his plate and nibbled on it. "Not yet anyway, but it doesn't add up."

Jenna poured maple syrup over a pile of hotcakes and sucked a drop from her finger. "How so?"

"Willow instigated the plans to go on vacation with her friends. A girls' week in Vegas. Who takes their own life the night before a trip of a lifetime?" Wolfe shook his head. "You'll need to cast your eyes over the scene. I figure it's a homicide."

"I know that look. What else aren't you telling us?" Kane sat down at the table and stared at him. "What is it?"

"Her husband's Purple Heart medal was attached to her PJs, which might offer an insight into her state of mind. You see, some people cherish a medal awarded for being wounded or killed in action, while others see it as a constant reminder that their loved one is maimed or dead, but that wasn't what made me question the scene. A couple of things that Mrs. Walker mentioned I dismissed as an overactive imagination." Wolfe's lips quivered at the corners as if he fought to contain a smile. "I figure y'all go a little crazy around Halloween in Black Rock Falls."

Huffing out an annoyed sigh, Jenna leaned back in her chair and stared at him. "If you figure this poor woman was murdered, then everything is relevant. Give it up, Shane. What did Mrs. Walker say that was so darn funny?"

"She figured Willow's husband was haunting her." Wolfe stared at her. "Willow told Mrs. Walker that her husband had been calling her at midnight." He rolled his eyes upward as if seeking divine intervention. "She also told her friends she could hear him walking about the house at night and that her husband's ghost had been by to visit her."

"Where does she live?" Kane flicked a glance at Jenna before looking at Wolfe. "I'm assuming that she lives alone?"

"Yeah, she does and has since her husband died." Wolfe poured more coffee into his cup. "It's an old log-built two-story out at Twisted Tree Ridge. It's surrounded by forest and difficult to find. I can't figure out why a woman would want to live alone in an isolated place like that. Once the snow comes, she wouldn't be able to leave the mountain for weeks." He shrugged. "It's the people living in this town. You give the word *crazy* a whole new meaning."

Wagging her finger at him, Jenna frowned. "You're part of this town now too. So, what else did you see to drag you all the way back here to speak to us in person?"

"Two things." Wolfe swallowed a mouthful of hotcakes and licked the syrup from his lips. "One, she had a Glock in her nightstand and it's been fired recently. Secondly, she'd packed her bags and left them at the front door." He looked directly at Jenna. "Nobody packs their bags for a vacation and then takes an overdose. She knew darn well her friend was coming early the next morning, and if she'd planned on taking her own life, she'd have at least left her a note."

"I figure the so-called ghost killed her." Kane raised both eyebrows. "Seems to me someone has had access to her cabin for a time. It sounds as if Willow dismissed the noise as the wandering spirit of her late husband, and for whatever reason, someone wanted her dead."

TWO

The colors of fall surrounded Jenna as they drove up the mountain road. All shades of green through to gold patchworked the lowlands, and the forest was awash with pine cones in such plenty they spilled over the blacktop. Jenna turned to Kane. "Will we have time to stop on the way back and collect pine cones?"

"Sure." Kane smiled at her. "That reminds me. I'll need to haul that fallen tree back to the house and chop it up for firewood. It will last us through winter."

As the Beast wound its way up the narrowing, winding roads, the forest closed in around them, and the temperature dropped. Jenna zipped up her jacket and peered ahead. This part of the forest had been deprived of light and the trees were dark and twisted. Moss grew on the many boulders sent down the mountain during a prehistoric landslide to pepper the forest floor. Jenna shivered and glanced over one shoulder. Shadows shifted and it was as if someone were out there watching her. "This place is creepy. Why would anyone want to live up here all alone?"

"It was sure well named." Kane flicked on his headlights. "Twisted Tree Ridge. It reminds me of the grotto around the wishing well in town. Do you figure someone tried to poison the trees here as well?"

Jenna's mind went to their good friend Atohi Blackhawk, a Native American tracker, who'd told her many stories about the forest. "I doubt it. I can't see a reason. In town the story goes that the forest was poisoned when they were building Stanton Road. Here, the cabins are everywhere. Some are just for hunting, others were part of land claims back in the 1800s. I figure the old house belonging to Willow Smith was likely handed down through generations. It wouldn't be too difficult to trace the ownership."

"I'd like to know a little more about what happened to her husband." Kane turned onto a dirt road with grass growing between two worn wheel ruts. "Wolfe mentioned he was MIA and the entire team went missing over Halloween. It's going to be difficult getting information on the mission, darn near impossible." He shrugged. "It seems unusual to me that his wife remained here every Halloween if she believed he was haunting her."

As if cold fingers had brushed her spine, Jenna's skin prickled into goosebumps. "There's no way I'd stay up here in a haunted house." She rubbed her arms. "Atohi says that many spirits walk the forest, both good and bad. I mean, who told her it was her husband haunting her? Maybe it was an ax murderer from another century."

"Uh-huh." Kane slowed the Beast to a crawl as the driveway snaked ahead through overhanging branches. "I'm guessing you've heard stories about Twisted Tree Ridge and being here in the dark forest is spooking you?"

Right now, Jenna didn't want to be reminded about the things she'd heard. "Not here, but yeah, there are tons of stories about the older parts of Black Rock Falls." She cleared her throat. "The kids always talk about Damien's Hollow. You might recall, we had a callout one day last summer about a fight between a group of high school kids out there. They'd gone there to party?"

"Yeah, it seemed like a normal place to me." Kane pulled up outside an old two-story wooden house. "What was spooky about that place?"

Jenna pulled on surgical gloves and shrugged. "Yeah, but that was in daylight. Do you recall that old house, some ways from the clearing with the wall made from rocks? Well, the reason the place was called Damien's Hollow was that the guy who built the house went crazy. Every Halloween he'd wait for young couples to come by, hack off their heads with an ax, and display them on top of the wall. This guy, Damien, named his house 'The Hollow'. He died in 1890 and yet heads were found on that fence right through to the 1960s. Go figure." She turned to look at Kane's incredulous expression. "They say he still haunts the Hollow every Halloween—and yeah, just like the way the kids go to the Old Mitcham Ranch to scare themselves batshit crazy—they still head out to Damien's Hollow to hunt down the axman."

"Uh-huh." Kane shook his head slowly. "They really believe a ghost can wield an ax?" He snorted. "Trust me, it's no ghost. If it happens again, we'd have ourselves another psychopath on a killing spree."

Shrugging, Jenna sighed. "Have it your own way but strange things do happen. I've read about the owners asking the local priest to perform an exorcism. I figure it worked because the house was sold to a couple about seven years ago and nothing has happened to them." She followed Kane out of the truck and waited for him to open the door for Duke. "Maybe that's what this place needs. Perhaps we should ask Father Derry to come by."

"If someone is haunting this place"—Kane drew his weapon

so fast Jenna didn't see it leave the holster—"trust me, this is the only exorcism we need." He twirled the pistol in his fingers and holstered it with a grin.

Jenna rolled her eyes. "You've turned my deputies into gunslingers." She waved a hand at his low-slung holster. "Okay, so wearing all black and carrying your weapon on your hip is one thing, but what's with the Billy the Kid attitude?"

"Gun twirling is an art, Jenna." He tipped up the brim of his Stetson and winked at her. "Being fast on the draw and accurate is a skill our team needs for hunting down murderers. Think about it, some guys whittle and leave piles of wood shavings all over the house, but me, well, twirling my gun never hurt anyone or made a mess... and for Rio and me it makes us slide right into life here in Black Rock Falls. You did know that Rowley has been twirling his gun since he was a teenager?"

Amused, Jenna shook her head. "No, I figured he was copying you. You know, monkey see monkey do?"

"Nah, but I do have them stripping their weapons blind—and I mean all the available weapons. Being able to do that is essential in our line of work." Kane bent over to peer at the ground. He glanced up at her. "That and my mantra of *practice, practice, practice* at the range has them both fast and accurate. Same with the work we all do in the gym. We need to keep fit. The gun twirling is the light relief us guys like from time to time and it's great for the reflexes."

There's never been anything wrong with your reflexes, that's for darn sure. Pulling up her hood, Jenna scanned the remote yard. The house was old, with the timber weathered over decades. The front stoop sagged a little in the center but for its age the house looked in good shape. The dirt road leading to the house was neglected, but a thick gravel walkway at least eight feet wide surrounded the house. Garden beds made from local granite rocks ran along each side of the steps devoid of any plants. Old sacks covered the dirt as if trying to prevent weeds. Every window had shutters, but considering Willow was planning a vacation, she'd not closed one of them. She turned to Kane. "If you planned to go on vacation, wouldn't you lock up the house?" She indicated to the windows. "The shutters are open. If I were leaving on an early flight, I'd have closed them the night before to save time in the morning."

"The hinges look kinda rusty. Maybe they haven't shut for a time." Kane stared up at the building and then both ways. "If someone were hanging around last night, they might have left footprints."

Jenna nodded. "I was thinking the same and we should check the doors and windows for prints."

"I have the scanner in my pocket." Kane sighed and looked over one shoulder at her. "Why didn't she have a dog?" He rubbed his chin. "Do you know how many people are murdered in this town and they didn't have a dog? I mean apart from company, they're an early warning system."

Not having a pet before Duke and Pumpkin had arrived in her life, Jenna shrugged. "Maybe they're worried a dog might be eaten by the wildlife? Or perhaps they have a job that means the dog is left alone all the time... or they don't like dogs in the house. I don't know." She absently rubbed Duke's ears. "Let's get at it." She headed along one side of the house.

"I'm wondering who had the idea of filling the walkway with gravel?" Kane stared up at the windows as he walked. "It would be murder during winter. A snowplow, even like the one I fit to the front of the Beast would throw it all over and smash windows." He waved a hand toward the eight-inch-thick layer of gravel and shook his head. "It's impossible to find any footprints but it does make one heck of a noise walking on it. Maybe this was her way to hear anyone who came by?"

Jenna turned the corner and found the back door up three

cement steps. "Check the door handle and lock for prints." She bent to look at the lock closely. "No forced entry."

"And we have prints." Kane downloaded the prints to his phone and sent a copy to Wolfe. "I've asked Wolfe to see if he can get a match to the victim and the woman who found her."

Jenna tried the door and it opened with a soft whine. She glanced at Kane. "My ranch is isolated, but I'd never leave the doors unlocked, especially if I believed the house was haunted."

"Yeah, and if it were, the locked doors wouldn't prevent them going inside, would they?" Kane turned a serious look in her direction. "I've seen the movies. Ghosts can walk through walls, right? That's if you believe the hocus pocus." He moved up behind her. "Forget about ghosts. Someone might be in there just waiting for another victim."

Slowly, Jenna opened the door. It was cold inside, like walking into the morgue, and the hairs rose on the back of her neck. Kane was right, many killers return to the scene of the crime, and she paused on the top step, peering into a dimly lit kitchen. It was like stepping back in time. In the middle of the room sat a wooden table scrubbed clean over decades. The benches and cabinets all handmade from local timber. She edged into the kitchen and looked over her shoulder at Kane. "This place hasn't been updated since the last century. Apart from the clock on the wall, the refrigerator, and phone, everything else belongs in a museum."

"My grandma had one of those wood stoves. She kept it going all day." Kane rubbed the back of his neck. "Beeswax-polished floors. Just how old was Willow Smith?"

Jenna frowned. "Thirty-eight with a ton of spare time on her hands to keep the place in such good shape." She stared at the phone. "Does that thing still work?"

"I'll see." Kane lifted the receiver and dialed his number, his phone chimed. "Yeah, it works just fine." He stared out of the open door. "I don't figure anyone is here. Duke is bored and he'd bark if he heard or smelled anyone close by."

"Okay." Jenna pulled her weapon. "We'll clear the rooms as we go. I want to check out all the windows to look for any signs of a break-in."

"They didn't need to break in if Willow left the doors unlocked." Kane eased out into the hallway, and they moved along the wall. "Sheriff's department. Come out so we can see you before anyone gets hurt."

Kane's voice seemed to echo through the house. It took them a few minutes to search the lower floor and they walked back into the foyer. The house was the same throughout, furniture and fittings appeared to be antiques. A gust of wind rattled the shutters and the house let out a series of long moans. The front door rattled and Duke barked. Jenna spun around, staring into the shadowed rooms. "Now don't tell me that wasn't spooky. No wonder Willow believed the place was haunted."

"It's the wind, is all. This close to the mountain, it rushes down in gusts and curls around the house." Kane headed for the staircase. "An old house moves and creaks. It's normal. I'd bet my last dime the stairs squeak as well." He took a few steps and the old staircase seemed to complain about his weight. "There's good and bad in this happening. Maybe the noises frighten people, although you'd get used to it, but you'd be sure to know if someone was walking up the stairs." He ran a hand over the handrail "Look at this. You don't see craftmanship like this so much anymore."

Although Jenna appreciated the antique aesthetic of the house, she wouldn't want to live without the modern additions to her own period ranch house. The low light inside, despite the windows, made her claustrophobic. "It's beautifully crafted but it gives me the creeps. I keep figuring I'm going to open a door and find Whistler's Mother."

As they climbed the stairs an icy wind rushed past them and the front door rattled. Suddenly afraid, Jenna spun around, staring into the gloom. Shadows moved across the foyer windows. "Did you see that?" She turned to look at him but the room was empty. "Dave?"

THREE

Kane headed up the stairs, weapon drawn, and stood on the landing, sweeping his gun in an arc. The door to the room in front of him was open. Ahead he made out the main bedroom with an attached bathroom. The bed had been stripped and the yellow marker tags Wolfe had left behind littered the furniture, carpet, and walls. Moving slowly down the hallway, he opened each door. One bathroom and two bedrooms, both furnished, but the beds held nothing but mattresses, no blankets. Not one speck of dust covered the highly polished surfaces. He turned to look back at Jenna. Her face had paled but she held her M18 pistol steady with two hands. "It's just the wind, although I doubt Wolfe would have left a window open. Maybe someone's been by since he left?"

"It's miles from anywhere, and not the type of place for a social drop by, is it? I don't like it here." Jenna moved closer. "My gut feeling is to get the heck out of Dodge."

Kane peered inside the bedroom as a gust of wind caught the fine white drapes, making them lift high into the air and twist and turn before they dropped motionless back in place. "This is a murder scene. I'm curious about the window. It's the

old sash type that runs on a pulley system." He headed for the
window and pulled down the frame. It rattled against another
gust of wind and he turned and smiled at Jenna. "The window
catch is loose. It only takes a strong gust of wind to release it and
then, I figure, it slowly opens." He took a version of a Swiss
army knife from his pocket, found the tool he required, and
secured the catch. "That won't open again anytime soon." He
looked at Jenna. "No ghosts, just the wind, is all."

They processed the scene, collected fingerprints, and
searched the room. When Kane opened a photograph album,
he frowned at the images of what he recognized as a special
forces team, geared up and ready to head out on a mission. It
was an unspoken law that pictures of teams, especially in
uniform, were kept under wraps. Most teams had group
photographs, but at cookouts and in civvies. He'd spent his
fair share of time behind enemy lines, and in the event of
capture, this type of information could mean the difference
between life or death. He copied a few images of the team
with his phone, as classified information of this type often
went "missing" during an investigation. The powers that be
could swoop in at any second and remove sensitive information even after all this time. He pulled an evidence bag from
his pocket and pushed the album inside and added a small
box filled with letters. Seven years ago, people still liked to
send letters home and he wondered if Willow had received
her husband's death letter. The one all of them wrote to their
loved ones to be sent if they were killed in action. He'd
written one himself to his family and later to his sister. They'd
been destroyed the day he'd left active duty, but he could
recall every word.

"What are the spots on the wall?" Jenna was peering
intently at the discoloration beside the yellow stickers on the
wall. "They look like blood."

Kane turned to look at the dark marks. "Maybe. It's hard to

tell. Wolfe has obviously taken samples. Have you found anything interesting?"

"I've found her purse with her airline ticket." Jenna held up an evidence bag. "Her phone is here too and she had a wad of bills. The motive, if any, wasn't robbery." She blew out a breath. "Apart from that, absolutely nothing. One thing is strange. There's no TV, no laptop. Living here all alone, what did she do all day, apart from clean?"

Not finding anything else of interest, Kane shrugged. "We'll speak to her friend and find out more about her. She sounds like a recluse."

A metallic rattling came from downstairs, followed by a rush of cold wind. Duke barked and ran to the door. Kane dashed after him, weapon drawn, and turkey-peeked down the stairs to the foyer. The front door stood wide open and a gust of wind tumbled fall leaves across the polished wooden floor. "Sheriff's department. Show yourself before you get hurt."

"What is it?" Jenna pressed her back to the wall, gun drawn.

Kane scanned the lower floor, easing out onto the landing and moving forward one step at a time. "I can't see anyone. The front door is open." He glanced back at her. "If someone came inside, they didn't try and sneak in."

He looked at Duke, sitting nonchalantly by his feet. "Chase him down, Duke."

The dog looked at him, yawned, sniffed the air, and whined. Kane shrugged. "There's nobody there or he'd have taken off downstairs."

"You keep watching and I'll grab the evidence bags." Jenna holstered her weapon and turned away. "We'll do another sweep of the house just in case anyone is here." She stopped midstride and looked over her shoulder at him. "I didn't see a root cellar. Sometimes in these old places they're under the kitchen, hidden in the pantry."

Kane snorted. "Now you tell me." He waited for her to join

him and headed down the steps. "So that could have been someone leaving?"

"Or a ghost." Jenna gave him a sideways glance and raised her eyebrows. "You checked that door for prints inside and out and closed it, so don't tell me it wasn't shut. You'd never leave a door open with a killer possibly close by."

They moved down the stairs and the treads creaked underfoot. With each gust of wind, the house moaned like an old man and fall leaves danced in a rustling procession along the hallway toward the kitchen. Beside him Jenna stiffened and he glanced at her, surprised to find her so jumpy. "I shut the door and there's no ghost here, Jenna. You've always said dogs can sense things and look at Duke. He's just having fun being with us. He's not worried."

"My cop brain tells me it's not a ghost, but my scared-little-girl brain is hiding under the blankets convinced there's something bad in this house. I keep expecting something to jump out at us, Dave. Call it being stupid or gut instinct, whatever, but I'm darn sure it wasn't making so much noise when we arrived. It's as if it wants us to leave."

Kane stopped walking and stared at her. "What's gotten into you, Jenna? Wolfe said everyone goes a little crazy around Halloween in this town, but I've seen you at brutal crime scenes and you're detached. This is an overdose, suicide maybe, but not a bloodbath." He squeezed her shoulder. "It's just the wind, is all. This old house moves more than ours because of its age. The trees outside rub against it and the wind pushes through the blinds making the noises. It's not a ghost, okay?"

Kane checked each room again and found nothing. He closed each door behind him and crunched over dead curled leaves to the kitchen. He checked the pantry, searching the floor for an access into the cellar and found nothing. The idea of dropping into a dark cellar wasn't something he enjoyed. A remnant of a bad experience as a child had magnified since finding his sister slaughtered in his grandma's cellar. "Nothing here."

"Good." Jenna huffed out a sigh of relief. "Let's get the hell out of here."

Kane stood at the front door and peered around. "I'll be interested to see the images Rio has taken of the scene. The floor is so highly polished anyone walking in would have left footprints. Look, you can see where we've walked, other footprints, and the gurney. I know Wolfe and Rio would have worn booties, so we have the friend and the killer. Rio would have taken images of the floor for sure."

"Yeah, same with just before, if someone had come inside, they'd leave damp footprints." Jenna stared at the open front door as a blast of cold wind scattered more leaves throughout the house. "Take a look at the lock on the door as well."

After playing with the locking mechanism on the door, opening and shutting the door several times, he led Jenna outside, shut the door, and leaned on it. The sturdy thick door didn't move and the lock held tight. He turned the doorknob. The metal ring surrounds rattled, but the door opened without a sound. He frowned and looked at Jenna. "I have no idea why the door blew open. I shut it that's for darn sure."

A cold breeze rustled the trees and seemed to curl around them, lifting the edges of their jackets in a promise of winter. He scanned the forest surrounding the house and his gut tightened in a warning that someone was watching them. He shook the feeling away. There was no way this old place was going to drag him into its spooky spell. A few spots of rain brushed Kane's cheeks and he urged Jenna toward the Beast. "I smell rain. It's time to get off the mountain."

After securing Duke in the back seat, Kane slid behind the wheel. He headed down the old dirt track and turned on some tunes on the radio and hummed along. Although they complemented each other in their marriage and on the job, Jenna was his complete opposite in many things. She had a whimsical side that he loved, but he had no time for ghosts or things that went bump in the night, although if someone proved beyond doubt that lost souls roamed the earth seeking vengeance, he'd look at it logically. His life as a sniper sent behind enemy lines to take down enemies of the free world hadn't left him with any mental scars. It was a job and someone had to do it, and as sure as the sun came up each morning, if there were any vengeful ghosts out there, he'd have seen one by now. Jenna valued all life, even those of unstoppable murdering psychopaths, but he didn't possess that degree of forgiveness, especially when it came to child killers. It had taken Jenna's persuasive argument that they could learn more from a live psychopath than a dead one to change his mind, although he wouldn't hesitate to act if anyone were in mortal danger. He recalled that his mom had been a very sensible woman but had believed in fairies. She blamed them when socks vanished from the dryer and when things went missing from her sewing basket.

"You're miles away." Jenna touched his arm. "Thinking about the case?"

Kane turned onto the highway that wound down the mountain to join Stanton. "Yes and no. I've been thinking about my old life. My mom didn't believe in ghosts but she did believe in fairies." He shot her a glance to see if she'd find the notion amusing.

"Mine too." Jenna sighed. "The fairies took socks in winter to make sleeping bags and that's why they always go missing during the wash. I know you wouldn't consider such a thing, but where do the socks go? I've never found any."

Kane smiled at her. "Me either." He chuckled. "We had this cat when we were little kids. He was born on Christmas Day and we called him Nick, as in Saint Nicholas. My sister had scrunchies for her hair and she'd leave them on her nightstand, and in the morning, they'd be missing. My mom blamed the fairies, but I'd often seen the cat playing with them. Years later, like twenty years later, we pulled out a wall and found a great pile of them inside the heating vent. The cat had been collecting them for years."

"You figure it was the cat, huh?" Jenna grinned at him. "Maybe you found the fairies' stash."

Shaking his head, Kane looked at her. "Maybe I did."

"I know you're trying to lighten the mood, Dave, but I've been spooked since I stepped out of the truck." Jenna checked her watch. It was almost noon already. "We'll drop by Aunt Betty's Café and then I figure we should go and see what Wolfe's discovered. If there's something wrong, he'll have found it by now. I'll call Rio and ask him to upload the images of the scene to our files. We can go over them later."

Nodding, Kane cleared his throat. "Okay. I think you're right about the house. Something is wrong with that place. That's for darn sure. I agree with Wolfe and this case isn't sitting right with me either." He flicked her a glance. "A ghost didn't open the front door at Willow's house. It didn't open from a blast of wind either. Someone turned the knob. They'd have been able to do that and leave the door ajar and get away without us hearing. Sooner or later the wind would throw it open." He shrugged. "My gut instinct was in overdrive and I had the feeling someone was watching us. I didn't see anyone and Duke didn't react, but the forest is vast and anyone could be watching us through field glasses. If this is a rogue Seal, we're talking about an out-of-control, highly trained killing machine."

FOUR

Aunt Betty's Café was the hub of the town. Open seven days a week and serving meals from breakfast to late-night snacks, it also provided Jenna with information. The manager and good friend Susie Hartwig was always forthcoming about anything unusual happening around town. As they side-stepped the pile of pumpkins and ducked under the cobwebs surrounding the door, she made her way to the front counter. The diner was always busy, sometimes with a line of customers waiting for takeout going out the door and up the sidewalk. Ahead, Duke nosed his way around legs and sat at the counter and barked. As a police service dog, he was permitted to be inside the diner with his handler, and just about everyone in town knew him by name. He waited patiently for Susie to find him a treat, with his thick tail thumping against the tiled floor. The dog satisfied, Jenna perused the specials and sighed. "I'll have the home fries, sage and red wine sausage, with peppers, onions, mushrooms, topped with bacon gravy, and a fried egg."

"Make that two and a gallon of coffee." Kane sniffed. "Oh, and peach pie."

"Large size for you, Dave?" Susie grinned at him. "À la mode?"

"No ice cream this time." Kane chuckled. "I'm watching my weight."

Jenna snorted and headed for their reserved table. "Says the fat-burning machine. In all the years I've known you I've seen you thinner after an injury, but you never seem to carry any extra weight. Is it genetic?"

"I'm not sure." Kane frowned. "My dad was strong and my sister was always working out, so maybe." He removed his jacket and hung it over the back of the chair before sitting. "My mom, was my mom, you know. I never really noticed her body shape." He stared at her across the table. "You're always in great shape. Is it genetic for you?"

Leaning back and shaking her head, Jenna sighed. "The way we work out each morning, do our chores, and then sometimes work seven days or more without a break, I don't get the chance to get out of shape. I do watch what I eat so I can keep up with you."

"Uh-huh." Kane smiled as Suzie came by the table to fill their coffee cups and give them silverware for their meal. As she walked away, he shrugged. "I've always believed that humans are just like any other species. We come in all different shapes and sizes. Look at Duke. No matter what he eats or how much exercise he gets, he'll never resemble a Boston terrier. Cosmetic surgery isn't going to make a five-six guy look like me. He might grow muscle but he'll never be six-five. I figure people should stop worrying about body image and just eat sensibly. In truth, no one really cares what you look like, do they? The only critics are the reflection in the mirror."

Considering Kane's philosophy, Jenna leaned back in her chair as Susie came back with the meals. She smiled at her. "Thanks, Susie." As she walked away, Jenna picked up a fork, but her mind was back at the murder scene. "Wolfe mentioned

Willow's husband was MIA. How does that happen to an entire team? Captured?"

"Many things happen in war, Jenna." Kane looked perplexed. "I figure she'd know if he'd been captured. Where he'd been stationed, they didn't take many POWs, as in kept them locked up for the duration. They'd usually make videos online and execute them. That usually made the news." He ate slowly. "Carter would have been there at the time. Seal teams would have been deployed and he'd possibly have intel he could share." He narrowed his gaze. "Not specific but general. Possibly, if they ran over an IED, there wouldn't be much left to bring home. They'd have sent a cleanup crew to go look for them."

Stomach churning, Jenna swallowed the food in her mouth, all appetite suddenly gone. "I'll call Carter."

"No, don't." Kane's brow crinkled into a deep frown. "We'll have a nice meal and then head back to the office. I'll call him. He's more likely to open up to me a little, as we're brothers in arms. It's the code, Jenna. We don't discuss our missions, not ever."

Trying unsuccessfully to push the horrors of war from her mind, Jenna took a long drink of her coffee. "My first thought was to ask Wolfe but even he has his limits."

"Oh, he'd be able to get the information, but he won't." Kane refilled his cup from the pot Susie had left on the table and added the fixings. "If it were necessary to protect us, he'd go to the top but to chase down a dead man wouldn't be considered 'need to know.' Wolfe never strays from the path, Jenna, never cuts corners, always does everything according to the book." He gave her a long look. "That's why we can trust him with our lives. He'll never let us down."

Nodding, Jenna picked at her food. She trusted Wolfe and wouldn't normally compromise his position with the powers that be by asking him to overstep his mark. "Okay, but what if

Willow's husband took his own life? I could understand the reason if his team was all killed. Wolfe could find out, couldn't he?"

"Do you figure that makes a difference to security?" Kane shook his head.

Jenna shrugged. "It could be a reason Willow took her own life."

Kane snorted and shook his head. "Don't go there, Jenna. You couldn't possibly understand."

Jenna took in Kane's flash of annoyance. "Don't look at me like that. I know you donate to a foundation to prevent military suicide—but military trauma aside, if Willow truly believed she was being haunted by her husband, it would prove he was waiting for her on the other side. It could have pushed her over the edge."

"I see no reason in your thinking at all. She was planning a trip to Vegas. That would have been a complete turnaround." Kane dug into his peach pie. "It's common knowledge that grieving people think they see dead relatives at stores or driving by. I admit, I often felt Annie close by. Well, I did until I visited her grave and told her I'd found you. It wasn't what you consider being haunted."

"Ha!" Jenna poked him in the arm. "You've just admitted you believe in ghosts."

"Not at all." Kane sipped his coffee. "I believe there's more to life than just now and that we go to a better place. It's a fact, energy can't be destroyed but it can be changed into another form, and as we're energy, then we must go somewhere, *but* ghosts that hurt and frighten people usually prove to be real—as in arrestable." He gave her a long look. "I feel you when you're away from me. It's like a warmth in my chest, a feeling of well-being. I still had that when Annie died and it helped me through the grief of losing her. It's as if they're in the next room and you can sense them there. It's hard to explain."

The memory of losing her parents rocked Jenna to the heart and she nodded. "Yeah, I know what you mean and it's nothing like being haunted. For me personally, there's too much evidence for the existence of ghosts, and too many tales of people being hurt by them, for me not to believe they exist." She pushed away her plate. "If you're done, we should drop by the morgue and get an update."

"Talking about Shane"—Kane's mouth twitched up at the corners—"have you noticed a difference in him since he came back from vacation?"

Jenna smiled. "You mean his Texas drawl is back? Yeah, I noticed. He also regained his sense of humor. We'll have to make sure he visits his family more often."

"I'm wondering if he was a man on a mission." Kane winked at her. "I have the feeling he has found someone. Maybe he was running it past his folks?"

The possibility of the serious, old-school Wolfe having a romance was intriguing. "Maybe you should ask him?" At Kane's aghast expression, she giggled. "No? Well, you should call Carter while we're there. You'll be sure no one is listening in Wolfe's office."

"Nah, I'll call him from our office." Kane stood and dropped bills on the table. "It might take a time to explain."

Ten minutes later they walked inside the medical examiner's office as Wolfe emerged from an examination room. Jenna followed him to his office and waited for him to pull up files on his computer. "Did you find anything?"

"I located her next of kin, two cousins, out at Blackwater, although they didn't seem too interested in the fact she'd died. Willow rarely contacted them at all. I sent an image of her to them. The body, as you know, is undamaged and Emily made her look presentable for the photographs. We struck gold when we found them. They're the children of Willow's aunt, and one of them had a sample of their DNA on file. I found a mitochondrial match and they both completed the paperwork to verify the identity and gave permission for an autopsy."

Almost bursting with the need for Wolfe to get to the point, Jenna nodded. "Have you completed the autopsy?"

"Nope." Wolfe leaned back in his chair and shook his head. "I know you expect me to do things around here yesterday but there are procedures to follow." He held up one finger to stop her next question. "I have completed a preliminary examination, but you'll need to look at the crime scene photographs I took before I removed the body. You have what Rio recorded but I have a few more for you to see." He tapped on his computer keyboard and turned the screen toward them. "See the empty pill bottle on its side beside the bed? The cup with the sticky drink residue?" He raised an eyebrow. "Two things alerted me the moment I set eyes on them. First, when people take a deliberate overdose, they rarely dissolve the pills in a drink. They usually swallow as many pills as they can and wash them down. The sticky residue tells me there was a ton of sugar in the drink. I checked out the pill bottle. It had only her prints on it and was a prescription for one hundred barbiturates and it was dispensed two days ago. I called the pharmacist and he recalls Willow dropping by and mentioning her trip and saying she'd always had a problem sleeping in strange places and would be taking them with her. The last prescription she'd filled had been eight months previously. This tells me she doesn't need to take the pills nightly."

"Where is this getting us, Shane?" Kane rubbed his chin. "Did she take her own life or not?"

"There you go again, rushing along at a thousand miles an hour." Wolfe shook his head slowly. "Listen. Taking all what I've said into consideration, what do you figure happened?"

"Did you find residue from the pills on the bedside table or any spilled on the floor? When people overdose, they often just upend the bottle into their mouths and some spill." Kane peered at the images using his fingers to expand the view. "I don't see anything here, or on the floor."

"There weren't any." Wolfe looked at Kane and smiled. "I figured the same, as the drug kicks in they tend to spill some of the pills. If someone added enough medication to her drink to kill her, it wouldn't take an entire bottle. Ten pills of that strength would be enough. The initial effect would be sleep, especially if she'd sipped the drink." He looked from one to the other. "The moment I received the permission to conduct an autopsy, I did a preliminary examination of the stomach contents. There are no undissolved pills in her stomach and if she'd taken fifty, they wouldn't have all dissolved. She had no food in her stomach. The small residue was from a chocolate drink and it contained the drug." He cleared his throat. "Conclusions?"

Feeling like she was back at Quantico, Jenna glanced at Kane and then back to Wolfe. "Sounds like murder to me. When will you have the proof?"

"I'll be conducting the full autopsy at ten tomorrow." Wolfe turned the computer screen back to face him. "I tested for only the one specific drug. I'll run a full toxicology screen. If this poor woman was seeing ghosts and hearing her dead husband, she might have been given a hallucinogenic. I figure you should hunt down her phone records. From what her friend told me, the calls at midnight came through on the landline."

Jenna stood. "Okay, we'll get at it, but we'll need more information on her husband. What if he isn't MIA?"

"That would be hard to prove and what would be the motive to kill his wife?" Kane removed his Stetson, scratched his head, and replaced it. "If he suddenly showed, the military would keep him for a time to debrief him and ensure he hadn't turned rogue. If he wanted to leave his wife, he wouldn't need to kill her, and from the ton of letters I found from him right up to his disappearance, it seems to me they were close. I'll look through them later to be sure, but I don't figure it's the husband."

Jenna thought for a beat. "The cousins didn't get along with Willow and they'd inherit her estate, so that's a motive. We'll need to discover if she had anything other than the house to leave them." She smiled at Wolfe. "Thanks. I've learned a lot today."

"Good." Wolfe pushed up from his chair. "I know you appreciate me setting out the facts. You're the investigators and needed a starting point. As ME, nothing is proved until I've completed the autopsy and have the results of the tests."

Jenna headed for the door. "Okay, do you want us back here in the morning?"

"Ten if you decide to attend, but it's not necessary." Wolfe followed them out the door. "With a badge-holding deputy as an assistant, I could just send you my report, and if I find anything we haven't already discussed, I'd call you."

Running the things to do through her mind, she shook her head. "Unless something comes up, we'll be there. Thanks."

FIVE

Kane sat at his desk in Jenna's office as she brought Rowley and Rio up to speed on the case. Discussing missions with Carter would be difficult. He understood Carter suffered PTSD after a ton of kids had been killed during his last deployment. Bringing back memories might cause a great deal of harm. He ran a plan of approach through his mind, to maybe avoid any problems while Jenna issued orders to her deputies.

"Rowley, find the carrier for Willow Smith's landline and get her call records. We need to find out if she received any calls at midnight as she claimed." Jenna turned to Rio. "Wolfe has just sent through the images he took at the scene of the meds he found. They're in the case files. Find out who prescribed the drug and go see the doctor. I want to know what other drugs she'd been prescribed over the last year."

"Copy that." Rio followed Rowley out the door.

"I'll put on a pot of coffee." Jenna smiled at him. "Unless you'd prefer, I'll go downstairs while you call Carter."

Kane frowned. "You know the deal, Jenna. You're ex-FBI. To keep you safe, I won't ever discuss my missions or anyone else's with you."

"Okay, okay." Jenna held up both hands. "Come on, Duke, let's take a walk." She patted her thigh and, with Duke at her side, headed out the door, closing it silently behind her.

Kane made the call. "Hi there. We have an interesting case." He gave Carter the facts. "I figure you were around at the time the team went MIA. I don't want specifics, but is there any chance any of them might have survived?"

"Yeah, I was on active duty with my team when that went down." Carter cleared his throat. *"Just give me a moment."*

Kane heard Carter's cowboy boots clicking over the tiled floor, a door opening and closing. He waited and soon Carter's voice came back on the line.

"Are you alone?" The sound of the creak of a chair and an exhale of breath as Carter sat down came through the earpiece. *"I'm not breaking protocol, not even for you, Dave."*

Kane nodded to himself. He'd been right about Carter. "I know the deal and I'm alone. I wouldn't ask if it weren't a priority."

"It was a routine patrol, nothin' special, but they all ended up angels." Carter paused for long seconds. *"Or so we were led to believe. Guys go out, they come back, and you know as well as I do that what happens in the team stays in the team. We don't know who does what. It's safer that way, but the way it was handled made me suspicious. The scuttlebutt was that they ran into a spread of IEDs. It wasn't our AOC but they sent us out to recon the area."*

Kane ran a hand down his face. He didn't want to ask the question. He'd seen the damage from an improvised explosive device. They killed or disabled in horrific ways. Hidden on roads, inside soda cans, and in doorways, they often went undetected. "What did you find that sent up a red flag?"

"That's the problem." Carter moved the phone and it scratched over his chin. *"I figure you've seen what happens to a man when he steps on an IED? There was nothin' there, zip,*

nada. I walked away from a similar situation, but they'd sent kids out to get candy from us and they'd rigged them. The bodies were gone but the heads were all over. It was a massacre. Here's the thing: When we went out with the medics after the other mission looking for survivors, we found nothin' but craters."

Running the scenario through his mind, Kane sucked in a deep breath. Reliving the memory that had caused Carter's PTSD was dangerous. He phrased his questions with care. "POWs?"

"Unlikely. If they'd captured that many men, they'd have used them for propaganda or trade. More likely they'd have beheaded them on social media. If they'd died in the explosion, somehow someone had a cleanup crew out there before we were deployed. It never sat well with me and never will, but that has to be six or seven years ago. If they're alive, we'd have heard somethin' by now." He sighed. *"As far as I'm aware, they're all listed as MIA."*

Kane considered his answer. His deployment had been very different from Carter's. He'd spent most of his time alone with Wolfe in his ear, a sniper rifle, and a backpack. Occasionally he'd have a spotter, but he'd always figured he was there just in case he froze and didn't take the shot. It happened to others but never to him. His time in the Secret Service had given him insight into things he'd prefer not to know, but making an entire team vanish on a mission wasn't one of them. He'd need to dig deeper. Something wasn't right. That was for darn sure. "It stinks on ice. I can't imagine any type of IED able to vaporize an entire team without leaving a trace. It sounds more like nuclear, and they didn't have those weapons in the desert."

"Or it was a mass desertion." Carter growled deep in his throat. *"If it was, I sure hope none of them cross my path. I don't have much time for people who turn their backs on their country."*

Kane stared at the ceiling as memories flooded back. Unfortunately, when men couldn't cope with war they deserted or killed themselves after witnessing atrocities, but those trained at the highest level usually held it together on a mission. Their troubles began, most times, when they returned home. They didn't have the outlet most high-pressure occupations enjoyed of being able to talk through what was worrying them or causing the nightmares with those closest to them. All they had was a military shrink. As good as these doctors were, it wasn't the same as unloading problems to the sympathetic ear of a loved one. For most, the thought of reliving the memories became too much to bear. The problem was empathy and everyone had it. It was just some of them, like him, had a switch. Once deployed, the machine kicked in, shielding their minds from harm. Others suffered irreparable damage. Carter had suffered and it had taken him two years to get his head straight. "How would they get back into the country?"

"They'd have needed help, which means they might not be MIA at all, if you get my meaning." Carter lowered his voice. *"I'm not high enough on the chain of command to give you an answer, but I've seen a ton of explosions and there's always debris. Sure, there's never much left, but there's always a trace. We found the casings of the IEDs, but not even a fragment of a helmet. All the IEDs were exploded. We found nothin' else at all, which is another anomaly. Seems to me it's a cover-up, but for what reason remains a mystery, and I'm darn sure they don't want us askin' about it."*

Kane rubbed the back of his neck. How could a potential overdose become so complicated? He touched the pumpkin lantern Jenna had placed on his desk and it lit up and wailed like a ghoul. "It would be pointless trying to get any info out of the military. I guess we'll just keep hunting down suspects. Maybe it was someone playing a cruel trick."

"Well, it's the right time of year for it." Carter's footsteps came down the line. *"We might be able to hunt down where the*

MIA Seals' wives live. If this is a homicide, it might have happened before."

With brutal serial killer attacks, this is the first thing Kane would have on his list, but Willow Smith's murder had been almost gentle, personal, as if the killer had known her. He gathered his thoughts. "Yeah, thanks that would be great. Are you coming to town for the Halloween Ball?"

"Wouldn't miss it." Carter chuckled. *"Black Rock Falls is my kinda town and I'm sure Jo would want Jaime to be out trick-or-treating with Wolfe's daughters. Snakeskin Gully is kinda tame at Halloween."*

Kane smiled. "Great! We'll have the cottage made up and stocked with beer and steaks."

"Now you're talkin'." Carter's mood had lifted considerably. *"I'll talk to Jo about Halloween and one of us will get back to you if Kalo hunts down those leads we spoke about. Catch you later."* The line went dead.

Running the conversation through his mind, Kane thought for a beat and then called Wolfe. He explained the situation. "Carter is going to hunt down where the team lived or at least where their wives live now."

"Many would have lived near the base, but that doesn't mean they didn't purchase a home during their tour of duty. I sure did and know many who've made the same investment. Problem is, you'd need the names of the men in the platoon and that's not going to happen." Wolfe paused a beat and then breathed out a long sigh. *"At this stage of the investigation, I don't have enough evidence to ruffle the feathers of the powers that be. Carter will have no chance of hunting down their wives. I don't know why you didn't discuss this with me first. Now if I make inquiries as well, red flags will go up in the Department of Defense and they'll haul us all in. We might never see the light of day again if this is sensitive."*

Kane quickly thumbed a message to Carter to hold all

communication with the DOD and asked him instead to get Kalo to hunt down apparent suicide victims in surrounding counties. He sucked in a deep breath and let it out slowly. "Okay, I've asked Carter to stand down. I guess now we wait for answers."

"Just hope you don't find any other apparent suicides connected to this platoon or I'll be ordering exhumation orders and calling in a forensic anthropologist." Wolfe sighed. *"It takes so much red tape to get a team from Helena and they're stretched to the limit now. I'm thinking of asking Dr. Norrell Larson to join my team. She'd use Black Rock Falls as her base and be available for other counties in this part of the state to relieve some of the workload on Helena."*

Biting back a grin, Kane tried to keep his voice serious. He knew darn well Wolfe had nurtured a friendship with Dr. Norrell Larson, and he'd hoped the few times they'd been together had maybe sparked an interest between them. He'd met Norrell during a conference. Super intelligent, she'd excelled and was at the top of her field. He hadn't imagined Wolfe would have considered her as anything more than a colleague, but he'd noticed a new bounce in his step after he'd visited the ME's offices in Helena. Norrell was more than ten years Wolfe's junior, with white-blonde hair and sky-blue eyes. She was, in fact, stunning. "Uh-huh."

"Don't get all judgmental on me now." Wolfe barked a laugh. *"I need a forensic anthropologist and Norrell is looking for the opportunity to lead her own team. It will be a tight squeeze for a few weeks, is all. I already have approval to expand the ME's office into the old bank building next door. The funding is there, and as it's only a refurbishment, it will be finished in no time at all. It would mean when Emily finishes her degree she can join the team. You know she has a hankering to work in forensic anthropology. It would be perfect for everyone."*

Kane cleared his throat. "I figured you might make a move on her. She kinda fits into your lifestyle."

"*I knew y'all believed I was chasing tail.*" Wolfe went suddenly serious. "*I don't deny the visits to Helena were to see her, but, and I do mean but, the main reason was to see if we could get along. I needed to know if we were on the same wavelength. I'm radically enthusiastic about advancements and seek out new technology and she's the same. She'll bring a fresh new insight into my world.*"

Kane headed for the coffee machine and, placing the phone on speaker, went about filling it. "So, you don't find her attractive or someone you might want to start a relationship with?"

"*I don't recall me ever asking your intentions with Jenna.*" Wolfe cleared his throat. "*Yeah, I do find her attractive, but do you figure she'd consider someone of my age as relationship material?*"

Kane chuckled. "What are you? Forty-two? I've known many men who don't even consider marriage until they're in their forties. Look at Carter. He's, what, thirty and hasn't had the urge to run out and marry. Heck, he hasn't had his first relationship yet and, trust me, women find older men attractive and dependable. And she's not exactly a teenager, is she?"

"*Nope she's thirty and she knows her own mind.*" Wolfe said nothing for a long moment. "*I'm not planning on rushing in and spoiling things. I'm old-school, but if I see any sparks between us, I'll throw the dice and see what happens. Right now, we're just friends, is all.*" He sighed. "*There are so many single men around town. Take Carter, for instance. It would be just my luck the moment he sees her, he decides she's the one he's been searching for all his life.*"

Shaking his head, Kane watched the first few drops of liquid drip from the pot, filling the room with the smell of the delicious brew. His special blend. "Then she wouldn't be the woman for you, would she? You guys are worlds apart and I know Carter met her at the last conference and struck out. I don't figure she'd be interested in him." He took down two cups from the shelf. "Has she ever been married?"

"I've never asked. It's not as if we're dating. I know she doesn't have kids. She's very interested in mine though and wants to meet them." Wolfe sighed. *"Maybe it's because she wants to join the team."* He suddenly changed the subject. *"Okay, I'll get at it. Don't forget the autopsy is at ten tomorrow."* Kane could hear Wolfe's daughter Emily in the background. *"Emily says to say hello. I'll see you in the morning."* He disconnected.

A knock came on the door and Jenna stuck her head around. Kane smiled at her. "You're just in time for coffee."

"Good." Jenna placed two takeout bags on the desk. "I dropped by the cookie store and they now have a selection of brownies. I figured you'd like to try them."

Kane's stomach gave an appreciative growl as he bent to rub Duke's ears. "Thanks. I've been speaking to Carter and Wolfe about the circumstances around Smith's team going MIA. We'd be stepping on toes if we made inquiries. It's a mission no one is willing to talk about, especially as we have nothing to suggest it's Oliver Smith."

"So, what did they suggest?" Jenna poured two cups of coffee, added the fixings, and returned to sit at Kane's desk.

Kane opened the bag and inhaled a fudge brownie. "Ah... they suggested we hunt down similar cases of suicide and especially wives of men in the military. Carter is on it." He sighed and nibbled at the delight. "If they're the same MO as our case, Wolfe will have the bodies exhumed and he'll bring Dr. Norrell Larson onto his team. That deal is already done. We'll have our own forensic anthropologist on call, although like Wolfe, she'll be working all over when necessary. I don't figure we have too many unmarked graves here for her to investigate."

"There you go tempting fate again." Jenna dropped into a

chair and reached for a bag. "These are called chocolate crumble, double choc chip cookies. I don't really care if I spoil my dinner. I'm having one." She waved one under Kane's nose. "We might as well head home. It will take time for the guys to hunt down the information I need, and if they find anything, they'll call. There's nothing we can do to move the case forward without more evidence of a crime. If Wolfe decides Willow was murdered, we'll hunt down Willow Smith's friends. We already know one, so I'll ask her for a list. It will be interesting to discover what they know but that can wait for tomorrow." She nibbled on a cookie, staring into space, and then looked at him. "Isn't Dr. Norrell Larson the woman Wolfe keeps slipping off to meet in Helena?"

Kane swallowed a mouthful of brownie and nodded. "Yeah, that's her."

"Hmm, interesting." Jenna sighed. "You've mentioned her before and I think you used the word *stunning*. I hope she won't become a problem. It seems to me every time a good-looking woman comes into town, people start dying."

Trying not to spit a mouthful of coffee over the table, he swallowed hard and gasped. Gathering himself, he grinned at her. "It seems like you've started a trend."

SIX

It had taken courage for Christy Miller to go ahead and purchase the house at Death Drop Gully after Hank had gone MIA during his last deployment in Afghanistan. It was one of those beautiful houses built after the Second World War, when people had hope for a brighter future and the skills and time necessary to produce fine craftsmanship. It seemed like a lifetime ago since she'd last visited it with Hank. Childhood sweethearts, they'd drive up and picnic on the rocks overlooking Death Drop Gully. He'd proposed sitting on the brick wall surrounding Valley View, the old house boarded up for decades after its owner died and left it to a distant relative to fall into disrepair. Hank had promised to buy the house for her when he left the service and they'd made plans to restore it to its former glory.

Each year at Halloween, memories flooded back, beautiful memories of their life together. She'd never have another man in her life, and purchasing Valley View and restoring it had been a panacea for her loss. Being an only child in a large family, she'd found her name mentioned on the wills of relatives who'd passed, leaving her with a considerable fortune. They'd never had kids, postponing everything until his last tour of duty was over. It had been easier when the house was filled with contractors, but as the years went by and Hank never returned, she'd become a recluse. All alone, she rattled around the house trying to keep busy, but had recently taken a positive step and joined an art class in Black Rock Falls. She'd met a nice group of people. Of late, she'd been hiking up the mountain to Death Drop Gully to sketch and take photographs. She wanted to paint a picture of the place that Hank had loved so much and hang it above her fireplace.

It seemed right somehow, to wait for midnight each night over the week before Halloween and light a candle to commemorate Hank's ultimate sacrifice to his country. The soldiers in their dress uniform hadn't given her much information apart from he'd died at midnight at Halloween and more details would follow. They never arrived, nor did his body.

She set the alarm as always to wake her at eleven-fifty and snuggled into bed. When the alarm woke her, she'd go downstairs and light a candle in the front window, wait for midnight to pass, and tell Hank how much she missed him. She never cried and always allowed her mind to remember the good times they'd had together. Her beloved husband wouldn't like to see her sad. As usual the alarm buzzed, and she dragged herself from a dream. Fully awake, she pulled on a gown and pushed her feet into slippers before heading downstairs. She switched on lights, and only the groan from the furnace in the cellar filled the night. It was strange but she'd always been comfortable in the house. Alone maybe, but few people would venture in this direction and she had an arsenal of weapons and knew how to use them if anyone dropped by with the intent to break in. Confident, she went downstairs and straight to the table to light the candle. Outside the moon was high in the sky and she could hear the hoot of an owl in the forest. Before she had time to open her mouth, a scratchy sound came from the cellar. She turned and listened intently, sure she could hear someone calling her name.

Confused, she headed for the cellar door and turned the knob. The scratchy sound came again, and using the switch outside on the wall, she flooded the interior with light. From her position at the top of the stairs she could see the furnace and the bench along the wall where she stored her tools. The noise came again, scratchy and distorted.

"Christy, can you hear me?"

Heart pounding, she stared in disbelief at an old military-style walkie-talkie sitting on the bench. Hank had used more sophisticated forms of communication. She moved hesitantly toward the disjointed scratchy voice and her gaze settled on her husband's Purple Heart medal. It had never been out of the case and was now tossed on the bench as if it held no value. Suddenly frightened, she grasped it to her chest and looked all around, but the cellar was empty.

"Christy, can you hear me?"

She gasped as an indistinctive voice came from the walkie-talkie. "This is madness. I'm no fool."

Grabbing the device, she stared at it, trying to make out how it worked. Without warning, it sprung to life again. She gaped at it, fingers trembling. If this were a Halloween prank, it wasn't funny.

"Remember where we used to go for picnics? Come to me. I've waited so long to hold you in my arms again. I have only one chance to see you again. It has to be tonight. Hurry."

Grabbing up the walkie-talkie, she pressed the button. "Who is this? This isn't funny."

"Remember the flowers I put in your hair before I deployed? It's me, Christy. Come to me and wear the medal so I know it's really you. Hurry, I don't have much time."

Christy dropped the walkie-talkie and it bounced across the bench. Only Hank would know about that intimate moment.

She vividly recalled the wildflowers he'd collected. He'd used his phone to take a photograph of her. They'd spent a few precious hours together before he'd deployed for hopefully the last time. They'd walked along the riverbank alongside the base and made plans to buy Valley View when he returned. Fingers trembling, she stared at the medal and, closing her hands around it, ran up the steps and headed for her bedroom. If someone were playing tricks on her, they'd picked the wrong person. The forest didn't scare her at night, but the wildlife could be a problem. She dressed in warm clothing, boots, and a woolen hat. After staring at the medal for some moments, she pinned it to her shirt. After putting on a warm jacket, she threw a rifle over one shoulder and, stuffing her phone in one pocket, grabbed a flashlight and slipped out of the front door.

She'd walked the path a thousand times but never at night. A shiver of apprehension slid over her as the dark forest closed in around her small beam of light. The anger at being played for a fool ebbed as she climbed higher toward the top of the gully. In daylight the view from the top was spectacular and now in fall a paintbox array of colors flooded the town below and spread across the panoramic view of the lowlands like an old master's painting.

At night it was as if all the life had been sucked out of the scenery, leaving behind a negative image. No longer luscious greens and golds, the filtered moonlight had turned the forest around her dark and threatening. Small noises amplified the squeaks of rodents trapped between an owl's beak, more like the screams of the tormented. The cold night air brushed her cheeks, but a trickle of sweat ran between her shoulder blades. Deep inside, a voice told her to turn back, but the stubborn, self-reliant person she'd become since Hank had died won over. If she didn't face this mischief maker now, she'd be plagued by them for the rest of her life. The flashlight dimmed and she tapped it against one hand and then continued to climb higher.

Soon the path would widen and the plateau above the gully would come into view.

With a narrow beam of light to follow, branches snagged at her clothes and whipped at her cheeks. She blundered through cobwebs and tripped on the uneven path. As she reached the summit her flashlight weakened to a glow and panic gripped her. She slapped it against her palm, but the weak light flickered and died. She shook her head and went to her jacket pocket to pull out her phone. She stared at the blank screen in disbelief. How would she find her way back in the dark? She stared at the sky. It would be past one by now and a long cold wait until sunrise.

A rustling of leaves close by startled her. She slid the rifle from her shoulder and held it high, tucked into one shoulder. "Okay, enough of your games. Come out where I can see you."

Her heart missed a beat as she looked around and, seeing the outline of a man dressed in full combat gear, standing just within the perimeter of the trees, she took aim. "Do you think this is funny?"

"Shoot if you must, but you can't kill someone twice, Christy." A soft chuckle drifted on the breeze, so low she could hardly make it out.

Had the voice come from somewhere behind her? Confused, she scanned the area, moving her rifle in an arc. The chuckling came again and, not wanting to take her eyes off the man in the trees, she took a few steps backward. She glanced to her right and the next second a black shape lunged from the trees on her left and snatched the rifle from her hands and disappeared without a sound. Horrified, she swung her gaze around, but the man in combat gear hadn't moved. The hairs on the back of her neck prickled in warning as the other man stood there taunting her with low chuckles. Defenseless, terror gripped her by the throat and she took another step away from him. This had gone way past a prank. She pulled out the flashlight to use as a weapon. "I'm here like you asked. The Hank I remember would never have frightened me like this. Does it take two cowards to frighten a defenseless widow? This is a very poor Halloween joke."

A cold wind rushed up from the gully, lifting her hair. She glanced over one shoulder and froze in horror at the gaping hole behind her. In the dark she'd ventured too close to the edge of the gully. One more step would mean a fall to certain death, but in front of her she faced an unknown threat. She stared into the blackness. "Okay, you've had your fun. What do you want? Money? Name your price."

Nothing.

Time seemed to stand still as if they enjoyed frightening her. The trees moved in the wind, scattering shadows, and making it impossible to see. Yet, someone had taken her rifle and the military man was still standing in the bushes watching. Trembling, she stared from the military man and back into the dark forest too afraid to move. The next second something came flying toward her and hit her full on the face. Pain shot through her nose and she staggered back. Blood filled her mouth as her feet slipped on the loose soil. Dropping the flashlight, she cartwheeled her arms to regain her balance, grabbing at bushes, anything to regain her footing, but stepped into air and fell backward into nothing. Screaming, she tumbled over and over through the darkness. Seconds later, she seemed to fly with her arms and legs spread out like a skydiver. The sides of the canyon glistened in the moonlight as she landed on her back in a rush of agony and then the pain vanished. She couldn't move, not even her eyes. The sky in all its dark beauty filled her vision. An image of Hank smiling at her flashed across her mind as the stars faded to black.

SEVEN

TUESDAY

The seasons in Black Rock Falls were spectacular and varied. The remarkable change of colors from the lush greens of early summer to an often dry and wildfire-dangerous fall had to be seen to be believed. Jenna had lived through dry Indian summers to cold windy days and misty nights followed by snow. The one thing about living in an alpine region was that snow arrived without warning and she'd wake up to an eerie white light to discover the landscape had changed overnight. Living in this remarkable town had another bonus, the sunsets and sunrises changed their colors during the year. The sunsets and then twilights were something she loved. After work, especially in summer, she had time to take long rides and allow the horses to amble along the trails all through her ranch.

It had been wonderful to discover Kane also enjoyed her love of nature, and driving to the highest point on their ranch just to take photographs of the sunsets or sunrises had been a wonderful distraction from the reality of living in Serial Killer Central. Although, the week before Halloween had started cold and windy, it hadn't prevented the townsfolk from adorning Main and all the local houses with elaborate decorations. Pumpkins, ghouls, skeletons with flashing red eyes, and mutilated corpses uttering moans when people walked by littered the storefronts and front yards. Aunt Betty's Café this year was covered in cobwebs and huge spiders. It had a special menu with pumpkin pie, eyeball tarts, and severed-finger hotdogs. The residents of Black Rock Falls loved Halloween and so did Jenna. She'd embraced it and wallowed in the tradition. Walking through town and watching the faces of the children as they moved from house to house trick-or-treating was a delight, and she wouldn't miss it.

As they turned into Main just before eight, mist swirled across the road to be whipped up into ghostly figures as each vehicle passed by. The shapes moved in a procession along the sidewalk to drift into alleyways and then vanished as the wind whisked them up into the atmosphere. It was as if the mist, which rose from the river from dusk until dawn, was adding its part to the celebrations. It sure made goosebumps rise on her flesh each time she watched it crawl along the sidewalk making anyone walking by appear to float along without legs. Jenna shivered and dragged her attention away from the spooky view to look at Kane. "I'll call a meeting before we drop by Wolfe's office for the autopsy. I want to see if Rowley and Rio have chased down any leads."

"That sounds like a plan." Kane drove into his spot outside the sheriff's department. "You're looking pale again. Is everything okay?"

Jenna pulled her hoodie over her hat and smiled at him. "It's just Halloween. I know it's crazy, but with the mist and all the decorations it's creepy. I love it—but it seems to push up my spooky meter and I start imagining things, is all."

"Imagining what?" Kane cocked one eyebrow at her. "You're not seeing ghosts in slickers and cowboy hats again, are you?"

Jenna pulled a face. "Now that was real and you know it."

She grinned at him. "No, I'm not seeing things. I'm as sane as you are, but I believe in ghosts, which I guess for a sheriff isn't something I'd make public."

"Uh-huh." Kane slid from the truck and opened the back door to allow Duke to jump down. He looked at her. "I guess you'd better head into the office before the Three Horsemen of the Apocalypse ride into town."

Gathering her things, Jenna hurried up the steps as a blast of freezing air caught her open coat and seeped through her clothes, bringing with it tall swirls of mist. She swallowed hard. It was as if a ghost had walked straight through her. "Dave." She turned to look at him.

"Yeah?" He walked to her side with Duke at his heels.

Jenna slipped her arm through his and smiled. "Nothing. I just like you being close."

An unfamiliar noise in the office drifted down to her as she headed for the front desk to greet Maggie. She turned and stared up the stairs to her office with the conference room beyond and blinked. "Do we have visitors, this early?"

"That would be Rowley's twins. Sandy has caught that bug that's going around and so has her mother, so he had to bring the twins into the office. He's set them up in the conference room and said he'd work in there today." Maggie smiled. "I've organized babysitters. Emily is dropping by after the autopsy and her sister Julie will be by after school. He'll only be tied up for an hour or so in between. He said they sleep in the afternoon."

Jenna smiled. She and Kane were godparents to Vannah and Cooper. "Oh, I don't mind them being here at all. I'll go and see them." She turned to Kane. "Can you tell Rio about the meeting? We'll be in the conference room, I think."

"Sure." Kane nodded to Maggie and made his way to Rio's desk.

Jenna found the conference room transformed. One end held two traveling cots and was sectioned off using the barriers she'd seen at Rowley's ranch to prevent the active ten-month-olds from getting into danger. Toys were scattered across a rug and the twins sat in the middle happily chatting away to each other in a language only the two of them understood. They did talk remarkably well for babies and called her, "Dena." She didn't disturb them and turned to find Rowley working on his laptop. "Morning. I figure we'll have the meeting in here today."

"Sorry about the twins." Rowley shrugged. "I'd have taken personal time but I knew you needed me here. Sandy is spewing and her mom isn't well either, so I had no choice."

Jenna smiled at him. "That's fine." She looked over at the twins. "If we're blessed, I'm bringing our baby to the office. I'm planning on hiring a nanny so my work isn't affected too much. That room beside my office is twice the size of this one and I already have the plans to turn it into a nursery. It's bright and the right size for a bunch of kids to run around. I figure child-care is essential for a working family and it will be available to anyone in the department."

"I figure Sandy would make a great nanny." Rowley grinned at her. "She has the qualifications to run a kindergarten. She'd completed a course before we were married. It had always been a dream of hers but then we married and the twins came along. Caring for them is a full-time job in itself."

She glanced up as Kane and Rio, with Duke trailing behind, came into the room. To her surprise, Kane stepped over the barrier and sat on the floor to chat with the twins. She watched him dance teddy bears and sing a nursery rhyme before she turned back to the others. "Okay what have you got for me?"

"The meds came from Doc Brown. I went to see him, and after some persuasion, he informed me that he'd given Willow Smith one prescription for phenobarbital eight months ago and another recently. She'd had antibiotics but nothing else signifi-cant. She was in good health. So, we can assume the bottle held two-hundred capsules, less what she took the first night, and the bottle found beside the bed was empty. I checked the house for drugs and apart from Tylenol the place was clean." Rio frowned. "Phenobarbital is a medication rarely prescribed for sedation these days, mainly because it's too easy to overdose. It was popular at one time but now I figured it was used for epilepsy."

Jenna blinked. "How do you know so much about drugs?"

"Oh, I've been reading autopsy reports going back to the mid-1960s." Rio shrugged. "I find them interesting. Phenobarbital was given out like candy and many people overdosed, mainly because they mixed it with other drugs. Which makes me wonder why Doc Brown would prescribe that drug when there's a ton of safer drugs available now."

"Did you ask him?" Kane left the twins and sat at the long table.

"No." Rio straightened. "It's not my place to question an MD about his prescribing practices. I figured that question should be asked by Wolfe. Him being a doctor and all."

"I'm sure he'll look right into it. Old autopsies, huh? Some of the old Hollywood stars' deaths are interesting. They sure did things differently back then. Thank God for DNA." Kane shook his head and made notes.

"I've filed the statement from Marsha Walker, the woman who found her dead." Rio scrolled through his files. "She arrived to collect Mrs. Smith, went inside. The door is never locked and she called out, got no answer. Went upstairs and found her dead. She touched Willow Smith's cheek, found her to be cold. She went straight outside and called 911." He glanced up at Jenna. "She mentioned Willow had been receiving calls at midnight. She figured it was a prank."

"Thanks. We'll go and speak to her." Jenna looked from one to the other. "Okay, moving right along. Rowley did you find the carrier for Willow Smith's landline and get them to send over her call records?"

"Yeah, I'm looking at them now." Rowley glanced up from his screen. "They've only just arrived."

Impatient, Jenna twirled her pen through her fingers and stared at him. "Did she receive a call at midnight over the last few days as she claimed?"

"One second." Rowley scrolled through the screen. "Yeah, three calls on the landline and all from her number." He raised his eyebrows. "That can't be right, can it?"

"A burner phone often displays the number it's calling on the caller ID." Kane glanced up from his screen. "It's another reason why they're untraceable, and if a person did know the number, most people using a burner toss it into the trash after they've used it once."

Jenna's phone chimed and she glanced at the caller ID. It was Carter. "Morning, Ty. Do you have anything for me today?"

"Morning, Jenna, I figure you have me on speaker, so I'll need to speak to Kane when we're done here. It's a private matter." Carter sounded agitated and a scrape of a chair and then footsteps on tile came through the speaker. *"Kalo found two apparent suicides involving the wives of enlisted men last Halloween. One in Helena and the other in Louan. The one in Louan had a twist: Both mother and daughter took their own lives."* He cleared his throat. *"My concern is why this is happening in Montana. Seal teams comprise men from all over the US, not from one state. I do have a theory, but it touches on classified information, which I'm unable to divulge."*

Jenna shot a long meaningful glance at Kane. "Okay, send me what details you can and we'll chase down a link between them... if there is one." She handed her phone to Kane. "Don't forget we have an autopsy at ten."

"I'm all over it." Kane stood and left the room.

Running through her notes, Jenna turned to Rowley. "Okay, when the details come in about those cases, see what you can find and hunt down Willow Smith's friends. We'll need to speak to them." She smiled at the twins playing happily and looked back at him. "If the twins get restless, call Deputy Walters and ask him to take over the research. The twins take priority, so take what time you need."

"Once they've eaten, they'll sleep for a time." Rowley held up crossed fingers. "They're not teething right now and seem content. I shouldn't be held up for too long getting them fed and settled. Later Emily and Julie will take turns helping out."

"That works for me and order takeout for lunch. Put it on the tab." Jenna turned to Rio. "You'll want to be at the autopsy?"

"Yeah, but I'll help out here if you need me." Rio frowned. "I can work fine from Wolfe's findings."

Jenna checked her watch and collected her things. "That's why we have Walters on standby. He might be semiretired but he's always there when we need him. You might as well head off now. I'll wait for Kane."

"Sure." Rio closed his laptop and looked at her. "I hope Wolfe finds some answers."

Jenna slipped past him and hurried to her office. Kane would be inside speaking to Carter, and she leaned against the wall and waited for him to finish. The door opened and Kane beckoned her inside. She shut the door behind her and stared at him. "What?"

"The wives were married to the men in the same team." Kane dashed a hand through his hair. "The one that vanished on Halloween night."

Jenna stared at him in disbelief. "Oh, please don't tell me Kalo hacked the Department of Defense?"

"No, Carter couldn't risk sending up red flags by allowing Kalo to hack classified documents. These cases were sealed for a reason and we can't go there." Kane lifted his black Stetson from the desk and slid it on. "Kalo found another way. He hunted down the lists of military burials around the time Oliver Smith was buried and cross-referenced them to the names of the women who'd taken their own lives."

Jenna shrugged. "That doesn't prove these men were in the mysterious vanishing team. You don't have their names apart from Oliver Smith, do you?"

"I have a photograph of the team. I copied it from an album in Willow's house and probably broke every rule in the book by sending it to Kalo." Kane narrowed his gaze. "Bobby used the women's last names to do a photo ID match. That's how he found the connection." He frowned. "Before you ask, no he hasn't gotten the names of the other team members yet. It's a work in progress and, with no information at all, he's flying blind. Carter assures me Kalo will find them, but it means searching databases across the country. These guys could have come from any state."

Running the information through her mind, Jenna leaned against the desk thinking. She glanced up at Kane. "Which makes me wonder why three of the wives decided to settle in Montana after their husbands died?"

"I was trying to figure that out too." Kane scratched his cheek. "There's only Malmstrom Air Force Base in Montana, so they wouldn't have been stationed here. That's not saying they couldn't have spent time here. A hunting vacation, fishing, or whatever. The teams are like brothers and it wouldn't be out of the question."

"We know Oliver Smith was raised here and Willow too, so he might have encouraged the members of his team to visit. If they did vacation in Montana, the chances of meeting their wives here would have been a possibility and where do women usually go if their husbands die?" Jenna straightened. "They go home to their friends and family."

"Uh-huh." Kane pushed his phone inside his pocket and then reached for their jackets. "Willow's close friends will know, and I found old letters at the house. Finding them was gold, especially if they're from before she married Oliver. I'll take a closer look at the photo album too. There were tons of group shots with Oliver and Willow along with his team. We should recognize areas around or in Black Rock Falls, and then we'll know at least some of them visited Montana."

EIGHT

Dr. Shane Wolfe stared at the results on his screen and shook his head. Nothing was adding up in the Willow Smith case. Blood tests don't lie and are often the frontline in the search for the truth in homicide cases. As ME, if he noticed an irregularity by an MD that led to death, it was his duty to investigate and report any suspicious findings to the state medical board. Somewhat reluctantly, he reached for his phone and called Doc Brown. He gave his name to the receptionist, mentioned it was urgent, and waited some time before the doctor picked up. "Morning. One of your patients, Willow Smith out of Twisted Tree Ridge, is currently in the morgue awaiting autopsy. I found an empty bottle of phenobarbital at the scene, prescribed by you. Did you at any time consider Mrs. Smith to be suicidal?"

"Suicidal?" Doc Brown was obviously shocked by the news. *"Not a chance. She came by a couple of days ago. She'd stepped on a nail and I gave her a prescription for antibiotics as a precaution. Her shots were up to date. She was chatting about a trip to Las Vegas over Halloween. She was excited and happy. She needed something to help her sleep, is all."*

Wolfe listened intently. The elderly doctor was well liked in town. He cleared his throat. "Why did you prescribe pheno-barbital?"

"She was suffering anxiety again. Her husband died at Halloween and I considered it appropriate at the time."

Wolfe rolled his eyes to the ceiling. "I'm wondering why you prescribed an outdated drug to this patient when there are more suitable and safer medications on the market. Was there any particular reason to use this drug?"

"I don't recall a particular reason. I've prescribed it many a time with no problems at all." Doc Brown's chair creaked and fingers could be heard drumming on the table.

Staring at the blood results on his screen, Wolfe bit back a snort of anger. "Well, let's hope no more of your patients end up in the morgue from an overdose. You know any cases of suspicious deaths I find are forwarded to the Montana Board of Medical Examiners for review. Thank you kindly for your time." He disconnected and pushed to his feet with a sigh.

Voices in the hallway announced the arrival of Jenna and Kane. He opened his office door to see Rio following them along the passageway. "You're ten minutes early." He smiled at them. "Slow day?" He waved them toward an examination room. "Get suited up. We'll be in examination room two today."

He swiped his ID and the doors whooshed open. His assistant and badge-holding deputy, Colt Webber, had everything prepared. He gave him a nod and slipped into a plastic apron. The smell from the chilled body crawled up his nose. He'd never get used to the smell of an autopsy and was actually glad that sensory adaptation to his work environment hadn't occurred. Some odors were important pointers to know how a person had died. The phenomenon was quite common. Many people adapted to smell and often lived in stink in their own homes without realizing just how bad it was. One killer, many years ago, placed the bodies of the women he'd murdered in the walls and under the floorboards of his home. He'd gone about his daily life, sleeping and eating apparently unaware of the stench of death seeping through the walls.

He glanced at the sheet-covered body with only the bluish discolored toes and obligatory toe tag showing. The day he'd viewed Willow Smith, there'd been no odors. The woman appeared to be asleep. That in itself sent up a red flag. He reached for the medicated salve and swiped some under his nose, pushed on a face mask, and pulled on surgical gloves. He went to the screen array and pulled up the X-rays he'd taken of the victim, plus MRI images and crime scene photographs. He turned as the door opened and Jenna and her team walked in. "Y'all be wondering why my first instinct about this case was homicide."

"You've mentioned not finding undissolved pills in her stomach." Jenna leaned against the counter. "Rio told me just before that phenobarbital isn't used much and it doesn't take a great quantity to kill. She could have just dissolved the pills in the drink. How would we know?"

Wolfe peered at her over the top of his mask. The way Jenna's mind worked intrigued him. She covered all angles. "I don't have all the toxicology reports back yet, but I know the concentration of the drug in the chocolate drink would substantiate the entire bottle would have been dissolved. At first, the scene itself wasn't right. In the majority of cases involving an overdose, the dying isn't easy. Once a ton of pills hit the stomach, most will vomit and experience cramping in the legs and they're usually found in a fetal or distorted position. I found Willow with her head on the pillow, arms across her chest and legs straight as if she'd been posed. There was no sign of vomit or bodily fluids, which in itself is unusual."

"You mentioned finding bed linen in the dryer." Kane's brow wrinkled. "Do you figure someone cleaned up the crime scene?"

"And washed the sheets?" Jenna's eyes grew round. "He cared how she looked when she was found. So, he isn't a psychopath or he'd just kill and leave. This shows empathy toward his victim."

"I don't agree. That's cold and calculated." Kane shook his head. "The killer wanted it to look like a suicide, all nice and neat. He expected her to go to sleep and die. I figure he hasn't tried this method of killing before. Maybe when she started spewing, he panicked."

Loving the discussion, Wolfe nodded. "I knew you would come around to my way of thinking." He turned to the screens. "All indications show she's in the normal parameters for a woman of her age. I did an MRI, taking particular note of her brain. She's been having hallucinations, hearing things, and seeing ghosts according to her friend."

"What did you find?" Jenna moved to his side. "Her house was kinda spooky."

Wolfe pointed to the MRI scans on a screen. "There's nothing to indicate any problems with her brain. No tumors or blood clots. I've run a tox screen for specific hallucinogenic substances, including toadstools and plants, but the thing with ingesting a hallucinogenic is the hallucinations don't just happen at night. They'd be causing her problems at other times as well." He shrugged. "I asked specifically if Willow had mentioned seeing things at other times and her friend confirmed that she'd only ever mentioned seeing her husband's ghost at night."

"I know the results will take time." Jenna folded her arms across her chest. "We're stuck between a rock and a hard place if we can't get information on her husband's team. The files are sealed. We can't even get names." She flicked a glance at Kane. "Why isn't it the same as the 'once you're dead you don't have any rights' rule?"

"Why are you looking at me?" Kane shrugged. "I don't have all the answers, Jenna."

"Well, we can't even make up a suspects list without knowing the couple's friends." She turned back to Wolfe. "How can I make a case against anyone?"

Wolfe wasn't sure if the murder of the wife of a man MIA would be reason to open a sealed file. He opened his hands. "I can't give you a solution, Jenna. You can't really pin this on anyone in the military, there's no proof. It could be anyone with an ax to grind with Willow Smith, someone to inherit her money, perhaps. The only choice you have if you insist on heading down the military path for suspects, is to chase down the men and women who signed up at the same time as her husband. If they all went through boot camp together, they might know something."

"I'm convinced it's someone in the military. Kane will explain my theory later to you. Maybe I can discover if any of them left the service and now live in Montana." Jenna nodded slowly and stared at him. "Is there any reason we need to be here for the completion of the autopsy?" She shrugged. "It seems to me we have all the relevant information we need until further results show."

Wolfe nodded. "I'd say, from the initial findings, the cause of death would indicate an overdose administered by persons unknown. I'll complete a full examination to exclude any other causes and call you if I discover anything."

"Thanks." Jenna turned to Rio. "Head back to the office and assist Rowley." She looked at Kane. "I'll wait in Wolfe's office for you."

Wolfe nodded. "Have a coffee while you're waiting. I have a new pod flavor to try. Get at it."

"I will. Thanks. I love trying new flavors." Jenna walked out, peeling off her gloves.

Concerned that Kane might want to divulge sensitive information, he glanced at Webber. "Go call the lab and tell them I want to know the second the results come through for Willow Smith's bloods."

He waited for Webber to leave and turned to Kane. "Okay, what's going on here?"

"Kalo found three apparent suicides in Montana." Kane stared at him over his face mask. "One is a mother and daughter. All were married to men who went MIA. We discovered they belonged to the same darn team that went MIA over Halloween."

Alarmed, Wolfe walked to the door and hit the locking mechanism. If anyone overheard their conversation and repeated it, all hell would break loose. He spun around to stare at Kane. "Have you lost your mind? Did you ask Kalo to hack the files?"

"Nope." Kane leaned nonchalantly against the counter. "The information came from a general search. If what happened to these men is classified, then all the paraphernalia surrounding them should have been destroyed." He shook his head. "I found photographs of Oliver Smith's team at the house. Kalo chased down military funerals around the time Oliver Smith was buried. All it took to discover their names was to use the dead women's last names and run the team images through facial recognition." He shrugged. "We don't have the entire team, only those buried at the same time as Smith."

Shaking his head in disbelief, Wolfe stared into space to get his head around the information Kane had dumped on him. "So, you'll need me to discover proof of foul play and to reopen the cases. It won't be a problem to access the autopsy reports and case files. If I believe they're homicides and related to the Smith case, I'll be able to request exhumation orders for the women buried in other counties within Montana. I'll finish up here and then get at it." He thought for a beat. "You'll need Jo and Carter. You don't have jurisdiction in the other counties."

"We've asked other counties to share information before without a problem. I could ask them to send over the case files. It would save time." Kane removed his face mask and gloves. "Don't you figure they'd cooperate?"

Wolfe lifted one shoulder. "You could run into roadblocks if you disagree with the local law enforcement's findings. Not every sheriff is as cooperative as Jenna."

"Okay. I'll call Carter and you'll need a forensic anthropologist. Will Dr. Norrell Larson be available at short notice?" Kane pulled a wipe from a packet on the bench and rubbed the salve from under his nose.

Wolfe gave him a long stare. "There y'all go again jumping the gun." He shook his head. "First, I'll request the case files and autopsy reports of the alleged victims and study the findings. I'll need a darn good reason to ask a judge to issue an exhumation order. I don't figure the relatives will be too happy either, so don't expect it to happen overnight." He cleared his throat. "If and when we get the order, then I'll call Norrell. I'll need her team to supervise the exhumations and conduct the necessary examinations. I'll be there as well and between us we'll determine causes of death."

"Time is an issue, Shane. If we had the names of the other men in the team, we might save the next victim. It will be someone living local, that's for darn sure."

Wolfe walked to the gurney and pulled back the sheet. He stared at Kane. "Four possible homicides might make the right people listen to me. They know I have the clearance to handle sensitive information discreetly. I'll see what I can do." He looked at Kane and shook his head. "Making waves is dangerous."

"How so?" Kane narrowed his gaze. "Not a soul suspects either of us are anything different than a deputy and an ME."

Overwhelmed with the concern for his friend's safety, Wolfe stared at him. "When you were missing in Florida, I called it in. You're an asset and always will be. The knowledge you have inside your head could bring down governments even twenty years from now even if the slightest word got out." He rubbed the back of his neck. "Problem was that the contact on my secure line wasn't known to me. He sure as hell knew who Ninety-eight H was and wanted details. I disconnected and nuked the SIM but they had my code name." He leveled his gaze on Kane. "I couldn't risk calling anyone and made the trip to the White House to speak directly to POTUS. You have no idea how long they kept me waiting. I spoke to the press secretary, as he knows me on sight, and we went from there."

"Why haven't you mentioned this before?" Kane stared at him expressionless.

Wolfe stared right back at him. "Because I handled it. They discovered three rogues in our chain of command. The problem is every time I asked for a favor, it triggered an alarm. Agents good and bad were trying to figure out where the money was going and who was getting private jets, choppers, and huge budgets to run a nonmilitary facility. So, to avoid attention, we've been delegated to the black budget. Our funding is off the books and Black Rock Falls might as well be Area 51. We have a new contact, Blue Angel Five, for emergencies. You go through me as usual unless I'm compromised."

"These rogues, how much information did they get out?" Kane's brow furrowed. "Is Jenna in danger?"

Wolfe sighed. "Unknown. As you know, our agents are trained to the highest level, which means extracting information from them is practically impossible." He gave Kane a long look. "I don't have to tell you to watch your back, Dave, but these murders are too darn close to home."

"You think they're using the wives of guys MIA to set a trap for me?" Kane snorted. "One man or maybe two using women as collateral damage to lure me into a trap? What then? Do they figure they can capture me and make me talk? That's never gonna happen, Shane."

Over the last few weeks of constantly worrying about Kane's and Jenna's cover, Wolfe had considered every option including relocation. "Your life has changed. You have Jenna now and friends you never had before. These people would stop at nothing to capture you, including using your loved ones as bargaining chips. The bounty alone would be millions."

"They don't know where I am or what I look like." Kane rolled his shoulders. "I'm living in a town with a ton of men my size. If they did discover I live here, I don't figure they'd imagine I'd be living in plain sight. I've never backed down from a fight, Shane. If they plan to come into my town and take me down, well, they're going to discover I don't go down so easy. That's for darn sure."

Wolfe took in the set of Kane's shoulders, the steel determination in his eyes. He'd yet to see anyone intimidate him. "Okay, I'll make a few calls but watch your back."

NINE

It wasn't too difficult to read Kane's mood as Jenna climbed into the truck. "I'm guessing it didn't go too well."

"You could say that." Kane drummed his fingers on the steering wheel. "He figures we're creeping around the edges of legality and bringing attention to ourselves, which is dangerous." He turned to her. "He'll look into the other deaths. He might find enough evidence to reopen the cases. We'll have to wait and see."

Jenna snorted. "We don't have time to wait and see." She blew out a sigh. "Okay, while you were busy, I chased down the woman who found Willow. She's a stay-at-home mom, so we'll drop by and see what she can tell us about Willow Smith's friends." She added the coordinates to the GPS. "She's on Maple, so we can drop by Aunt Betty's for lunch on the way back to the office."

"Well, that will sure improve my day." Kane smiled at her and then shook his head. "You know, I can't get over Wolfe being my handler. He may be my best friend, but on the job, he's still a hard-ass. I've had four-stars assisting me in investigations, but I can't speak to them now that I'm officially dead... but I need solutions."

Frowning, Jenna stared at him. Something was wrong. She sensed anger boiling under the surface. "Wolfe offers solutions all the time. What's eating at you, Dave? It's not Wolfe, is it?"

"I guess not." Kane turned into Main and slowed as men carrying skeletons walked across the road. "If you work on the theory that one or more of the men MIA are alive, and maybe one of them is murdering their teammate's wives, it just goes against the code. I hate traitors, is all."

Jenna went through the glovebox searching for a statement book. "What code?"

"The unspoken code we have for each other in the military. I was more of a lone wolf, but when I used a spotter, I had his back and he had mine. Carter was in a Seal team. Those guys would take a bullet for each other, and if any of them died, making sure that their wives and kids were taken care of was a given." Kane hunched his shoulders. "Even contemplating there's a rogue out there seems impossible. I can't get my head around it. It shouldn't happen."

As they pulled to the curb outside a tidy red-brick, missing the extravagant Halloween decorations preferred by its neighbor, Jenna sucked in a deep breath. "It was just a theory. Maybe talking with Marsha Walker will shed some light on the case."

"I sure hope so." Kane climbed out of the Beast and looked at her across the hood. "Remind me to pick up something for Duke from Aunt Betty's. He'll be wanting a snack by the time we get back to the office."

Jenna chuckled. "I'm sure Maggie has that covered." She tucked the statement book under one arm and headed for Marsha Walker's front door.

She stood to one side as Kane rapped on the door. When a woman in her late thirties appeared, Jenna smiled at her. "Marsha Walker? I'm Sherriff Alton and this is Deputy Kane.

We're following up on the death of Willow Smith. Do you have the time to answer a few questions?"

"Yes, I'm Marsha Walker. Come in. I've just put on a pot of coffee." Marsha stood to one side and made a waving motion with one hand. "Straight down the hallway. The kitchen is okay, I hope?"

"That will be fine, ma'am." Kane led the way.

"Oh and watch out for Toby." Mrs. Walker gave Jenna an apologetic stare. "He's all bark and no bite."

A small mixed-breed dog charged down the hallway toward them, claws clicking against the polished wooden floor, hackles raised, all teeth and bulging eyes. It was barking up a storm. Jenna stopped in her tracks, but Kane just pointed at the dog and make a hissing sound. The little dog slid to a halt and then stared at him, sat down and didn't make a sound.

"Well, would you look at that?" Mrs. Walker bent to pick up the dog. "Toby doesn't like strangers and he doesn't usually stop barking."

Jenna stared at Mrs. Walker. "Deputy Kane has a way with dogs."

"I figure Toby has met his match, is all." Mrs. Walker chuckled. "He's trembling."

The house had the general untidiness of a house filled with kids. Discarded shoes and toys littered most areas. The smell of fresh coffee drifted from the kitchen and spotless benches sparkled in the sunlight streaming from the windows. Photographs, reminders, and other paraphernalia covered the refrigerator door. Jenna dropped a statement book on the kitchen table. "Do you mind if we sit down?"

"Go right ahead." Mrs. Walker deposited the dog on the floor and pulled cups from a shelf. She poured three cups of coffee and placed the fixings on the table. "It was a terrible shock finding Willow like that. I've never seen a dead body before." She pulled out a chair and sat down.

"How long have you known Willow?" Kane added the fixings to his cup.

"Since she moved to Black Rock Falls." Mrs. Walker added sugar to her coffee and stirred it slowly. "The house next door has been a rental for as long as I've been here. Willow and Oliver often stayed there for vacations. I met up with her again in Aunt Betty's Café when she inherited the house out at Twisted Tree Ridge."

Making notes, Jenna looked up at her. "Did she ever mention the reason she returned to Black Rock Falls after her husband went missing in action? She wasn't from around here originally, was she?"

"Nope out of Colorado. She won a scholarship to Montana State and made friends with a group of girls. One of them was seeing a Marine and she met Oliver on a blind date. They both married their Marines and lived on base, but Oliver and Hank being locals came here regular to hunt and fish, and Willow and Christy would come along with them." Mrs. Walker sighed. "They came to look over the house and sign the paperwork. The estate was handled by James Stone. You recall that lawyer who went bad?"

Swallowing hard and trying to push the memory of discharging her weapon at the murdering psychopath James Stone as a wildfire raged at her back, she nodded. "Yeah, I do. Please go on."

"Willow didn't know her aunt and was very surprised the estate didn't go to her cousins out of Blackwater. I figure it caused friction between them, because I called them this morning and they didn't seem interested in making funeral arrangements. They didn't seem to care she'd died at all." Eyes welling with tears, Mrs. Walker stared at her coffee cup and then back at Jenna. "What will happen to her now?"

"You needn't concern yourself with that. If they're her next of kin, then they're responsible. Leave it to us." Kane sipped his coffee. "We'll need to find her will. Whoever inherits her estate will be responsible for her burial. Did she ever mention which lawyer she was using?"

"Well, yes." Mrs. Walker looked surprised. "She went to see Samuel J. Cross recently about another matter, I believe. She mentioned he was the most unusual lawyer she's ever spoken to." She smiled. "She mentioned the cowboy hat, long hair, and boots. It was everything that she doesn't like about a man, but she found him incredibly charming and helpful."

Wondering how anyone could find Sam Cross charming, Jenna raised an eyebrow. "That's very helpful. Thank you. Do you know many of her other friends? Had you planned the trip to Vegas with a number of people?"

"Four of us were going." Mrs. Walker pulled a tissue from her pocket and dabbed at her damp eyes. "It had taken such a lot of planning. I had to make arrangements for my children for the week, same with Susan Watson, Willow and Christy don't work or have children. Of course, everyone is upset by what has happened. I know suicide has been mentioned, but I can't imagine why Willow would kill herself. She was excited about going to Vegas. We all were."

Jenna made a ton of notes and lifted her gaze back to her. "Is Christy the same person she knew at school?"

"Yeah. Christy Miller. She lives out of Death Drop Gully. She moved there after her husband died too. I believe Hank and Oliver were in the same regiment or whatever. The girls didn't say what their husbands did in the military, but I do know that Hank and Oliver went missing in action at the same time over Halloween."

"When was the last time that you spoke to Christy?" Kane gave Jenna a meaningful stare and then leaned back in his chair, making it creak.

"I called her and the others just after I found Willow. I was supposed to collect everyone and take them to the airport. I had to explain why I wouldn't be there." Mrs. Walker frowned. "I called Christy this morning, but she wasn't picking up."

A cold feeling crawled up Jenna's spine. "Does she live alone?"

"Yeah, she does. She would often visit the old house up there with Hank. It was built a very long time ago. Their dream was to purchase it and restore it to its former glory. Christy made that dream come true. Although, she doesn't often leave the house unless it's to go to the top of the gully to paint. She comes into town for some art classes occasionally, or when we can get together for a meal at Aunt Betty's Café." She wiped her eyes. "If she's not answering her phone, she'll be above the gully. There's a plateau there where she can set up her easel."

"And the other friend, Susan Watson?" Kane narrowed his gaze. "Does she have ties to the military?"

"No, she's married to a rancher." Mrs. Walker blinked a few times and cleared her throat. "I spoke to Susan this morning outside the school. She was heading to the general store."

Jenna had thought long and hard during the ride over about how to phrase the question of Willow's apparent hallucinations. She took a deep breath and looked at the emotional woman. "Did Willow ever mention to you about seeing ghosts in the house?"

"Yeah, she did and so did Christy the last time I spoke to her." Mrs. Walker sniffed. "I figured it was due to Halloween. They didn't mention it happening before. Willow said she could smell Oliver in the house and hear him walking around." She shuddered. "The old house she was living in creaked and whined all the time. It was the same with Christy. This is why she decided to go on the trip with us. Over the last week or so, she'd convinced herself that Hank was haunting the house. She said something about getting phone calls. I told her it was probably kids calling people at random to spook them." She shrugged. "Why she would even consider that her husband was haunting the house when she had renovated it from top to bottom makes no sense at all." She looked at Jenna with sad eyes. "I figured it was Willow putting suggestions into her mind. I've dropped by Christy's house many a time and never found anything creepy about it at all. I can't say the same for the museum that Willow lived in. It was like going back in time."

Suddenly having the urgent need to contact Christy, Jenna pushed the pad across the table to Mrs. Walker. Christy could be the link to the other men they've been chasing down. She would be able to give them a list of the other women in the group of friends at Montana State. She just hoped that they'd find her alive and well. If this was a serial killer they were chasing down, it might already be too late for Christy Miller. "Could you please read through my notes and sign them as a true record of our talk today? Also, can you give me Christy's details. I'd like to speak to her as well."

"That's fine." Mrs. Walker read over the statement, signed it at the bottom, and then added Christy's details. "If you need any more information, I'll be glad to help you."

Jenna stood. "Thanks for the coffee. We can see ourselves out." She gathered her things and headed down the passageway to the front door with Kane on her heels.

She turned as they reached the curb and touched his arm. "I'm concerned about Christy Miller. Death Drop Gully is some ways away. There's a road into the forest but it's a hike to the top. Most of the buildings are hunting cabins. We might be able to use a fire road to get closer but I'm not sure where her house is located. I don't recall anyone mentioning a big house up that way. If so, I figure it would be at the end of a private road."

"If she's an artist, it makes sense she might be out painting somewhere around the gully. There are a ton of picturesque areas of Stanton Forest and I know from speaking to Julie Wolfe that she often hikes all over the mountain with the local group of artists, sketching and photographing scenery." Kane pulled open the door to the Beast. "If you want to hike up there, we need to eat first and gather supplies. We'll need to bundle up and take our backpacks, bear spray, and a rifle, just in case we meet up with a hungry bear who decides we look just fine for dinner."

Unable to shake the gut feeling something wasn't right about Christy Miller, Jenna climbed into the Beast and stowed the statement book back in the glovebox. It was howling up a storm. High gusty winds often came around over Halloween. They might blow away the flow of mist from the river, but they cut through clothes like a knife made from ice. The icy chill would get through everything. She strapped in and leaned back with a sigh. "We've gotten a ton of information from Mrs. Walker. Now we have a clearer picture of how Oliver Smith's team came to know so many women from Montana."

"Yeah, if he'd met up with Willow and her friends on a furlough, he wouldn't have kept them secret from his team." Kane smiled at her. "They'd have planned a vacation during their downtime for sure and met up again. If any of them became serious, then of course, as you said before, when they went MIA, most women would return home. They'd want to be close to family, especially if they had kids. With the entire team MIA, they wouldn't have the support from the other members that usually happens when a member of the team is KIA." He flicked her a glance. "There's a Seal's foundation and many forms of assistance available, but that connection they have with members of the team would be missing. It would be very hard, and I'm not surprised the women stayed close together, in the same town or close by. Think of our team, what we do in our downtime, the cookouts, the hunting and fishing. It's much the same. The wives, families, and girlfriends are close."

Lost in thought of how terrible it would be to lose a member of their team, Jenna stared out of the window. "We have something in common with those women. We both left tragedy behind and came here not knowing anyone. It's hard to start over without a friend in the world, isn't it?"

"I figure you need a purpose to live." Kane turned into Main and pulled up outside Aunt Betty's Café. "I don't figure anyone should hide away and stop communicating. It seems to me this is what's happened, which means they didn't want any assistance from anyone. It would have been easy for me to close down and give up, but Wolfe was on my case, about some sheriff who needed my help. He didn't give me details, but insisted you were in danger and I was the only person he trusted to keep you safe." He chuckled. "Turned out he was right, huh?"

Jenna scowled at him. "I can take care of myself just fine." She zipped up her jacket. "I managed for two years before you arrived, but I admit having you around has its advantages."

"Uh-huh." Kane indicated to the spiderwebs draped around the front door of Aunt Betty's with his chin. "Watch out for the spiders. I'm sure I saw one of them move." He slipped out of the truck and hurried inside.

Smiling, Jenna watched him go. He always kept their conversation upbeat after an autopsy. She figured it was his way of dealing with death. She slid from the Beast and followed him into the diner. The smell of pulled pork filled the room and she could hear Kane's stomach growling in appreciation over the hum of conversation. She walked up behind him and peered at the specials menu. Her mouth watered at the selection and waited for Wendy, the assistant manager, to take their order. "The pulled-pork stacked potato with honey carrots and pan-fried mushrooms." She stared at the apple pies cooling on the racks. "Oh, and apple pie."

"Your appetite is improving. That's good. You can't go starving yourself before winter." Kane smiled at her and turned to Wendy. "I'll have the same but make mine two potatoes." He smiled. "Coffee too and I'll need takeout to go. Sandwiches and coffee in a Thermos for two. We're heading up the mountain."

"Sure, I'll have everything ready." Wendy smiled. "It won't be long."

Inhaling the tempting aromas, Jenna headed for their table at the back of the diner. She removed her jacket and sat down. "I'm not starving myself, Dave. I figure I had the bug going around. Unlike you, I seem to pick up everything."

"Your shots are up to date and we haven't been near anyone who's sick." Kane's gaze moved over her face. "You look better now too. Maybe it was something you ate?"

Jenna shrugged. "I feel fine now and just starving." She thought for a beat. "While we're waiting for our meal, I'll call Christy Miller. If she's okay, it will save us a long drive." She made the call but it went straight to voicemail. "This is Sheriff Jenna Alton. Would you please give me a call? Thank you." She disconnected. "Hmm, she's still not answering her phone."

"If she's painting, it would take all day." Kane smiled as Wendy poured two cups of coffee and placed the pot on the table. "She'd hike up the mountain and head back down before dark."

Jenna added the fixings to her coffee and stirred. "I still want to go and speak to her. I have this nagging feeling something isn't right. Living up there all alone, anything could happen."

The food arrived and they sat in silence for a time just enjoying the meal. She'd just finished the pulled-pork delight and was reaching for her pie when Kane's phone sounded an alarm and all hell broke loose. Outside, the Beast lit up with lights and sirens blasted. It was so loud Jenna couldn't hear what Kane was saying. She raised her voice. "What's happening?"

"Someone is trying to steal the Beast." Kane rolled his eyes, put down his fork, and stood.

Jenna followed him to the door. She turned to Wendy. "We'll be back to eat our pie."

Outside, Kane stared into his truck his expression like thunder. He used his phone to stop the noise and pulled open the door. Jenna moved to his side and stared at the sheet-white round-eyed youth. It was unusual for people to steal vehicles in Black Rock Falls. It happened but not often. She glanced at Kane. "He's just a kid."

"He's a thief." Kane leaned into the truck. "What kind of stupid steals a deputy's truck?"

"I didn't know it was a police vehicle." The young man pushed a lock of greasy hair into his hoodie. "You left it unlocked."

"Obviously, I don't need to lock it, do I?" Kane grabbed him by the arm and pulled him out. "What's your name and where do you live?"

"I don't have to tell you anything." The boy gave him a belligerent stare. "I want a lawyer."

"Fine." Kane stared at him. "When did you last eat?"

"I don't recall." The boy stared at his feet.

Catching Kane's interpretation of the incident, Jenna waved a hand toward Aunt Betty's Café. "We're right in the middle of eating our meal. Come inside and I'll get you something to eat and we'll talk. If you're in trouble, you came to the right place. We might hunt down criminals, but we also help people."

"That doesn't mean you're getting away with trying to steal my truck." Kane glared at him. "Right now, you need a darn good excuse to get back on my good side. Get inside the diner before I change my mind about feeding you." He dropped the boy's arm and used his phone to rearm his truck.

Confused, Jenna stared at the Beast and then back to Kane. "What just happened?" She raised one eyebrow. "How come it doesn't go apeshit when I open the door?"

"Smart keys. Our smartphones are programmed to identify the owner. It doesn't need a key to start it does it?" Kane smiled at her. "After Duke was taken from the back seat, I increased the security." He cleared his throat. "No one touches my wife, my dog, or my truck." He flicked her a glance. "Your phone gives you access, so does Wolfe's just in case."

Jenna stared at him. "And you didn't tell me this, why?"

"Don't sweat the small things, Jenna." Kane waved her inside. "What are we going to do with that boy?"

After a good deal of food, the boy gave his name as Jimmy Drew, a thirteen-year-old runaway from foster care in Blackwater. Seeing the condition of his clothes and shoes, Jenna assumed he'd been on his own for some time, but when she discovered he'd left three days earlier and hitched a ride on a truck into town just the day before, the lights and sirens going off on the Beast didn't come close to the warning bells sounding in her head. She'd seen the tragic results of unsupervised foster homes. Montana had a good reputation for the management of foster care and seeing this kid in poor condition troubled her. She moved away from the table and called Father Derry. He ran the homeless shelters in town and was also involved in the Her Broken Wings Foundation, a home for battered women and their children. She asked him to care for the boy for a short time, while she sorted out what to do with him. In normal circumstances, she'd call social services at once, but sending him back to his current foster care wasn't an option. She noticed Kane was making headway with the boy and returned to the table to listen in.

"Where were you planning on heading in my truck?" Kane leaned back in his chair and sipped his coffee.

"I wanted to find my mom." Jimmy flicked a glance at Jenna. "They took my brother and me away from her when she lost her job. They said it would be for a week or so, but it's been six months. I ran away to look for him. When they took us, I heard them mention Black Rock Falls and hitched rides until I got here. I've been sleeping in different barns and taking eggs from chicken coops. I hung around the school looking for my brother, but I haven't seen him. I was heading back home to find my mom."

Concerned, Jenna leaned forward. "Was that all that happened? Be truthful now. We're here to help not make judgements. Was your mom on drugs? Anything else we should know about what happened?"

"No, she's so not into drugs." Jimmy shook his head. "She lectures us all the time about them. My pa walked out a year ago. He emptied the bank accounts and left Mom with five bucks in her purse. We don't have any family to go to, but she worked two jobs to pay for everything and then she got sick and lost her jobs. It wasn't her fault." He looked wildly at Kane. "They took her to the free clinic and then they took us away. I don't know if she's okay. I can't find her anywhere. No one will tell me anything."

"Where were you living with your mom?" Kane's voice was soft and conversational. "In Blackwater?"

"Nope." Jimmy shook his head. "I'm from Idaho."

"Okay." Kane gave Jenna a meaningful stare. "Father Derry has a place where there's other kids. It's not foster care. It's a place where moms stay with their kids if they're in trouble. You'll be safe there and so will your mom and brother. You shouldn't have been taken out of the state. We'll hunt down your mom and find out what's happening." He pulled out his notebook. "I'm gonna need your details: your name, your mom's, and your old address, and your brother's name."

"You're not going to throw me in jail?" Jimmy's eyes widened.

"Not this time." Kane leaned forward in his chair. "Mess up again and you don't get another chance. Don't run away again. I'll find your mom and get this sorted. You have my word."

Jenna looked at the boy. "We don't allow families to be torn apart in Black Rock Falls and we protect anyone in danger. We use the foster system only as a last resort, and I personally make sure every kid in foster care is safe and well." She indicated to Kane. "You have Deputy Kane on your side now. He'll make sure everything is okay." She looked up as Father Derry came into the diner with a teenage boy at his side. "Ah, here is Father Derry now. Go with him and he'll give you a place to stay where there's other kids your age until we can find your mom and brother. We'll drop by and keep you up to date with our investigations."

"Hello, Jimmy." Father Derry smiled at the boy. "This here is Stu. He's staying at Her Broken Wings for a time too. He'll show you around." He wrinkled his nose. "You can choose some clothes and get cleaned up. The kids are decorating the yard for Halloween, if you want to join them."

"Okay." Jimmy looked at Jenna. "How do I find you?"

"I'm at the sheriff's department or you can call me or Deputy Kane anytime." She handed him her card. "But we'll be dropping by to make sure you're okay."

"Thanks." Jimmy looked at Kane as he turned to follow Father Derry. "I'm sorry about your truck." He pushed the card into his pocket and hurried out the door.

"It's amazing, isn't it?" Kane leaned back in his chair. "The way life goes, with problems we need to solve right in the middle of a homicide case. We sure need another deputy. I know you'd prefer another female, but after one gets murdered and then we had the Poppy problem, would you consider a guy? Even a rookie would help. We're over our heads right now and that kid needs our immediate attention."

Considering his request, Jenna nodded. "I'll think on it." She tried Chrissy Miller's number again. "Chrissy is not picking up. Grab your things. We'll head out there now to make sure she's okay."

TEN

Dead bodies are all around me. I can smell blood and loose bowels. The dead follow me, grinning from disfigured faces with sightless eyes, and point fingers or wave dismembered arms at me, mouthing words I can't hear. Some walk on stumps, others carry their guts in their arms, the entrails dangling behind them in a bloody trail. It's as if the Halloween decorations have come to life to haunt my every waking second. I bang my head against the tree to dislodge the images and peer again into the forest, but the trees have vanished. Before me a vista of golden sand spreads out littered with human debris. Cries pierce my ears. My team lies dead or dying. I lift my weapon as the enemy descends on us like a swarm of grasshoppers on a field of wheat. So many. Too many are running toward me, faces split in wide grins to grab the dying as trophies and laughing at me, the last man standing ready to inflict horrific death and humiliation.

My choice is clear.

Tears wet my cheeks but the sand shifts in a mirage caused by the heat. Am I in Montana or has Halloween transported me back to the desert again? I met her in Montana, fresh from the campus, all smiles and youthful exuberance. She was the most beautiful woman I'd ever seen. We made our vows together and I figured she'd wait for me until the end of time, but she died in shame because I survived in a hellhole. Now, in my dreams she turns her back on me, and when I call out her name, she turns to display blood dripping from slashed wrists. I was never able to explain what happened that night so long ago, when a full moon lit a Halloween sky so far from home. I never had the chance to clarify how bullets from my weapon riddled the bodies of my team. They haunt me now because they believe I saved myself, you see. On that Halloween night so far from home, I screamed out a slogan in Pashto and killed them all.

ELEVEN

Clouds covered the sky, moving at rapid speed, pushed along by wind gusts that whipped up the pine trees and spread brown needles across the blacktop. The scent of rain was in the air and with it the smell that promised early snowfall. Kane pushed the Beast up a narrow mountain road and glanced at Jenna. "Have you noticed everywhere we go of late has a really weird name? What is it with Black Rock Falls? We find a body at Twisted Tree Ridge and now we're heading for Death Drop Gully."

"I blame it on Halloween." Jenna shuddered. "Weird things always happen around this time of year. I figure the places were named by the old cowboys and if something weird happened there, that's the name they gave it. We've seen the twisted trees and the place we're heading to has a long history of people falling and dying."

Kane ran some of the names around town through his mind and nodded. "They either had no imagination whatsoever or a very good sense of humor."

"More like they came about in conversation. You know, something like, 'I went by that house, you know, the one where they found a headless man in a hollow.'" Jenna grinned at him. "Then after that, that place was called Headless Hollow."

The GPS instructed them to turn onto a dirt road running deep into the forest. Kane slowed and peered ahead. "I can't believe she lives alone up here."

"It's spooky." Jenna pulled her jacket around her. "It's only midafternoon and its already dark here. It's like driving into a cave made of trees." She looked at him. "There's a more direct road to the top of the gully. Well, it's one of the fire roads that runs off Stanton, but Christy Miller's house is some ways away from Death Drop Gully."

Kane flicked on his headlights. "Yeah, I checked out the hiking trails in this area and one of them goes alongside the gully and leads up to the plateau. The view there is spectacular, according to the Black Rock Falls Happy Trails website."

"I think I'll call Atohi. Oh, I'm not getting many bars." Jenna slipped the satellite sleeve onto her phone. "That's better." She leaned back in the seat. "Hey, Atohi, how are you? We're heading to Death Drop Gully. What do you know about it?"

"I'm fine, but what are you doing out at Death Drop Gully?" He chuckled. *"As superstitious as you are, that's not the place to be so close to Halloween."*

"Is there something I should know?" Jenna sounded serious.

"Not in relation to Halloween, although many throughout time have believed the dead cross over into the world of the living on the first of November, or at midnight on the thirty-first of October, and stay for a time." Atohi gave a low chuckle. *"For some, it's all about candy and dress-up; for others, Halloween is a time when the dead return. Your people celebrate but in truth you're in fear of the spirits. I welcome them like a reunion of old friends but even I wouldn't venture into Death Drop Gully at this time of year."*

"Why is that?" Jenna stared at Kane.

"Death Drop Gully isn't a place you should be right now because the people who died there did not die a peaceful death. They were shot by the owner of the house many years go and thrown into the gully to rot. The elders say they walk the forest seeking revenge."

"Is that how it got its name?" Jenna was looking nervous and chewing on her bottom lip.

Kane barked a laugh. "That's not a good story to hear right now." He squeezed Jenna's arm. "We're heading along a dark road through the forest to check on a woman who lives close by."

"It's not a story." Atohi cleared his throat. *"It was named by the locals after the massacre. We use a different name. Above the view is a place where tourists visit but below the sun refuses to shine and the trees close in all around in despair. All are ashamed to stand tall in the sun after watching what happened."* He paused a beat. *"Are you saying someone lives alone in the cursed house?"*

Kane stared at Jenna's concerned expression and stopped driving. "What do you mean, a cursed house?"

"The man who built that house was a murderer." Atohi made a noise of disgust. *"There's nothing you can do, Kane. This happened maybe one hundred and fifty years ago. It didn't work out so good for him. His wife could hear the dead calling out at night and refused to live in the house. She told everyone the dead had cursed the house and all who live within. Soon after she ran into the forest and was never seen again. They say you can still hear the sounds of the dying coming from the gully at this time of the year. The murderer boarded up the house and rode away, leaving everything behind. No family members have risked going inside because of the curse. From what I hear, it was passed down through generations but not one of the owners came to see it. I had no idea someone had purchased the house and lived there. It's not a place I'd visit."*

"So, he left it leaving all his possessions inside and no one disturbed it?" Jenna snorted. "That's so not human nature. Surely someone broke into it to steal some of the valuables. They'd be antiques and worth a fortune."

"Look around you." Atohi chuckled. *"Would you go there willingly? Can't you feel the evil around you?"*

"It is creepy." Jenna reached for a bottle of water and sipped it. "I didn't know there was a house here. It's so remote. I wonder how the people who purchased it found it in the first place?"

"I can't answer that. Perhaps the county clerk will have the information you seek. I have to go. I'm collecting groceries for my mom." Atohi chuckled. *"Watch out for the ghouls now."* He disconnected.

Noticing Jenna's eyes widen even more, Kane drove back onto the road. He needed to make light of the situation. If his wife believed in ghosts, well, he'd be understanding and support her strange notions, but the dead or the afterlife he believed in formed part of Scripture and held no fear for him. Although, he had to admit this place was dark and intimidating, but he'd been in worse places—up to his neck in a swamp came to mind—and sometimes being in a dark forest was an advantage, especially if he'd planned to hide or get the jump on someone. He guessed it was a personal preference, and if a dark creepy forest unnerved Jenna, he'd respect that and make sure she felt secure. "Let's hope we find Christy Miller peacefully painting close by. This near to Halloween, the townsfolk will blame the ghosts for dragging her away to the other side or whatever."

"I've never heard anything bad about Death Drop Gully." Jenna placed her phone into the consol. "In the sightseeing flyers, it's mentioned as a place to hike to see spectacular views and the trail is via the fire roads and a few mountain paths to the plateau." She gave a little shudder. "I guess people still hike through Bear Peak and that's a killing field." She glanced at him.

"One day when I have time, I might research the names of some of the places around here. Some of them are so weird they must have stories behind them."

Ahead, the road opened out into a clearing, and standing out in the middle in a pool of sunshine sat an unusual house. It seemed out of place and not in the usual style of anything he had seen in the locality. It was old but sturdy and every inch of the outside was covered with vines. A brick wall surrounded a neat garden and rose into an archway that led to a gravel footpath. At the end of the path two brick steps led to a vine-covered porch with a red front door. It was like stepping into another place and time.

Kane drove around to the side of the house and found a barn with the doors flung wide open to display a glistening white Chevrolet Equinox. He stopped on the driveway and turned to Jenna. "Maybe she's just not answering her phone. That vehicle was washed recently. It's windy here and there's not a speck of dust on it."

"The yard is immaculate and so is the barn." Jenna peered out of the window. "If she lives here alone, she must spend all of her time cleaning and tending the yard. I can't see a gardening service coming all the way up here."

Kane shrugged. "Maybe she keeps busy. It would be lonely living here all alone."

"Can you imagine this place at night?" Jenna glanced all around. "It's spooky in daylight and walking up to the plateau through the dark forest when it crowds in around you like that wouldn't be my idea of fun." She shivered. "It's so cold up here too and by the way the trees are bent over it must be windy all the time."

Kane slid from the seat and collected Duke. He looked at her as she came around the hood. "She'd lost her husband and renovated this house in his honor, so maybe she prefers to be alone." He glanced around the neat garden. "The place is in good shape. I figure she'd still have connections with the gardeners and contractors who worked for her at the time." He turned three-sixty degrees and scanned the area. The driveway went around the barn and disappeared into an open area of forest. "Look over there. I figure the GPS brought us by the fastest route, but I'm heading back that way. I bet that takes us around the bottom of the gully and leads right back to Stanton. It looks wide, and from what I can see, I'm sure that's not a dirt road."

"We'll ask Mrs. Walker if we see her." Jenna pulled on a woolen hat and tucked in her hair. "I can't see a truck loaded with building supplies getting through the road we came along." She turned toward the house. "I hope she's home. It's too cold for a trek up the mountain."

Kane walked to the barn and placed one hand on the hood of the truck. "It's cold, so she's been home for a time." He headed for the front door.

The house was shut up tight, the shutters on the windows pulled in against the weather. It was something most folks did at night. Opening them to let in the sunlight and some warmth was usual even in the mountains. Kane lifted the ornate brass knocker in the image of an owl and struck the matching plate three times. They waited, looking at each other, but no sound came from inside. He knocked again and after a few minutes of complete silence tried the doorknob. To his surprise, it turned and the door swung open without a sound to an entry with large granite flagstones. The floor led to a carpeted hallway with open doors on each side and ahead he made out a kitchen. He called out twice but silence greeted him. "The hall light is on. The front door is open. Maybe she went out for a spell last night and didn't come home." He turned to Jenna. "We'll clear the rooms. If she's not here, find something she's been wearing and we'll get Duke to track her."

"I'll go right and we'll both go upstairs." Jenna hurried off, moving swiftly into the first room. "Clear."

They cleared the house and went back downstairs. With the light also on in the kitchen, the thought the woman might have been stranded on the mountain overnight worried Kane. If she'd been injured, it would be difficult to survive overnight in the freezing temperatures. "It looks like a hike up the mountain. I'll grab our backpacks."

"I found a pair of socks in the laundry basket." Jenna waved an evidence bag. "Bring the Thermos. It's a long hike to the plateau from here. I'm surprised anyone would carry all their painting gear up there."

Kane shrugged. "She could work from photographs or sketches. A sketchbook and a pencil aren't heavy." He stared at the paintings adorning the walls. "However, she did it, she's good. Look at the pictures. They look like photographs." He led the way outside. "While you're waiting, go and look at the other side of the house in case she had a fall. Take Duke with you. I'll check out the barn. If we can't find her, I'll grab the Beast and drive to the trail and we'll head up the mountain."

TWELVE

Jenna followed the pathway around the other side of the house. She found a neat vegetable patch, dug over and waiting for planting after the snow. The back door led to a grassy backyard with a washing line with a few towels blowing in the wind. There was no sign of anyone and even the sounds of the forest were muted by the howling wind. She stared into the dark bent trees and couldn't push the warning from Atohi from her mind. The pines that stood so straight and tall on most parts of the mountain appeared stunted, bent, and covered in vines and dead vegetation. It was as if winter had come and stayed, forever robbing the forest of its lush green and pine scent. She shook her head. One spark, one careless hiker and the entire area would go up in smoke. It seemed from where she stood all she could see was dead leaves and browning pines. It was no wonder that Christy hiked to the plateau to view the spectacular scenery in her pictures. Living in the clearing and surrounded by a dying forest would be very depressing. She turned as Kane came around to the front of the house and went to meet him.

"It looks green here but why is the forest dying?"

"It's just fall, Jenna." Kane handed her a backpack. "It probably greens up after the melt, but I'd say the damage is done by the wind howling up from the gully. It's nonstop and must have been the same for years to bend the trees like that."

Unconvinced, Jenna shook her head as they moved out in search of the path up the mountain. "I figure it's more than that. Even in the middle of winter the pines around our house and in the mountains are green. This place looks as if it's been poisoned. I've lived here long enough to know that doesn't happen to pine trees unless they're dying. Brown like that, they're a fire hazard. I'll notify the forest wardens when I get back to the office, before we have another wildfire up here." She opened the evidence bag for Duke and offered it to him to smell. "Seek."

The dog took off at a trot and she followed Kane through the trees and along a well-worn pathway heading up the mountain. She hurried along behind him. "Well, at least we know she went this way recently."

The steep trail wound in and out of the forest. Going from dark to light and back again made the trail through the forest more foreboding. The quiet was getting to Jenna. It was like walking into a tomb and not at all like she had gotten used to. She missed the usual noisy birdsong and the odd glimpses of elk or bison as she crunched through a path covered with brown pine needles and negotiated vines she'd convinced herself had made it their business to strangle her at every turn. She stared into the shadows and, seeing nothing but darkness, followed closely behind Kane. As the path opened up to light ahead, the unmistakable smell of death rushed toward her in a howl of wind. "Oh, that doesn't smell good."

"It could be an animal." Kane pushed on ahead, holding back low branches for her. "It's coming from the gully. Maybe something fell over the edge." He waved a hand toward Duke. "He's still heading up the mountain, so I doubt it's Mrs. Miller."

As they came back out into the watery late afternoon sunshine, Jenna could see the side of the gully clearly for the first time. Made millions of years ago when a glacier cut a path through the mountain, it was one of many in Black Rock Falls. All were different sizes. Some, like this one, filled with water only after the melt but others had become part of the waterfall and river system all through the mountains and lowlands. The rock wall on either side of a steep ravine rose up to a plateau. The flattened-out area formed when a great chunk of the mountain broke away and tumbled down the gully, leaving behind what resembled a giant sofa. It was accessible to people willing to risk their lives to peer into the gully, but just above where the hiking path ended the forest wardens had erected a lookout. The pine fence blended well into the scenery and the plateau had become a popular tourist destination for photographers.

Curious, Jenna moved closer to the edge of the ravine. "Wait up. I want to see what's down there."

"Don't get so close. The edge isn't safe." Kane grabbed her arm. "Hold my hand if you must look and use me for an anchor."

Taking slow careful steps, Jenna eased to the edge and peered over. "Oh no. It's someone spread out on their back. It's too far away to make out who it is."

"From the smell, I'd say they're dead, Jenna." Kane pulled her back to the path. "I'll take a look."

Jenna held her breath as Kane crawled out headfirst onto a jutting boulder and peered over. She waited anxiously for him to reverse back to her. "What do you think?"

"It's hard to say." Kane frowned and rubbed his chin. "It's a body. I can't see a way into the gully either." He checked his backpack. "Dammit, my scope is in the Beast. Wait here. I'll run back and get it."

Jenna looked at him. "I'll come with you."

"I'll be faster alone and you need to call Wolfe." Kane

smiled at her. "You'll be fine. Sit down on that rock and catch your breath. You have Duke and a weapon. I'll be back before you know I'm gone." He bent to kiss her and then took off at a run.

Jenna stared after him and shrugged. She whistled for Duke and he came back and sat down beside her, his big brown intelligent eyes watching her face as if waiting for his next orders. "Lie down and have a rest. Dave will be back soon."

She smiled when Duke barked once and looked in the direction Kane had vanished, turned around three times, and lay down beside her with a long sigh. She patted him on the head and his long thick tail thumped in the grass. "You are such a good boy."

Pulling out her phone, she made the call to Wolfe and explained the situation. "It's hard to make out if it's male or female, and from here, we can't see a way into the ravine by foot."

"Okay. I'll contact search and rescue to see if we can figure out a way to retrieve the body." Wolfe tapped away on his keyboard. "I've just checked the weather. The wind gusts coming up from the gully and the narrow width will prohibit the use of a chopper. I'm looking at an arial shot of the gully. Even if the wind weren't a problem, I wouldn't like my chances of taking a chopper that close to a sheer rockface on both sides. I'll call Atohi as well. He knows ways in and out of places no one else has discovered yet. I hope we can make it there before dark. Leave it with me. I'll get back to you real soon."

Without warning, the hairs on the back of Jenna's neck prickled and she had the intense feeling of being watched. She glanced around, hoping to see Christy Miller walking down the path toward her but no one was there. She turned to look back down the path Kane had taken into the forest. A shadow moved out of sync with the movement caused by the constant wind gusts. "Dave is that you?"

Nothing.

The shadow moved again.

A crunching sound like boots on dried leaves came from deep in the forest and, alarmed, Jenna sprang to her feet. She glanced down at Duke, but the dog hadn't reacted. She took a few steps back down the pathway, peering into the darkness. The shadows striping the trail from random beams of sunlight would disguise anyone hiding in the forest, and their movements would be muffled by dying trees rustling under the onslaught of the relentless gusts of wind. Uncertainty gripped her and her heart rate picked up. She spun around as the sound of people moaning rushed toward her on the wind from the gully. Suddenly afraid, she backed out, turned, and froze. Something was coming down the pathway and it wasn't human. It shimmered like a mirage and seemed to dance toward her. Unable to believe her eyes, Jenna gaped at the sight. Was her mind playing tricks on her? Shaking her head to dislodge the image, Jenna stood transfixed as it moved closer. The illusion resembled a woman in a long dress running down the path, and as the sun hit her, she sparkled as if lit up by a million dust motes. Not a soul would believe she'd seen the ghost of the missing woman from so long ago. Trying not to panic, she held up her phone and took a video. She gasped as the apparition kept on coming toward her and then seemed to hover, twirling for a few seconds before picking up speed and running over the edge of the ravine.

The howling of angry spirits stopped at the same time and Jenna sat down hard on the rock. She rubbed Duke's head, glad to have him close. The dog hadn't reacted at all. Had she imagined it? Were Atohi's Halloween ghost stories getting to her? Trying to keep her hands from trembling, she played back the video just to make sure she hadn't lost her mind. It was all there, the image sparkling in the sunshine, the horrific moaning like people dying. The surreal experience had shaken her to the bone, and without the video no one would believe her, but now she had proof. A noise came from the forest again and, startled, Jenna sprang to her feet and drew her weapon. The crunch, crunch, crunch of boots on the dry forest floor was coming closer. Taking a deep breath, she lifted her M18 pistol and took aim.

THIRTEEN

Heart pounding, Jenna stared into the darkness. Beside her Duke barked and ran toward the pathway and was swallowed up by the gloom. She'd had the care of the dog for five minutes and had already allowed him to run into danger. "Duke, come here, boy."

"Hey, it's me. Lower your weapon." Kane emerged from the trees and held up both hands. "You look like you've seen a ghost. What happened?"

Heaving a sigh of relief, Jenna holstered her weapon. "I did see a ghost and now I know what happened to the last owner of the house. She ran over the edge of the gully. I saw her just before, wearing a long dress—and I heard the moaning. It was just like Atohi said, the moaning of lost souls."

"Uh-huh." Kane tilted his head to look at her his eyes sparkling with amusement.

Annoyed, Jenna thrust the phone into his hand. "I knew you'd do the 'uh-huh' thing. Look at the video."

She waited as Kane watched it a few times and then zoomed in to watch it again. "Well, now do you believe in ghosts?"

"Nope." Kane handed her back the phone. "I admit it is a spectacular phenomenon and I could see how being alone up here with Atohi's stories running around in your head and a dead body close by could spike your imagination, but it was just dust and leaves, Jenna. It was a dust devil, is all. Zoom in on the video and look closer. It's not a ghost, but I can honestly see how you'd believe it was supernatural." He frowned. "The moans are only the wind howling through the caves. You've heard that happen before, haven't you?"

Jenna took the phone from him and zoomed in on the video. This time she made out the swirling wind like a mini tornado dancing down the path carrying dust and leaves along with it. She looked at him and shrugged. "Just before, I could swear someone was watching me. I could see moving shadows."

"It's not a place a killer would hang out waiting for someone to walk by, and Duke would have alerted you if it had been a person. You know darn well he doesn't react to animals unless they're dangerous, and then he goes ballistic." Kane pulled his rifle scope from his jacket pocket and shook his head. "Halloween sure turns up the spook meter each year, but the townsfolk enjoy it. I figure this year I'll just go as me. Seems I scared the heck out of you before, so I won't need a costume."

Still shaken, Jenna stared at him and forced her head back into the game. "Enough about Halloween. Wolfe will be calling soon and he'll need information to retrieve the body, so let's get at it. Will you be able to make out who is lying in the gully from here and see how we can get them out?"

"I'll see." Kane went to the edge and belly-crawled out onto a ledge. He raised the scope to one eye. "Yeah, it's female. She'd have died on impact." He moved the scope around. "There are animal trails along the side of the gully but it's going to be difficult getting her out of there. We'll need to drop a couple of men down and rig up a pulley system to pull out the stretcher. The wind gusts are too unpredictable to risk a chopper retrieval."

Jenna sat back on her heels and waited for Kane to crawl from the ledge. She handed him her phone. "This is Christy Miller from the driver's license. Do you think it's her?"

"It's hard to tell. She's pretty banged up." Kane frowned at the image. "Maybe, she has the same hair color."

Jenna sighed. "That bad, huh?"

"Yeah." Kane handed her back the phone. "We'll need to find out where she went over. People who take their own lives often leave things behind, like their phone or a note." He sighed. "If she jumped."

Jenna led the way up the trail to the plateau. It was steep and the small rocks beneath her boots made the path slippery. She grasped on tree branches to steady herself. The higher they climbed the greener the forest became and the fresh wind from the snow-covered peaks no longer held the smell of death. "Do you think she might have been pushed?"

"I have no idea, but after finding her friend in a posed death scene, anything is possible." Kane moved beside her as the trail opened out. "People who tend a garden and make it ready for planting seem to be planning for the future. Christy Miller seemed to love the seclusion here, and she loved to paint the scenery. Obviously, the stories around the place haven't worried her before now. She's lived here for years." He shook his head. "If we discover she was getting phone calls from a dead husband too, then someone could have lured her up here and pushed her over the edge."

Jenna stopped walking and looked at him. "Why? Why would someone do this now? It's been years since their husbands died. If it is a revenge thing, why the wives? There isn't a logical MO."

"Since when have psychopathic killers been logical?" Kane raised one eyebrow. "With three women dying from the same group of friends, and now it seems that Mrs. Miller is splattered on the rocks in the gully, something weird is happening. Some old wound has been festering for years and has triggered a psychotic episode in someone close to these people. We just have to find out who it is and that will be difficult as all the players are dead and the DOD won't release the file on the incident."

Jenna thought for a beat. "There must be some returned soldiers living in Montana. I'm sure we have tons here in Black Rock Falls. I know there are some living off the grid in the mountains. Maybe some of them knew each other from boot camp?"

"Yeah, well, it's worth hunting them down." Kane stopped walking and stared into the forest. "I thought I heard something then as well." He laid one hand on her arm. "Watch my back." He took a flashlight from his backpack and slipped into the shadows.

Jenna pulled her weapon and peered into the gloom. She couldn't see or hear Kane moving through the forest and wondered how he managed to move without a sound. Moments later Kane appeared a little way up the pathway and beckoned her. "Did you see anyone?"

"Nope, but look here." Kane pointed to the forest floor. "Someone has been holed up here maybe to watch the house. Cigarette butts, and from the amount, I'd say he was here for a time." He pointed to six or so butts pushed into the patch of soil scratched out from beneath the coating of pine needles. "It looks like he intended to cover these up and something disturbed him." He pulled on surgical gloves, collected the butts and dropped them into an evidence bag. "If it's someone up to no good, we have his DNA."

Jenna stared at the butts. "Why would anyone hole up here?" She glanced around for bullet casings. "I don't see any brass, so he wasn't hunting." She straightened. "We'll search from here to the top of the gully and look for signs of a struggle. If she didn't jump, she was pushed." She glanced at Kane.

"What makes you believe she didn't fall from where we found her?"

"The wind is a factor." Kane stared into the distance as if calculating the drop. "The gusts are very strong and from the state of the body, she bounced some on the way down. So, I figure she fell or jumped from the top."

Scanning the side of the path as she walked, Jenna's mind went into overdrive. "So, if she came up here to paint or draw and somebody attacked her, she'd have left something behind and there should be signs of a struggle."

"I don't figure she came up here to paint, not in the dark. I believe she left at dusk last night, so around eight, and was expecting to return after dark. Why else would she leave the lights on?" Kane glanced at her. "Something important must have happened to drag her up the mountain at that time of night. I can't imagine anyone willingly walking up this path at dusk. It's hard enough to negotiate in daylight, not to mention the risk of becoming something's dinner."

Jenna's phone peeled out Wolfe's ringtone and she answered. "Hi, Shane."

"We're on our way." Jenna could hear the sound of an engine in the background. *"We'll be coming in via Stanton and taking the fire roads. It's a long hike from there, but Atohi is meeting us with horses at the end of the fire road. He wasn't happy going to that part of the forest, something about spirits out for revenge or something. No doubt y'all know what he's talking about. I'm bringing two search-and-rescue volunteers and Webber. Where are you?"*

Jenna glanced at Kane, who'd leaned closer to the phone to listen to the conversation. "Dave will explain."

"You'll need to set up a pulley system and then drop two men into the gully. The body is at the bottom, maybe fifteen feet down a sheer rockface." Kane cleared his throat. "We're doing recon around the plateau to see if we can find anything suspicious. We'll head down as soon as we're done and find a way into the gully from this side."

"Okay, I'll call when we arrive." Wolfe disconnected.

Jenna searched along the trail, and Kane walked along the edge of the gully, looking for any signs of a struggle. They climbed to the top and Jenna pointed to a flattened area of grass around the edge of the forest. "Someone waited here." She moved closer and peered at the footprints. "There are depressions in the pine needles but not clear enough to take a mold."

A bright flash of color peeked at her from beneath a tree. Jenna pulled on gloves and bent to pick up a candy wrapper. "I don't recognize the brand." She waved it at Kane. "Do you?"

"Yeah, vividly." Kane examined the wrapper and met her gaze. "It's been a while, but this was a staple during my time in service. It's military issue."

An ice-cold finger traced a path down Jenna's spine as she pushed the wrapper into a small evidence bag and turned to look at him. "You can creep around in the forest without making a sound, so that means someone like you would have the same abilities. I know I saw something in there before, or someone watching me. Even I know ghosts don't throw shadows."

"It keeps coming back to the military again." Kane scanned the immediate area. "Although, if he were trained to move with stealth, then he wouldn't be leaving cigarette butts or candy wrappers behind. Not when everyone in the military is on a DNA database somewhere. It all seems too darn easy, as if whoever is killing these women is leaving us clues. I'm starting to believe they're planting evidence to send us in the wrong direction." He peered over the edge of the ravine, sending pebbles tumbling down the sheer drop, so far away they made no sound when they landed. "Ah, I've found something." The wind lifted his hat as he leaned over and he held out one arm to stop her getting too close. "Maybe you should stay back there.

I'll take a video and some shots." He removed his Stetson and dropped it onto the ground.

Jenna planted her feet and grabbed the back of Kane's belt. "If it's not safe for me, it's not safe for you." She caught his disgruntled snort. "What do you see?"

"Jenna." Kane moved back to the path and turned to look at her. "I'll crawl on my belly to the edge. There are signs of someone trying to grab hold of the bushes. The branches are stripped bare and if the victim has plant residue on her palms, she tried to prevent herself falling." He frowned and his eyes looked troubled. "Sure, she could have walked off the edge in the dark, but she didn't. There's a flashlight just over the edge in the long grass. I'll see if I can reach it."

Jenna shook her head. "And have you fall into the gully? No darn way. We'll wait for backup and use a rope."

"Look." Kane rested both hands on her shoulders. "If you're concerned, sit down and grab my feet when I'm in position. Worse case, I slide on the pebbles and you'll act as an anchor." He pressed a kiss on her head. "No one is coming up here and we're wasting precious daylight. Let's get at it."

Heart pounding as Kane crawled on his belly over the edge of the gully, she took a firm grip of his legs, dug in her heels, and leaned back, not that she could have taken his weight if he'd fallen over the edge. Deep down, she understood he only tolerated her assistance to make her feel better. The evidence collected, Kane backed away from the edge and Jenna heaved a sigh of relief. "What did you see?"

"Like I said." Kane handed her the flashlight and his phone and then retrieved his hat and pushed it on. "There's no doubt she fell, and the evidence indicates she tried to save herself. What we don't know is if she fell or was pushed." He rolled to his feet and offered her his hand. "One thing for darn sure, she didn't jump willingly."

Pulled to her feet, Jenna peered at the video and then the

images. "Hmm, these look conclusive. We need her phone records. I want to know if someone was calling her last night as well." She passed back the phone. "Would anyone be stupid enough to head up here at midnight?"

"Think about it, Jenna. If I were MIA and I called you at midnight and told you I was at the top of the gully and injured or whatever, or even if I told you to come and help me, would you think twice about it?" Kane examined her face, his eyebrows raised in question. "Well, would you?"

Without hesitation, Jenna shook her head. "No, if you called, I'd come. Nothing could stop me. I'd run up here."

"Yeah, and that's what this killer is banking on." Kane shook his head and his eyes flashed with anger. "It's not bad enough a man dies in action, but to know a predator is using his wife's love for him as a tool for his own twisted fantasy is taking it to a new low. When we find this guy, he'll be sorry he messed with me."

FOURTEEN

I see him, moving through the forest, fast and silent. I've seen men like him before, worked beside them, but this one is special. The woman he protects, the sheriff of Black Rock Falls, was so close I could have touched her but I moved away. When she walked into the forest holding her weapon in steady hands, it was plain that she'd shoot me without a second thought. I have too much to do to provoke her, so I wait, hiding in shadows, fighting back the ghosts haunting me.

Last night I neglected to remove the evidence of my being here, but the excitement of watching Christy Miller fall and hearing her wailing screams of terror pushed reason from my mind. I relived the thrill all the way home and then later as my mind replayed the scene, I realized I'd messed up big time. I rushed to the plateau, taking the backroad and leaving my truck hidden in the trees, and hiked to Death Drop Gully. Finding the sheriff and her deputy on the trail was a surprise and dashed any hope I had of seeing Christy's broken body. Now all I can do is hide in the forest and wait.

He is back now, and slides from predator to protector in seconds. In the forest, a man who can move like a cat through dry leaves without making a sound and carrying no scent is an alpha. Only a head shot will take him down. That would be difficult for someone like me. Right now, my hands shake and I have difficulty distinguishing between realities, but as the faces of the dead or dying are not with me today, I know the scene before me is real. I've lost the chance to collect all traces of me from the mountain but not from the house. The walkie-talkie is still in Christy's basement. I must move ahead of the sheriff and retrieve it before they return to the house, but that's not going to be easy—not now with the deputy so close.

See how he stands over the sheriff, guarding her like a wild cat? He senses I'm here. His eyes slide from side to side as he watches his periphery while offering her comfort. Only a fool would risk his anger. He would be relentless and the encounter final for any man who touched what was his. His body language tells her all is well, but she doesn't see him like I do. I know men like him.

FIFTEEN

Skin prickling, Kane checked the slide of his weapon in its holster and scanned the forest. His gut instinct told him, like Jenna, that someone was watching them. With the wind at his back, he sniffed the air. Usually, a person would give away their position by their smell. Using unscented deodorant prevented the odor of sweat but the smell of fear leaked out from every pore of a person's body. Human scent also came from behind the ears, scalp, and groin, to name a few places and if someone were hiding in the shadows, he'd disguised his scent well enough to fool Duke. Using animal musk would do that easily enough. He tried to rationalize his concerns. It could be a hiker just watching police procedure or it could be the killer returning to the crime. If he'd killed Christy Miller last night, the need to view his kill might be overpowering. He held out his left hand and grasped Jenna's. "Come on, we'll need to find a way through to the bottom of the gully. Wolfe will be there soon."

It didn't take them too long to arrive at the bottom of the trail. Kane gave Duke a drink of water and then hoisted him into the back seat of the Beast and clipped in his harness.

"Okay, I guess we drive around the back of the house and see where the road takes us." He climbed behind the wheel and smiled at Jenna. "I can't wait to show that video to Carter." He snorted with laughter. "We've seen a ton of strange things in the desert, mirages and the like, but I figure your one beats them all."

"I knew you'd tease me about that video. Next it will be all over the media." She glared at him. "Don't even think about it, Dave." She waved a hand at him. "Drive. If the GPS can't help, I'll find a map on my phone." She bent over the screen.

The dirt road wound through the stunted forest for half a mile before it met the fire road. The wide-open road was bathed in afternoon sunlight and Kane accelerated when the GPS started to give instructions to Lower Death Drop Gully. It turned out to be a small area deep in the forest with a few hunting cabins spread out on each side of the fire road. He stared at the GPS screen. "If we keep going this way, we'll end up where Wolfe left his van. There must be a way through the forest to the end of the gully without traveling in a complete circle."

"Wait up." Jenna stared at the screen. "Pull over and look at this." She held out her phone. "This is an aerial shot taken for fire and rescue. Back a ways there was a small clearing. It didn't look like a road but it might be a pastoral trail to the end of the gully."

Kane stared at the screen. "If it widens out some, we might get the Beast through." He turned the truck around. "Or we'll hike. We have provisions in our packs but I'll grab a rifle. Just in case we're being stalked, and I don't like the idea of running into a bear looking to store fat for winter. They'll be hunting at this time of the afternoon for sure." He smiled at her. "There's a pepper ball gun in the back. We'll take that as well."

"I just hope we don't meet a bear." Jenna pushed her phone

into her pocket. "The smell of a dead body might attract one or a mountain lion."

The idea of encountering dangerous wildlife always concerned him when they went into the forest after a corpse, but killing them wasn't on his agenda. He preferred to run them off and allow them to live free. "That's just nature. We'll work around it. We always do. We're the intruders here, not them. Being aware is the recipe for staying safe and we sure are aware of the dangers in the forest."

Moving slowly, Kane finally found the clearing and stopped to peer into the trees. It was impossible to see anything past a few feet but what he could see was rough and steep. He switched on the headlights and the halogen beams illuminated a path ahead. It was overgrown but still visible. "Okay, let's see where this trail leads us. We'll clear any fallen logs as we go."

"It looks steep and rugged." Jenna looked anxious. "You spent all your downtime fitting the new engine and all the other stuff to the Beast. Doesn't it need time to settle in or whatever before it tackles terrain like that?" She indicated the rough trail ahead. Deep ruts crisscrossed the dirt road and boulders stuck out all over. Dead branches littered the trail. "What if you get a flat or two flats? What do we do then?"

Over the time the Beast was in Kane's new garage, built especially to carry out repairs and to house his vehicle out of the snow, Jenna had been a frequent visitor during the installation of the new engine. It was obvious her knowledge of anything concerning vehicles was limited. The specifications of the engine and what it could do were classified, as the Beast was in fact a military vehicle, so Kane had worked alone with occasional assistance from Wolfe. He'd not only replaced the engine but upgraded everything. It now went faster and was safer than before. The vehicle was bombproof, the body and windows bulletproof, and now it had more gadgets than he'd ever use. He glanced at Jenna and smiled. "The Beast can handle rough terrain, no problem, and we also have a RunFlat system, so if we get a flat, I can drive about one hundred miles before I need to change the tire." He headed into the bushes and the Beast tipped to one side and then to another as it bumped over the rocks.

"That's good to know." Jenna gripped the handle above the door. "I'm not sure Duke agrees. He's being jostled all over."

The wind howled around them, moving the wind-bent trees and making their shadows resemble a team of soldiers creeping through the forest carrying backpacks. Kane glanced at Jenna's transfixed stare. She'd noticed the resemblance as well. "Do the shadows bother you?"

"Do you mean, do they look like the MIA team following us through the forest?" Jenna turned to look at him. "Yeah, they do and it's creepy. I'm expecting cadaverous, flesh-eating zombies to stagger out in front of the truck at any moment."

Kane chuckled. "Uh-huh." His phone chimed and the panel in the dash lit up. He accepted the call from Wolfe. "Did you find the location of the body?"

"Yeah, we're here." The wind buffeting Wolfe's phone could be clearly heard through the speaker. *"It's going to be tough getting in and out of the gully. I doubt these guys have tackled something like this before. How far away are you? I might need your assistance."*

Kane drove up a steep incline and then the track leveled out and he could make out a break in the trees. "I'm not sure. We're on a track heading in your general direction."

"I can hear an engine. Sound your horn."

Kane complied and could hear it returned through the speakers. "Ah, so we're close by. I figure we'll be breaking out of the trees to your left anytime soon."

"Come out real slow. There's a clearing and about ten feet spare before you'll hit the edge of the gully." Wolfe's boots crunched on gravel. *"I can see your headlights. Slow down. The*

*long grass is obscuring the edge. There's no telling where it starts.
I can't see and I'm standing close by."*

Slowing the Beast to a crawl, Kane edged the truck out into
the weak sunlight and stopped on a grassy knoll. Just ahead the
gully opened up, its ragged sharp edge only a few feet away. To
his right he could make out Wolfe. On the perimeter of the
forest Colt Webber and two strangers in search-and-rescue
jackets were busy setting up a pulley system around a large pine
tree. He disconnected from the call and turned to Jenna. "I
figure we might have ended up in the ravine if Wolfe hadn't
arrived first. I still can't make out the edge through the long
grass and I know it's there."

"Close call." Jenna turned to look at Duke. "Maybe we
should leave Duke in the truck. He might fall over the edge. It
looks real sketchy to me."

Kane smiled at her and slid from the truck. "Yeah, he'll be
fine in here. He'll let me know if he needs a potty break." The
stink of death blasted him on the wind and he frowned. "Oh,
man, it stinks up here." He directed her around the back of the
truck. "Keep on this side of the truck and away from where the
grass obscures the edge. Walk along the tree line. Well inside
the tree line would be safer. Wolfe said the edge was ragged, so
it might be unstable all over this area. We'll head to the rocks
where Wolfe is waiting and I'll go down with him to retrieve the
body. I don't want him dropping down there with people he
hasn't climbed with before. Anything might happen."

"Trust me, I know about the edges of ravines." Jenna went
to the back of the truck to gather their equipment. "You didn't
know at the time, but when James Stone shot you in the head, I
climbed down the edge of a ravine to get to you. It's not something I'll forget in a hurry. Especially when I found you, I had
him shooting at me and you aiming your weapon at me too."

The time she mentioned was a little fuzzy but he did have
some memory of seeing her coming through the trees, all

scraped and dirty from the climb. She must have loved him then to have risked her life for him. Oh, boy he'd been such a jerk back then. Why she'd given him the time of day he'd never understand. He cupped her cheek and looked into her eyes. "Yeah, I'm really sorry about that. It seems amnesia is my Kryptonite. I'm a lucky man to have you, Jenna. I still can't believe you risked marrying me."

"I'm stubborn when it comes to getting what I want." Jenna let out a long sigh. "Right now, I want you to watch your step down there. Can you imagine me trying to drive the Beast home from here? It would be like driving an eighteen-wheeler along train tracks."

Laughing, he took the forensics kit from her and a helmet and gloves. "I'll be more careful this time—promise."

He glanced over at Wolfe, who gave him a cold stare. He understood his friend and assumed a serious expression. The body of Christy Miller deserved his respect and he'd give it, but keeping things light around Jenna was also a consideration. She'd had a nasty scare in the forest, followed by a drive straight from hell. In the field during his deployments, he'd faced many atrocities and moving the conversation away from the horror had kept him and his team sane. He led the way around the edge of the clearing and went to Wolfe's side. He explained what they'd found around the plateau. "There weren't absolute signs of a struggle—it's just rock up there—but finding a flashlight would indicate to me she didn't stumble around in the dark and walk over the edge." He pulled out his phone and displayed the stripped plants. "This looks to me as if she tried to stop herself from falling."

"It sure looks suspicious to me." Wolfe scrolled through the images. "Did you find anything at the house?"

Kane took back his phone and nodded. "Yeah, she left the lights on, which tells me she intended to return home, plus she'd prepared a garden bed for spring planting. She was thinking about the future. We checked out each room and she didn't leave a note. I figure someone lured her to the plateau and pushed her into the ravine."

"Hmm." Wolfe scratched his head. "They usually leave notes stuck on the refrigerator, on the kitchen table, on a desk, or on the pillow of their bed. They want them to be found and most people want to have the last word." He heaved a sigh, coughed, and pulled a mask from his pocket. "I guess we'd better get at it. It's messy. I don't figure the volunteers will be able to handle it. We'll go down with Webber. Blackhawk is tending the horses back a ways. He rigged up a travois to carry the stretcher back to my van. He refuses to enter the gully." He looked at Jenna. "I'll need you on the com to communicate with us and supervise the men." He handed Kane a climbing harness. "Put this on."

"From the evidence to date, we figure the killer is involved somehow with the military." Jenna looked from one to the other. "I'll call Rowley and have him hunt down any vets in the local area. We need a list of suspects and I believe that's the place to start."

"That sounds like a plan." Wolfe pulled on a helmet and then climbed into a harness and tied the straps. "It could also be a survivalist."

"Maybe, but someone knows these women, and both victims are widows of the same team MIA. In my book that's just too much of a coincidence." Jenna pulled out her phone. "I know people at boot camp can be spread all over, but it makes sense the guys from Black Rock Falls would have a connection. Maybe they were buddies. I'll start there, at boot camp and see how we go."

Concentrating on the job at hand, Kane went through his usual checks by making sure the ropes had been secured correctly. He gave the others final instructions. Having Jenna up top was a safeguard, but he wanted her in a harness and attached to a tree if she intended to stand on the edge and watch the retrieval. She never panicked in a dangerous situation and could handle just about anything—well, apart from ghosts. He smiled to himself and glanced over to her and gave her the thumbs-up. The sides of the gully were fragile with numerous cracks and loose boulders hanging by a thread, making the body retrieval dangerous. Wolfe would be fine but Webber didn't have their training, and as this was Kane's domain, he was ultimately responsible for getting the team down and back. He inspected everyone's gear one last time. Satisfied, he gave Jenna a nod and dropped over the edge.

SIXTEEN

Standing as close as she dared to the edge of the gully, Jenna's stomach went into freefall as the team dropped over the edge, rappelling down the rough sides of the gully into deep shadows and disappearing for a time into dense vegetation. Kane's voice came through her com for her to send down the basket stretcher. She instructed the search-and-rescue men to send it down and pulled out her phone. She called Rowley and explained what had happened. To make a list of possible suspects she'd need a list of Marines living in Montana across a wide time frame, and calculated an estimated time including possible tours of duty, time in basic training, plus the time passed since the men went MIA. "Okay, so we need the names of all the Marines currently living in Montana who attended boot camp between seven and sixteen years ago."

"I wouldn't know where to start." Rowley's chair creaked and she could hear his fingers drumming on the table.

Jenna thought for a beat. "You'll need to contact the Marine Corps at Quantico. They have a personnel locator, but they don't give out addresses, and as far as I'm aware there is no database." She chewed on her bottom lip. "I guess you could ask Carter."

"What about the Department of Military Affairs?" Rio's voice came through the speaker. *"I'll contact them. As it's a police matter, they might help."*

With her attention fixed on the team in the gully, Jenna shook her head. "I'm not sure but you could try." Down in the gully, Kane had emerged from the cover of the trees carrying one end of the stretcher. "I'll leave it with you. You might have more luck speaking to some of the townsfolk: Susie Hartwig at Aunt Betty's, the general store, the sporting stores. They might know someone in the military. Once you find one of them, you might be lucky and they'll know someone else who served around the same time. I'd imagine the men would be aged anywhere from thirty to forty-five."

"Okay, I'll make the calls." Rowley's chair scraped. *"Do you mind if I head on home when I'm done. The twins are getting restless."*

Jenna had completely forgotten the twins were at the office. "Yeah, sure. You must be exhausted. I hope Sandy is feeling better soon. I've got to go." She disconnected and watched the men in the gully heading across the rocky terrain to the body.

The next moment her phone chimed and she pulled it out of her pocket. It was Agent Jo Wells from Snakeskin Gully. "Hi, Jo."

"It sounds like you're in a wind tunnel. Is this an inconvenient time?"

Jenna kept her eyes on Kane and the others as they headed toward the body. "I'm watching a body retrieval in the mountains and it's windy up here. What's up?"

"Maybe nothing." Jo cleared her throat. *"Have you seen Carter? Has he dropped by lately?"*

Surprised, Jenna pressed the phone harder to her ear to make sure she was hearing her. "No. Is he missing?" She thought for a second. "I spoke to him this morning. He called Dave. Why? What's wrong?"

"Maybe nothing, maybe something. I'm not sure." Jo sighed and paused for a time as if choosing her words with care. *"It's just that he always tells me where he's going. Of late, he just keeps disappearing without a word, and when he comes back, it's as if he's been on a secret mission. It's so out of character. One minute he's here, next he's off in the chopper. He left the office this morning and hasn't returned. On Friday he went missing and showed Monday morning. I know it's his downtime but he usually checks in. I'm not calling him without a reason and we haven't had any callouts for days. I can't look like I'm checking up on him because, in truth, I'm not and it's not in my job description to be hunting him down. It's just I'm concerned he might be having PTSD episodes. On Monday when he showed he looked and smelled like he'd been sleeping rough. You know what he's like. He might dress like a cowboy but he's all designer jeans and snakeskin boots. It's not like him. Something's up."*

Rubbing her chin, Jenna sighed. "You're between a rock and a hard place as his boss and can't really be checking up on him during his downtime. It's not as if you're involved in a relationship. Maybe he's just gone fishing or hunting?"

"Yeah, maybe, but he usually plans everything and is buzzing with all the details. Most times he asks one of the local deputies to go with him. He hasn't even mentioned anything to Kalo." Jo sounded very concerned. *"This case you're on right now, could anything he discussed with Kane have triggered an episode in Carter? It is military based, isn't it?"*

Unable to give specifics, Jenna swallowed hard. "I'm not sure what they discussed. This case is very strange. The first woman who died told her friends she was getting calls from her husband. He went MIA seven years ago. Wolfe has proved she was given a drug overdose and now we have a woman's body in the gully and her husband was one of the team as well."

"Did the entire team go MIA?"

Jenna stared into the gully as Wolfe bagged the hands of the victim. A headache threatened and she rubbed her temple in slow circles, unsure of how much information she should divulge. "I'm not sure. The file is sealed and we don't have any solid information."

"If the file is sealed, then there's a cover-up. Something bad happened. That might be it, and knowing Dave as I do, if he discovered anything he shouldn't have, he'd keep it between him and Carter. They're both from military backgrounds and it's part of the code." Jo tapped away on her keypad. *"I still have access to many areas. They didn't take that away from me when I came here. I'll see what I can find. How long ago?"*

Jenna stared into space, suddenly oblivious to the body retrieval. She could give the information she'd gained from the victim's friend because it was obviously common knowledge. "The first victim's husband went MIA seven years ago." She blinked at the sound of voices as the men at the top of the gully shouted at each other over the wind. "What happened to Carter? Can you give me any details?"

"According to what Carter told me, and it's no secret, I know he's discussed it with Dave, he was the only survivor when his team went down during his last deployment. It was a group of kids asking his team for candy. Carter said he went back to the truck to get more from his supply and the kids were rigged with explosives. It hit him hard and he was out of commission for a time. Once he had his head back on and passed the psych tests, he joined the FBI and then an incident involving kids triggered an episode that sent him off the grid for two years. That's when I found him and persuaded him to join me. At the time he was fine and he's been fine since. If he is having an episode, he needs help."

Concerned, Jenna chewed on her fingers, the implications of Carter going AWOL was unfathomable. "He seemed okay to me, but I'll speak to Dave when we're done here and I'll call you later. If Carter shows here, I'll let you know."

"Thanks, I'd appreciate it. Bye for now." Jo disconnected.

Jenna touched her earbud. "Is everything okay down there?"

"Yeah, but she's a mess." Kane cleared his throat. *"One thing, she does have plant residue and deep cuts in her palms. There's no way she jumped."*

SEVENTEEN

There was more on Wolfe's mind than the broken body of the victim, and after a cursory examination of the remains of Christy Miller, he sent Webber to search the area toward the top of the gully and headed south with Kane. There weren't many places they could speak without being overheard. He looked at Kane. "Turn off your com for a few seconds. We need to discuss something."

"Okay." Kane turned the switch on his powerpack and raised one eyebrow. "What's up?"

Wolfe kept walking as he scanned the area for evidence. "I've been having problems with security." He glanced at Kane. "I mean, I've tried a few times to reach our contacts and found someone on the line I didn't know."

"Don't you get briefed about any changes as they happen?" Kane frowned.

Wolfe bent to examine a spot of blood on a boulder and pulled a collection kit from his bag. "Yeah, and you know I'm required to report regular. Something wasn't right, so I used the emergency protocol, the one I use if you're compromised. The call went straight to POTUS." He winced. "He wasn't amused but that changed when I explained. It seems for the last six months or so we've had an unknown security breach in the White House."

"How bad?" Kane flicked him a glance. "Does POTUS need me in DC or do I just need to watch my back?"

Trying to appear nonchalant, Wolfe shrugged. "Unknown at this time. The wheels are in motion to find who is rerouting the phone calls. We have a new number. Well, I have a new number. You can't call at all. Any problems, you go through me. Right now, the call I made when you went missing on your honeymoon could have alerted the mole that you were alive. When I made contact, I mentioned your code name. I knew something was up at the get-go and destroyed the SIM in my burner. I know they couldn't trace the call. I used my code name. I'm not in hiding and use my real name and profession. If they're in deep and discover who I am, it won't take them long to track me down and then possibly find you and Jenna."

"What did they advise we do?" Kane bent to look at the rocks.

Wolfe turned to head back to the body. "Nothing. They said to stand down and they'd inform me when they'd apprehended the mole." He looked at Kane. "I was on the phone for all of ten seconds, and it's been some time since I made the call and mentioned you, so we might have dodged a bullet. I figured it was need-to-know as the mole is still out there."

"You should have told me at the time." Kane rubbed the back of his neck. "I could be in a sniper's sights right now."

Wolfe shook his head. "They wouldn't want you dead—well, not until they've extracted all the information inside your head."

"That's outdated." Kane shook his head slowly. "Surely by now there's no bounty on my head."

He wished he could give Kane good news, but he met his gaze and shook his head. "The vendettas they have against the men who took down their leaders will be passed down through generations. They want to get even. They want revenge for every target you neutralized. It will never go away, Dave." He cleared his throat. "You're not alone. There are more like you in similar situations." He sighed. "It's a case of not trusting anyone new in town."

"No one is going to take me alive." Kane gave him a sideways glance. "Many have tried." He sighed. "Don't mention any of this to Jenna. She needs to live a normal life, well, as normal as possible in Serial Killer Central."

Wolfe nodded. "That's a given." He waved a hand toward the corpse. "I'd better get at it."

Christy Miller lay on her back, arms and legs spread as if she'd been trying to form a snow angel in the rocky bottom of the gully. He discounted the damage done by critters overnight nibbling at her extremities and bent over her to look closely. Long hair spread out around her in a sea of red, disguising her smashed skull, and from the angle of her neck, that along with what he could see in a visual sweep told him just about every bone in her body was broken. From the pool of blood, death hadn't been instant and she'd been alive during the fall. He'd need to do an intrahepatic probe to check the body temperature while she was in situ and unzipped her jacket. Pinned to her shirt was a Purple Heart medal with her husband's name inscribed. He turned to Kane. "This is interesting. Take a shot of this and I'll bag it. I'll look for fingerprints when I get it back to the lab. Two dead women both wearing their husband's Purple Heart. This case is getting more twisted by the second." He pulled out his equipment and frowned down at the body.

"It sure is." Kane took the photos. "How do you figure she fell this far? From the wind gusts, it's possible they influenced her trajectory."

The wind was a factor. Wolfe looked up and then back to Kane. "I'm looking at the gully through the eyes of a pilot. I know the speed of the wind gusts and figure if she fell from the plateau, she'd have been carried here. Most people bounce when they hit the ground but she appears to have landed on her back."

"Yeah, the wind is a factor." Kane stared up the gully. "It's not so windy here, so it must rise in an arc. She rode the arc and then dropped straight down. She looks startled and I've never seen an expression like that in a dead person's eyes before. It's chilling."

After taking the temperature of the liver, Wolfe bent close and examined the victim's eyes. "It's caused by the head injury and rigor. The plant residue on the palms and the deep cuts leave no doubt in my mind. She didn't try to take her own life. She fell or was pushed. We have evidence that someone was at the plateau recently and she's wearing the medal, which is more than a coincidence. I'm leaning toward homicide in this case, but I need more proof. For now, this will be an open case. There's not much doubt what killed her. See what you can find at the house for a DNA profile. A hairbrush would be good. Once I've established her ID, I'll need next-of-kin details to obtain permission for an autopsy, but I don't figure I'll be able to add to the obvious." He straightened. "Until then, my hands are tied."

"We'll head back to the house once we've finished here." Kane activated his com. "Jenna, we'll need to return to the house. Wolfe needs DNA to verify this is Christy Miller." He nodded and gave him the thumbs-up. "She recalls seeing a hair-brush in the bathroom."

Wolfe laid out a body bag and sighed. "If there's some crazy off-the-grid vet out there playing games with war widows, we need to find him. These women have been through enough, this is madness."

EIGHTEEN

An icy wind blasted through Jenna's clothes, raising goosebumps on her flesh. The chill surrounded her before darting into the forest to lift fallen leaves and whisper through the trees like a naughty spirit. She glanced behind her more than once, hearing sounds that made no earthly sense. The creaking of dry boughs and the moans as the wind moved through the caves in the gully could be mistaken for people dying. It was no wonder Blackhawk refused to come into the gully. With such a brutal history, it wasn't surprising that people believed the cries came from tormented spirits—and she had no proof they didn't. She gave herself a mental shake. Kane would call her thoughts madness, figments of an overactive imagination, or Halloween fever. She guessed he'd been in so many horrific situations, lived through bloodshed, and seen death all around him that the idea of a ghostly apparition seemed tame to him. He often said it was the living that she should fear and not the dead. Perhaps he was right after all.

Below in the gully, Kane and Webber carried the stretcher to the base of the rock wall, attached the ropes, and the search-and-rescue team hauled it up to the top and carried it into the forest. They would load it onto the travois and then wait for Wolfe and Webber to join them before returning to the van. She'd hoped she would be following them back to town, but now they'd have to negotiate the rugged pathway back to Christy's house to collect DNA samples.

Watching Kane doing anything physical always amazed her. The steep climb up to the top of the gully looked impossible but he negotiated it without seemingly breaking a sweat. Using the ropes and scaling the rockface like a lizard, he scrambled up without a problem. Wolfe followed behind slower, and when Kane pulled him over the top, he stood bent over, hands on his knees for a time, catching his breath. Webber was struggling and, despite being the youngest and a fit young man, had slipped twice. He dangled by his harness and appeared to be too exhausted to continue when Kane took hold of the rope and hauled him to the top. Jenna shook her head. Kane never ceased to amaze her. She walked up to him and handed out bottled water from her backpack. "That climb didn't faze you at all. How do you do it so easily?"

"That?" Kane flashed her a bright smile. "It was a walk in the park." He chuckled. "That's why I work out daily, to keep in shape. The rest is technique learned over many years. I've climbed out of deeper holes than that in basic training." He removed his harness and gathered up the ropes. "It helps that I'm good with heights. Being afraid uses up too much energy." He looked around. "Is Atohi a no-show?"

Jenna shrugged. "He refuses to come into the gully, and I don't blame him. This has to be one of the creepiest places I've visited in a long time. It's as if someone is whispering behind you one minute and then the long *wooing* sounds, like ghosts in horror movies, come at you from the gully. It's not a place I'd like to visit again anytime soon. With all the strange noises coming in a continuous stream, anyone could be hiding in the forest and you'd never hear them."

"It's just the wind, Jenna." Kane sipped from the bottle of water.

Jenna shrugged and looked at Wolfe. "Find anything interesting?"

"She was wearing a Purple Heart medal, same as the last victim, and I figure she died from the fall, but I'll confirm once I have her on the slab." Wolfe removed his harness and emptied the bottle of water in a few gulps.

Frowning, Jenna glanced over her shoulder as a chill ran through her. "Oh, that's another direct link to both victims. It sounds to me like someone was instructing them to wear the medal. It's darn-right creepy." She took in Wolfe's pained expression. "You look exhausted. Are you okay?"

"I'm fine. It was a difficult climb, is all. The wind was trying to pluck me off the rock wall and throw me down into the gully." Wolfe stretched, arching his back. "I'm sure glad you encouraged me to buy a hot tub. I'm going to need it tonight after riding back to the van. It's been a time since I rode a horse and climbed a mountain. My muscles are toast." He removed his helmet and glared at Kane's grin. "You can wipe that grin off your face, Dave. I don't need to be combat ready. Y'all know, I'm just a smalltown ME."

"You're doing okay." Kane slapped him on the back. "If you don't need us, we'll head back to the victim's house. The roads in and out on the other side of the gully are barely tracks and the one we took to get here tips at a forty-five-degree angle on one side in some parts. It's going to be one heck of a ride in the dark, even in the Beast."

"We can take it from here." Wolfe picked up his forensics kit. "Be careful, the killer might be watching in the forest. I've felt like I've had eyes on me all day." He gave them a wave and followed Webber into the forest.

Jenna led the way back to the Beast and put Duke on a leash to walk him while Kane did a very cautious Y-turn to get the truck headed in the right direction. The sun had dropped over the mountains, but twilight would last another two hours or so. She waited for Duke to lap up his water and hoisted him back on the seat, stowing the empty bowl in a plastic container Kane had that contained everything Duke needed for a road trip. She picked her way around the hood and climbed inside. She buckled up and smiled at Kane as he eased the truck back down the steep trail. "It never ceases to amaze me how you manage to climb up the sides of mountains. It's as if it's no effort at all."

"It isn't really." Kane shrugged. "It comes down to survival. The training I received gave me many skills. I'd never know if I had to carry a wounded asset five miles to safety or carry equipment if the truck broke down. We were conditioned to handle any scenario in any weather. It was all necessary to become part of the team."

Jenna had seen him in many precarious situations. "I've had training but nothing like yours. You can throw yourself into anything without even thinking about it."

"It just means I'm not losing my edge." Kane peered ahead into the gloom. "I don't intend to. Many say this is a young man's game, but I get tougher as I age. It's the same with torture. If ever I'm in that situation, I'll die before I give anyone more than my name. I'm confident they haven't made a torture device that can beat me."

Heart pounding, Jenna chewed on her bottom lip. "They do have something to use to beat you."

"Impossible." Kane's brow furrowed. "What?"

A cold chill ran down Jenna's back. "Me."

"You don't have to worry about anyone taking you." Kane shook his head slowly. "I could envisage two scenarios: the first is that they'd have to kill me to get to you, and the second is we both go down in a hail of bullets."

Jenna shuddered. "Oh, that makes me feel so much better."

"What made you think about foreign threats?" Kane negotiated around a large boulder and bounced over uneven ground that suddenly sloped away into shadows, emerging out of the range of the headlights like pools of dark water.

Holding her breath as the back wheel spun in nothingness for a few seconds, before Kane managed to get back on the road, she blew out a breath and looked at him. "Oh, I had a call from Jo. Seems like Carter keeps on going missing. He's acting really strange—secretive and quiet. It made me think of you in the service and the bounty on your head."

"What specifically was Jo concerned about?" Kane slowed to a crawl and the Beast started to slide down the pebble-laden trail.

Gritting her teeth and trying not to look petrified, Jenna held on tight. "She asked if what you discussed with Carter could have triggered a PTSD episode. She explained what had happened to him on his last deployment. Now he's acting strange. She wanted make sure he was okay. I didn't say anything apart from what's common knowledge."

"It's probably nothing." Kane shrugged. "Discussing missions might have triggered something, I don't know. He could be dwelling on the past. You know yourself how PTSD can creep back suddenly without warning. Maybe when the pressure increases, Carter needs some alone time. He seemed fine when I spoke to him. Don't worry. I'll call him later."

NINETEEN

The truck bumped along the uneven trail until they finally reached the fire road. It wasn't much longer before Kane parked outside Christy Miller's house. Jenna grabbed her flashlight and led the way to the front door. As they stepped under the front porch, the smell of fresh coffee greeted them. Jenna turned to look at Kane and lowered her voice to just above a whisper. "I can smell coffee. Someone's here or has been here recently." She pocketed her flashlight and pulled her weapon. "There's no vehicle outside."

"It can't be Christy." Kane slid his weapon from the holster on his thigh. "Only her killer would know she's not here."

Jenna stood to one side as Kane turned the doorknob and eased open the door. Jenna peeked inside and saw no one, but the kitchen and hall lights were blazing. "Sheriff's department. Show yourselves. We're armed."

Nothing.

She called out again.

Not as much as a creak of a floorboard.

Heart thumping, Jenna eased along the wall and indicated to Kane to clear the rooms on his side of the house. She slid into a study. A desk sat in shadows and was large enough to conceal someone. She flicked on the light and scanned the room, listening intently before taking a step inside. She checked under the desk and turned on an antique desk lamp. After searching the drawers, she turned to leave when a gust of wind buffeted the house. The old house moaned its complaint, the creaks like whispers inside the walls. The hairs on the back of her neck prickled and, sure someone was behind her, she turned in time to hear footsteps crunching in the gravel outside the window. The next second the door to the study slammed shut and the light flickered and went out, plunging her into darkness. The blackness swallowed her and every horror movie she'd ever watched flashed through her mind. Sucking in a shuddering breath, she pulled out her flashlight and headed for the door. She stopped midstride and gaped at the doorknob as it slowly turned. Without a sound the door swung open and a dark figure filled the entrance.

Jenna drew her weapon. "One more step and I'll shoot."

"I hope not."

She recognized Kane's voice and holstered her pistol. She aimed the flashlight at him and made out Kane's unimpressed unblinking expression. "There's someone outside. They ran past the window and the next moment the lights went out."

She pushed past him and headed for the front door. Behind her she could hear Kane, but as she reached the front door, his hand closed around her arm and he swung her against him.

"Wait! It could be the killer or just someone living off the grid. Maybe they come inside when Christy is away and help themselves to her food. We have no way of knowing."

Jenna stared at him. Her instinct was to hunt the person down. She swallowed the need and thought it through. "I figure someone has been following us all day. I had the feeling we were being watched. If so, they would have believed we'd left when we took the backroad."

"Exactly and he might shoot the moment we poke our heads out the door." Kane loosened his grip. He peeked around the door and scanned the area. "He's nowhere in sight, and I didn't see which way he went. He has a three-sixty-degree direction advantage and locating him would be impossible in the dark. We'll go after him if you insist, but we have no idea where to start looking. He knows the forest and will have the advantage. Going into the forest at dusk to hunt him down would be suicide. I'm not planning on becoming a victim today. What about you?"

Heart pounding, Jenna nodded. "Yeah, you're right. He's already in the wind. The moment we go into the forest we'll have a target on our backs." She shone the flashlight up the hallway. "Can you get the lights back on?"

"I'll go and see if they have a reset switch in the box in the utility room." Kane pulled out his flashlight and turned to look at her. "Coming?"

She followed him through the house and a few moments later the lights came back on. "How the heck did he trip the switch?"

"That was a coincidence." Kane shrugged. "Likely a faulty light in the study, is all. Lucky for him, it gave him time to get away."

Jenna slipped the flashlight back inside her pocket. "We'll search the house. He might have left prints. The hairbrush was in the bathroom, we'll go there last."

They swept the house and found no trace of anything missing. The only anomaly was the back door was wide open and the thick gravel had been disturbed, but no footprints were evident. Whoever had been there had vanished into the forest and blended in like a shadow. Jenna collected the hairbrush and emptied the bathroom trash into an evidence bag. Used tissues could carry DNA as well. As they walked into the kitchen, the coffee pot spat and gurgled into the pot. One cup sat on the bench beside a sugar bowl.

"It seems like whoever was here planned to stay for a time." Kane pulled on surgical gloves, lifted the pot and sniffed. "I can't smell poison. He poured a little into a cup and stared at it. "I'll leave it to cool and take a sample with us. I could sure do with a coffee right now. My energy level is getting low."

Surprised by his admission, Jenna stared at him. "We have a coffee plunger in the back of the Beast with our supplies. We'll take a break. I'm cold and a hot beverage would be nice right now. Even in this creepy house."

"Okay." Kane poured the coffee down the sink, emptied the pot, cleaned the filter and stared at her. "Yeah, that would be nice. It's a long drive home. The water supply should be fine. Run the tap for a while, wash out the kettle, and boil it again. I'll go and get the fingerprint scanner and the coffee."

Jenna shook her head. "Wait here while I refill the kettle. I'm not staying in this house alone. We'll bring Duke in too, just in case someone tries to sneak in the house again."

When they returned, they took a short break and then searched the house, including the loft, scanning almost every surface for prints, coming up with the same ones over and over. The kitchen was the same. Whoever had come inside had been wearing gloves. As she searched, Jenna was extra careful this time, checking for notes or any indication that Christy had been receiving calls from her dead husband. Apart from the empty case that once held the Purple Heart and Christy's purse, which held the house keys, the only things they found of interest were images of Christy's husband. When Kane compared them to the photographs taken from Willow Smith's house, he confirmed that Hank Miller was part of the same team that went MIA on that fateful Halloween night seven years ago. Jenna bagged everything and deposited the pile of evidence on the kitchen table before looking around. "I think that's everything but there has to be a cellar. Have you seen another door anywhere?"

"There has to be one. I looked in the kitchen. Maybe it's in the utility room?" Kane led the way and turned to look at her. "There's a door in here. How did we miss this?"

The idea of going into the cellar didn't appeal to Jenna at all. "It's probably just a broom closet."

"Nope, it's a cellar." Kane's mouth twitched into a smile. "I'll wait here and watch your back. You're not worried about going down into a dark cellar in a creepy house, are you?"

"Yeah, I am." Jenna poked him in the chest. "You wouldn't allow me to go down there alone anyway. Look for a light switch."

"Found it." Kane grasped a string hanging from the ceiling and pulled. A light came on above them and lit up the room down a short flight of stairs. "It looks clean and tidy." He bent to wedge something under the door to keep it open. "Cellar doors should open outward. If anyone ever gets trapped inside, it's easier to get out."

Jenna smiled to herself. "If that shuts on us and we're trapped, I figure there won't be much left of it after you're finished. You'd shoot your way out."

"Maybe I'd try and kick out a panel to open it first." Kane headed down the stairs and scanned the room. "No sign of entry from outside. It's clean down here. Nothing looks disturbed." He turned to look at her and frowned. "He could still be out there waiting for us to leave."

Jenna stared into space. "We could drive away and then sneak back and watch the house, but if he is military trained like you figure, he might be expecting that move. He might also have night-vision goggles and just be waiting to take us down." She sighed. "It's Catch-22. Seems we'll be walking into a trap either way." She tapped her bottom lip thinking. "We could use the wall around the house as a shield to get to the Beast?"

"That sounds like a plan." Kane took her hand and pulled her back up the stairs. "I'll organize the evidence bags if you fill the to-go cups with coffee for the ride home. I'll make his life difficult by locking the front and back doors when we leave. If we leave it open and people discover Christy is dead, the house will be stripped clean in a week."

After filling their to-go cups with coffee and grabbing their backpacks, Jenna waited for Kane to lock up and then they slipped out of the back door, locking it behind them. Keeping to the bushes they made their way to the Beast. Safe inside the bulletproof shield, she clipped in her seatbelt and Kane slid behind the wheel. She turned to pat Duke and stared out of the back window. The wind rustled through the trees and a strange mist had risen and was curling its way toward them. She pointed to the phenomenon. "Oh, that doesn't look good."

"It will sure make the journey down the mountain difficult." Kane started the engine and headed toward the road. With the headlights blazing, they drove into the darkness of the shrouded trail.

TWENTY

Using every ounce of concentration, Jenna tried to ignore the tendrils of mist trying to reach out like long silver fingers to grab her through the windows as they moved deeper into the forest. The twisted black trees bent over the trail and as the mist swirled it was as if they were driving through a coven of witches standing around a steaming cauldron. The moans of the trees as their branches rubbed together in the continuous wind sounded like the hags' wails and seemed to seep into the truck over the noise of the Beast's engine. In the darkness red and yellow eyes reflected in the headlights. Swallowing the sudden rush of fear of being trapped in the endless dark tunnel, Jenna looked for a distraction and stared at her phone, scrolling through the files to see if her deputies had added any information. As usual, all their day's work was listed and up to date. Although Rowley had made countless calls and found zip on the names of military personnel active or retired in Black Rock Falls, he had discovered a women's support group for widows of men MIA. Jenna opened Rio's files. He'd spoken to Susie Hartwig, the manager of Aunt Betty's Café, and had a page of notes. She glanced at Kane, whose silence when driving meant the way ahead was difficult to navigate and, due to the mist, the large boulders and sudden drops on one side of the road had become invisible in the steep incline. They crawled along, bumping over fallen logs and exposed tree roots. "Can you talk?"

"Yeah, I'm good but I can't risk taking my eyes off the road. It's like a minefield out there." Kane slowed to a crawl and eased the truck around a huge boulder. "I don't recall this many obstacles on the way here." He cleared his throat. "Problem?"

"The opposite." Jenna lifted her phone and blinked as the vehicle's jerky movements made the screen wobble in her hand. "Rio spoke to Susie Hartwig and she was very helpful. She's given him the names of all the ex-servicemen she knows. He has a list. Six or more would be around the right age and he's hunted down their addresses. We'll be good to go first thing in the morning." She gripped the seat as Kane went so close to the edge of a drop into a swirling mist-filled abyss on her side of the truck she couldn't take a breath.

"We'll try talking to them tomorrow." Kane hunched over the wheel peering into the darkness. "Anything else?"

As the Beast reached the end of the steep hill and the next part of the dirt road evened out, she blew out a long breath. "Yeah, Rowley found a support group for war widows. We might be lucky and find someone who knows both women. I'm going to the beauty parlor as well. I need my bangs trimmed and they'll fit me in. I might be able to get someone to talk. Sometimes acting like a normal person works better than being sheriff in that situation."

"Whatever works." Kane burst out of the dark tunnel and into the twilight. "I'm sure glad we're in the Beast. We'd be sitting ducks if anyone decided to play target practice with us in a normal truck."

Moving her gaze around the unfamiliar terrain, Jenna shivered. "When I purchased my ranch, it was isolated and I like that about it. The house had a good feeling when I first laid eyes on it, as if it had contained a loving family. I don't know how to explain it. When I walked inside, I had the strange feeling I belonged there." She reached for her to-go cup of coffee. "At Christy Miller's house, even though it's obvious she's lovingly restored the old home, it felt darn-right spooky. The moment I walked inside it was like I had a hundred eyes on me. I'm sure the man who killed all the Native Americans was so evil he left some of it behind in the house."

"I figure Blackhawk's stories and the drive through the forest have sent your imagination into overdrive." Kane scanned the way ahead. "I didn't find the house creepy, but I admit I wouldn't risk driving up and down that road every time I went to town, although by the wear on the backroad, I'd say Christy used it often and then took the fire road to Stanton. It would take longer but it would be safer."

Somewhere deep inside, she liked that nothing seemed to spook Kane, but she shook her head. "You admitted to me you felt someone watching us in the forest. The next minute we have footsteps and doors slamming, lights going out with no real explanation. We never caught sight of anyone did we? For me, that's creepy, especially around Halloween. You have to admit strange things happen around Halloween."

"They do bring out the crazies in Black Rock Falls, that's for sure." Kane flashed her a grin. "I find it highly amusing but that's not the same as feeling someone was watching us today. I still believe someone was in the forest. I don't think it was a sniper or we'd have bullets pinging off the truck, but someone was out there and they are highly trained. A Seal maybe or special ops. Whoever it is, he's good at concealing his movements and only a few are capable of moving with stealth like that."

Not convinced about Kane's observation of the house but agreeing with his assessment of the person in the forest, Jenna nodded. "We'll need to speak to the men on Rio's list."

"Yeah." Kane scratched his cheek. "While you're in the beauty parlor, I'll hunt down the first man on our list who lives in town. Maybe I'll be able to put him more at ease if I go alone. I'll ask if there's a group of ex-military that meets somewhere in town. The one thing about servicemen: they like the company of others of like mind. It's a brotherhood, so we have a chance they'll know each other. I figure they don't make a big deal about their meeting place or we'd have heard about them before now."

Jenna thought for a while and then snapped her fingers. "When Antlers opened up, they put up flyers about meeting rooms. The quilting circle moved there recently after the murders of some of their members. They figured it was safer. I recall speaking to someone about it a month or so ago. So maybe they offer a group a room for free if they have lunch at the restaurant?"

"They would more likely meet at the Triple Z Bar." Kane swung her a gaze. "I'd say some of them live off the grid and don't get duded up for places like Antlers or the Cattleman's Hotel just to meet the guys."

Fog still swirled around them, but the way ahead was almost normal. Jenna sighed. "It's way past dinner. The horses will be wondering where we've been. Don't head back to the office. Maggie will have closed up by now. We might as well go on home."

"The stalls are clean and I filled the mangers. All we have to do is move the horses into the barn and then I'll cook dinner." Kane smiled at her. "You pull out the steaks, and I'll handle the horses."

Jenna grinned. "Deal."

TWENTY-ONE

Waking in darkness to the tinny ringing of the old wall phone in the kitchen, Evelyn Brown stared at the bedroom door. She never used the landline unless the cellphone signal was weak, and hearing it ring in the middle of the night had startled her. Fearing something had happened to her parents, she grabbed her cellphone from the bedside table, ran down the stairs, and headed for the kitchen, only to have the infernal ringing stop the moment she entered the room. Panic gripped her and she called her father. The phone seemed to ring forever before he picked up. "Is everything okay? I had a call but they disconnected before I could get there."

"Yeah, your mother and I are just fine. We were asleep." Her father yawned explosively. *"I'll go and check the doors and windows. Stay on the line. I'll be back soon."*

Evelyn could hear her father shuffling in his slippers from room to room. He'd never wanted a cellphone, saying they were intrusive. She'd dragged her father out of bed to answer her frantic call for no reason. When he picked up the receiver, and insisted everything was fine, she blew out a long relieved breath.

"I'm glad you're okay. It must have been a wrong number. I'm sorry to have woken you."

"Don't be sorry. It's nice to know you care. Sleep tight, princess."

"Night, Dad." Evelyn disconnected.

Feeling a little silly, she went to the sink for a drink of water. As she lifted her gaze to peer into the backyard, every hair on her skin stood to attention at the sight of a military man, staring at her from the perimeter of the forest. She shook her head, refusing to believe someone was out there watching her. The mist had rolled in, making the forest appear surreal and playing tricks on her. She stared transfixed as the shadowy figure moved against the direction of the wind. She couldn't make out what was out there. The next moment, green eyes flashed in the darkness, a second before the bulky shadow vanished like a ghost into the trees. Heart hammering, she extinguished the lights and, peering around the refrigerator, scanned the view from the kitchen window. Leaves twirled across the lawn, lifting in gusts of wind as if skating across a lake of mist, and the trees appeared to shiver under the icy-cold blasts. Shadows moved, but nothing appeared to be in the shape of a man. Unsettled, she went to the gun safe and collected her Glock. After making sure the doors and windows were shut tight, she locked her bedroom door and slipped back into bed.

Seconds later the phone in the kitchen rang again. Sitting bolt upright, she swung her legs from the bed and sneaked downstairs using only the moonlight to guide her steps. Grabbing at the receiver, she pressed it to her ear. "Who is this?"

Nothing.

Suddenly afraid, Evelyn listened. Was that someone breathing, listening to her? "Who is this?"

Her skin pebbled as a low chuckle filled her ear. It was almost intimate. Skin crawling, she slammed down the receiver and pressed her back to the wall, trying to think straight. What possible fun could anyone get from waking her in the middle of the night? Had she upset someone at work? Perhaps dating a guy in her office had caused a problem, but he'd insisted he had no one in his life. Or did she have a stalker?

Suddenly vulnerable, she touched the heavy Glock weighing down the pocket of her gown. No one could get inside to hurt her but the blinds on every window had been pulled wide. There were no neighbors close enough to look inside and she loved the views. One of her joys had been looking at the garden at night. It was spectacular, seeing the moon high above the mountains and forest, but she'd forgo the view and close all the shutters and blinds before dark from now on. It was so quiet in the house, the usual screeches and moans aside. She'd always felt safe. As she made her way back to the stairs, she heard the sound of tires on the gravel of her driveway. A vehicle's door slammed shut. Aiming her pistol with both hands, she hurried down the hallway and peered out the window.

Nothing.

She moved from window to window but only the swirling mist tormented by the gusts of wind into ghostly shapes marched toward her. With the howls from the forest the driveway resembled a scene from a horror movie. Swallowing her fear, she headed for the stairs.

The phone rang again.

Looking over one shoulder, she ran back to the kitchen and gabbed up the phone. "I'm armed, so you've been warned. Stop calling me and get the hell off my property."

"I just wanted to hear your voice again. It's been a long time hasn't it, Evie?"

Evelyn didn't recognize the muffled voice. "Who is this?"

"Will. I'm back. Let me in. It's cold outside."

Shocked to the bone, Evelyn's fingers closed around the handle of her Glock. "Will is dead, you sick freak."

Ice filled her veins as she dropped the phone into the cradle and headed back to her room. As she reached the bottom of the stairs, a soft chuckle came close by. She spun around waving the Glock to sweep the area and saw no one. Only the shadows of the trees moved in the wind.

The phone rang again.

Evelyn dashed up the stairs into her room, turned on the light, and locked the door. Trembling, she stared around. The door was thick but she needed extra protection and tested the weight of a chest of drawers but could barely lift it. Dropping her Glock back into the pocket of her gown, she bent and pulled out the drawers. Using every ounce of strength, she heaved the furniture in front of the door, and slid back the drawers. Leaning back against the wall, she heaved in deep breaths. Above her, the ceiling creaked and footsteps moved from one side to the other. She gaped in disbelief. *How could anyone get inside?* Her heart was beating so hard she could hear it in her ears. The footsteps came again, slow, methodical, back and forth, back and forth.

Someone was in the loft.

Panic had her by the throat and she searched her pockets for her phone to call 911 and came up empty-handed. Evelyn stared around the room and her heart sank. She'd left her phone on the kitchen table. Sweating with fear, Evelyn climbed into bed, pushed the Glock under the pillow, and stared at the ceiling. It was going to be a long sleepless night and the freak could play games and call as many times as he wanted but he'd be wasting his time. She wouldn't be moving until daylight.

The following morning, Jenna set Rio and Rowley the task of conducting background checks on the retired military personnel Susie Hartwig had supplied. While they were busy, she called the beauty parlor to save valuable time and was relieved to find they'd be able to fit her in within the hour. With luck, she'd obtain some valuable information from the stylists about the victims. She leaned on her desk and listened as Kane contacted Carter. He'd called him the previous evening and the call had gone to voicemail. It was strange that Carter hadn't returned his call. He'd left a message he'd be calling this morning.

"Hey. Where have you been? I've been trying to contact you." Kane raised an eyebrow at Jenna and put his phone on speaker. "Jenna is here. We have a second victim connected to the first. We've identified Christy Miller's husband as—"

"Sergeant Hank Miller. Yeah, I remember him." Carter sounded perfectly normal. "I'm in town, taking some personal time. I'm not needed in Snakeskin Gully. It's as quiet as a tomb there right now and I had a hankering for a steak at Antlers. I'll be here for at least a week."

Anxious for any information to help solve the case and

maybe save the killer's next victim, Jenna leaned forward. "Ty, it's Jenna. Can you tell us who else was in the team? Do you know if any of them got out alive? We believe one of them is involved in murdering these women. If you have any information, we need to know."

"You know darn well it's classified." Carter's boots clattered over what sounded like a tiled floor. "I wish I could give you a list of the people I recall from that time, but my hands are tied. I'm an FBI agent and divulging that information would be a national security breach. They'd come for me and I'd rot in the federal pen. I'm walking a thin line by confirming what you know to be a fact, and that should be good enough, Jenna."

Shaking her head in frustration, Jenna stared at Kane's phone. "Even if it means another woman might die?"

"That's not my problem." Carter blew out a long breath. "I've gotta go. I'm going hunting. If you're talking to Jo, tell her my phone will be off, but I'll check my messages and get back to her if she needs me."

"Wait up." Kane looked at Jenna and pressed a finger to his lips. "Is everything okay? I mean talking about the missions the other day hasn't triggered an episode, has it? I'm always here to talk if you need help."

"Oh man, I take a few days' leave and the phones start running hot sayin' I've lost my mind." Carter's footsteps stopped and a vehicle door opened and slammed shut, an engine roared into life. "I figure Jo is the neurotic one. She's my boss and going behind my back checkin' up on me. I figure she called Jenna and made a noise about me going missin'—right? I have accrued three years annual leave and I'm taking two weeks that's owed me, is all. I dropped into the office a few times last week to make sure she was okay and got the third degree, so I took the chopper and came here. Now you guys are on my back too." He cleared his throat. "Y'all should know, sometimes a man just needs some alone time. I'll catch you later." He disconnected.

Jenna stared at Kane. "Oh, that went well."

"Don't be so tough on him. It wouldn't have been easy for him to settle back into work after two years off the grid. Now he's stuck in an office for weeks at a time staring at the walls." Kane pushed his phone into his pocket and leaned back in his chair. "He's an outdoors man and likes to be in the forest hunting and fishing. He did that to survive for two years, and from what he said, it was the best time of his life."

Recalling what Kane had told her about his time as a sniper, she shrugged. "You were a lone wolf during your missions, but you manage just fine without going AWOL."

"He's hardly AWOL. He took leave and, yeah, it was hard for me to become part of a new team after a few years alone in the desert, but I did have Wolfe in my ear during that time and an evac team to drag my sorry butt out of danger zones. By the time I came here I'd blended back into society, but the sniper is never far away." He smiled at her. "Somedays I can just about reach out and touch him."

Jenna frowned. "Carter is different than you; he's still carrying his ghosts, isn't he?"

"Maybe, it's not something you can forget in a hurry. Some guys just get the thousand-mile stare and others PTSD. Some, like me, handle the killing and bloodshed. Everyone is different, but most Seal teams are conditioned to perform, but people all have a breaking point." Kane pulled a notebook out of his drawer and pushed it into his pocket. "Basically, from what I know about Carter is that he's a player. He loves women and they love him. He's not attracted to Jo and he's trapped in a small town with no chance of meeting anyone. He needs some time to blow off steam, is all."

Jenna stood and collected her things. "You're saying there's no bars in Snakeskin Gully where he could hang out?"

"Hmm." Kane stood and raised both eyebrows. "Not many FBI agents hang out with the locals. I don't believe he'd fit in, and if he started chasing after their womenfolk, well, he might find himself in big trouble." He checked his weapon and then pushed on his black Stetson. "I'll drop you by the beauty parlor. Call me when you're done. I'm heading out to speak to Luke Thompson out of Dead-End Road, a Marine who served in Afghanistan around the same time as Miller."

Concern for Kane gnawed at her. Interviewing potential serial killers wasn't something she wanted any of her deputies to do alone. She pulled on her coat and nodded. "Why don't you take Rio with you for backup? You have no idea who you're dealing with and walking into a man's yard without notice could be dangerous."

"Nah, I can take care of myself." Kane whistled for Duke and then followed her out of the door. "He isn't expecting me and it usually takes people a few seconds to react if they're planning on doing some damage. That's all the time I need."

Jenna walked beside him down the stairs. "Yeah, but he's ex-military and might be just like you. If so, he'd keep himself in shape. If he's our killer, he might be a bigger threat than you think."

"Maybe, but I don't think so." Kane gave Maggie a nod as they passed the counter and, after rounding a man paying a fine, pushed open the glass doors. "I checked him out. He's ten years older than me and a writer. He self-publishes war stories, so he sits on his butt all day in front of a laptop. I figure I'll have the jump on him if he starts anything." He hoisted Duke into the back seat of the Beast and clipped in his harness. "And I'll have Duke, attack dog extraordinaire." He grinned at her from the back seat before straightening and getting behind the wheel. "You know he won't allow anyone to get the jump on me."

Shaking her head, Jenna sighed. "Okay, you know your limitations." She waved at Wendy, from Aunt Betty's Café. She was dropping by with a pile of takeout for her deputies. Her attention moved to Kane when his stomach growled. "It's only a couple of hours since breakfast. We'll have a break after we've spoken to a few people. Eat your energy bars."

"Yes, ma'am." Kane backed out of the space and headed down Main. "I'm surprised Wolfe hasn't called with an update. He usually conducts his autopsies around ten."

Admiring a few superbly carved pumpkins, displayed artistically on the steps of the town hall, Jenna turned back to look at him. "I guess he wanted to confirm the victim's ID and contact the next of kin before he started. He can't say it's a homicide without proof, so he needs the next of kin's permission. If he has none, then he uses his discretion."

"Maybe it's just as well the autopsy was delayed. You're still pale." Kane examined her face. "Still feeling sick?"

Waking and rushing to the bathroom to spew hadn't been her idea of fun and in truth, the idea of witnessing an autopsy made her stomach roll. She shook her head. "I'm fine."

Putting the autopsy out of her mind for a moment, Jenna pointed and laughed at some of the bizarre decorations adorning Main. She'd noticed the increase in zombies over the last few years, and this year automatons with jerky movements hung around every other lamppost, and in between black-eyed ghosts wailed as the vehicles drove by. The stores had gotten into the spirit of the celebrations with witches, cobwebs, and spiders being the most popular themes, along with the usual men with axes through their heads and severed hands crawling inside storefront windows. Unlike some towns, the stores in Black Rock Falls remained open until late each Halloween and handed out candy by the bucketload to passing children. The parade of trick-or-treaters started around seven and went from the sheriff's department right through to Antlers and beyond to some of the outlying houses. The kids walked down one side of Main and up the other. The night culminated in a costume-themed ball at the town hall. It was a night Jenna hated to miss, but every year something happened around Halloween to spoil it. It seemed that this year was no exception.

As they pulled up in front of the beauty parlor, she turned to Kane. "I shouldn't be more than thirty minutes. If you get delayed, call me. I'll walk back to the office."

"If that happens, go to Aunt Betty's and I'll meet you there. It's too cold and windy to be walking all the way back to the office." Kane smiled at her. "Good luck on your fact-finding mission."

Jenna opened the door and chuckled. "Aunt Betty's, huh? Any excuse for a bite to eat, right? Okay, I'll see you soon." She slipped out of the door and hurried into the beauty parlor without looking back. Kane believed he was indestructible, but he was just a man and Wolfe had warned her not to become his Achilles heel. If he were worried about dying and leaving her alone, he'd lose his edge. He could never know how much she worried about him. *Just don't run into a serial killer, Dave—not when you're alone.*

TWENTY-THREE

After making sure Jenna was safe inside the door, Kane entered the address into the GPS and headed out of town. Dead-End Road was about ten minutes away in the lowlands and Luke Thompson's ranch house sat right in the middle of acres of golden grasslands. To his right, deer barely visible in the tall waving grass popped out their heads to watch him drive by, and on his left, a herd of bison grazed as they moved slowly up a rise. He smiled seeing the freedom of wildlife in their natural surroundings. There were no closed gates here to hamper their movements. He found the driveway to Thompson's ranch, slowed to read the name on the gate, and drove inside. The property wasn't posted with warning signs, so when the ranch house came into view he sounded his horn. He scanned the area. A few chickens fluttered away, squawking as he slowed before the front door, and two old hunting dogs lifted their heads to look at him from their place on the porch.

As Kane slipped from the Beast, he moved his jacket away from his holster, putting it out there in plain sight. This wasn't unusual, in Black Rock Falls many men carried weapons and most knew him by sight. The dogs looked harmless enough, so he let Duke down from the back seat and told him to stay before ambling to the front porch. The door opened before he made it to the steps and a tall thick-set man pushed open the screen door. "Morning. You'll be Luke Thompson?"

"Yeah, that's me. What brings you out this way, Deputy?" Thompson leaned one shoulder against the doorframe and raised both eyebrows.

Watching the man's eyes for any sign of hostility, Kane smiled. "I've been hunting down the local vet's organization in town and Susie out of Aunt Betty's gave me your name. She figured you might be able to help me."

"Why now?" Thompson straightened and walked out onto the porch, letting the screen door slam behind him. "You've been in town for a time and haven't hunted us down."

Kane leaned his back against the porch railing and shrugged. "I didn't know there were any of us in town. Well, not until this week when we found the body of Willow Smith. A friend of hers mentioned a few men retired here after their time in Afghanistan."

"That would have been Oliver's wife. You know she went crazy? Said she heard voices and had phone calls from him." Thompson rubbed his chin. "How did she die?"

"That's undetermined." Kane watched his body language closely. "How did you know her?"

"I didn't know her at all." Thompson cleared his throat. "One of the guys mentioned it at a meeting, is all. We talked about how the wives of those who are MIA are stuck between a rock and a hard place. Most won't get on with their lives because they believe their husbands are going to come home." He gave Kane a long look. "We know that ain't gonna happen, right?"

Kane nodded. "Not much chance if there's no record of them as a POW. So how many ex-servicemen do you figure are in Black Rock Falls?"

"I couldn't tell you. We have six to ten at our meetings at any one time. There are more scattered around. They're all different ages. One of the old guys served in Vietnam. There are more than I can count who don't socialize, like yourself. Some are living in town, but many are off the grid. They've been living in the forest since they were shipped home and they don't want to be found."

Needing more information, Kane took a chance. "I used to know some of the guys from that time too. Do you know any men who attend the meetings and were in Afghanistan about seven years ago?"

"Yeah." Thompson stared into space for a long minute before coming back to himself. "Ah... let me see now. That would be Riley Sutton out of Gallows Hill, Mark Pittman out of Damien's Hollow, and Marco Myers out of The Devil's Cross-roads. Any of those names ring a bell?"

Kane shook his head, repeating the names over in his mind. "Can't say that they do. I figured we could have crossed paths, but there were a ton of teams coming in and out at that time."

"There were indeed." Thompson gave Kane a long hard look. "Seal?"

Kane nodded. "Yeah."

"So, what makes you want to mix with us all of a sudden like?" Thompson dropped into an old chair on the porch, picked up a knife from a small table, and started whittling a piece of wood shaped like a naked woman.

Unconcerned but not stupid, Kane kept his eyes on the knife. He needed information and had no idea who this man had known. He'd be playing against the odds if he made up a story about knowing any of the men Thompson had mentioned. He'd just have to wing it. "I know Oliver Smith's team went MIA and I know his wife, Willow, was friends with Christy Miller, who purchased a house out at Death Drop Gully, but her husband, Hank, didn't come from these parts. I knew some of the guys from that team married girls from Montana, but I didn't know any of them had settled here." He brushed the end of his nose. "Do you know how many of the wives of the men in Oliver's team live here?"

"Why? You planning on offering them a shoulder to cry on?" Thompson paused his whittling and stared at him.

Kane barked a laugh. "Nope, I just married Sheriff Alton and I don't figure she'd appreciate it."

"Why then?" Thompson frowned.

Kane had no choice but to show his cards. "Christy was found at the bottom of Death Drop Gully yesterday. I'm trying to locate her family or friends and have come up with zip."

"That's strange. I heard that two other wives of the men in the same team had died but not here. Helena, maybe?" Thompson leaned back in his chair, making it groan. "You figure they were linked? I'm sayin' that because I was an MP and my mind is always in police mode. I'm sure you understand."

As criminals, particularly psychopaths, like to insert themselves into crime investigations so that they can relive the thrill, Kane nodded. "Yeah, but we don't think these are murders, more like suicide. I just need close contacts, is all. We found little information at their houses."

"There are two other wives I know of in town." Thompson smiled. "You're wondering how almost an entire team ended up in Montana, right? I knew Oliver from school and we talked the guys into taking a furlough in Montana. We met a group of girls from Montana State and went on a cookout. Eight or so of the guys hooked up that weekend. More guys went back next leave. It was a honey hole of beautiful women and relationships were formed—you know the deal. Oliver was always raving on about Black Rock Falls and they'd come here to hunt or fish. It seemed they wanted to make this town their home after leaving the service. It would be a place they could all be together. I left soon after to join the MPs, but I do recall William Brown made plans to marry a girl named Evelyn. She lived with her folks out at Creeping Vine Trail, but they died during his last tour. Evelyn inherited the house and I know for sure Will had plans to live out at Creeping Vine Trail when his tour of duty was over. He'd never wanted to stay on and become a desk jockey, so had forgone the chance of a pension to leave and work as a civilian. Both these guys never came home, so maybe their wives are still friends, being as they were at school together and all. It's a long-shot but the best I can do. The guys meet first Friday of the month out at the Triple Z Bar. You're welcome to drop by. We drink and play pool, talk about old times, is all. No shrinks allowed." He chuckled.

Pulling out his notebook and jotting down the names of the men and their locations. Kane added the new information and smiled. "Thanks. I might take you up on that if I get the time." He straightened. "I'll go and hunt down these women. Chances are they'll be able to help me find relatives."

"Anytime." Thompson dropped the wood and knife on the table and turned to go inside. "If you find out what happened to Oliver's team, let me know. When I asked, I hit a brick wall."

After folding his notebook and pushing it back inside his pocket, Kane turned to leave. "Yeah sure." He headed to the truck, hoisted Duke into the back seat, and then glanced over his shoulder, but Thompson had gone back inside. "What did you make of him?" He rubbed Duke's ears. The dog growled and pushed his nose into Kane's hand. "Yeah, I agree. He's one to watch. Let's go get Jenna and then see what Susie has for you at Aunt Betty's today." He laughed when Duke barked in reply and his tail thumped on the seat in excitement. Kane took a long look over one shoulder at the closed door. He noticed the drapes on one window twitch. Thompson was watching him. Feeling eyes on his back, he climbed behind the wheel, spun the Beast around, and headed back to town.

TWENTY-FOUR

It was a surreal morning, sitting in the beauty parlor having her hair trimmed by a witch in a tall hat with attached black matted hair, wearing a long black gown and green face paint. Cobwebs hung from the mirrors and bats from the ceiling. The smell from the concoction of shampoos and hairspray made her queasy and almost made her believe they had a cauldron bubbling out back. Amid the sound of hairdryers and light conversation, Jenna tried to slide in questions about the two victims. The stylist knew both of them, but when Jenna asked if Willow or Christy had ever mentioned anything unusual happening at home, like strange phone calls, she'd received a roll of the eyes. "It's just one of Willow's other friends mentioned phone calls late at night, is all."

"Yeah, Willow figured it was Oliver." The stylist flashed the scissors and smoothed Jenna's hair with a comb. "She dropped by a few days ago all skittish and needing company. I washed and dried her hair and she told me. It's seven years this Halloween since Oliver died. She was convinced he was trying to contact her from beyond the grave. She said he'd been calling on the stroke of midnight." She shrugged. "She always gets a little crazy around this time of year, but not like this. She was leaving here and dropping by Doc Brown's to get something for her nerves before heading off for a week in Vegas." She brushed the hair from Jenna's shoulders and removed the cape. "There, you're all done and just in time too. I see a handsome man leaning against a black truck just outside." She winked at Jenna. "You must have been at the front of the lucky line to have married him."

Laughing, Jenna followed her to the counter, pulling a credit card from her pocket. "Yeah, it's been kind of like winning the lottery. I count my blessings every day." She handed the stylist her card. "Thanks for fitting me in when you're so busy."

"We all understand your time is limited, Sheriff." The stylist smiled and handed back her card. "I hope we'll see you at the ball."

Jenna smiled. "I hope so too."

As she stepped outside, Duke ran to meet her, tail circling like a propeller and making little doggy dance steps. He barked as if telling her about his morning and then dashed back to Kane. She smiled at Kane. He always looked so relaxed, leaning against the Beast, dressed all in black, his long open coat flowing in the wind like Dracula's cape. "I hope I didn't keep you waiting long."

"Nah, a few minutes, is all." Kane flashed her a white smile and tipped his head one way and then the other. "Hmm, you look good." He opened the door to the Beast and waved her inside. "Your carriage awaits, ma'am."

Surprised he'd noticed, she climbed inside and fastened her seatbelt. With Duke settled in the back seat, she waited for Kane to get behind the wheel. As they blended into the traffic, Duke stood and thrust his head out of the open window. She laughed at the way his mouth flapped in the wind as if he were singing along to the tunes on the radio. "Duke's happy today."

"I told him we were going to see Susie at Aunt Betty's." Kane chuckled. "He's been trying to run there since we arrived at the beauty parlor. I think he was trying to tell you to hurry when you came out."

Amused, Jenna shook her head. "Atohi was right when he said you two were meant to be together. He understands what you say and you both have an unhealthy attachment to Aunt Betty's Café."

"We both just appreciate good food, is all." Kane slowed to find a parking space near the diner. "I could smell apple pie cooking all the way here." He parked the Beast and climbed out, going straight to the back to get Duke.

A very social dog, Duke would wag his tail at people passing by but usually remained at Kane's side, only stopping if he came across a small child intent on pulling his ears. Jenna smiled as he danced across the sidewalk and nosed his way inside the door. "Did you forget to feed him this morning?"

"No, but coming here is a special treat on Wednesdays." Kane headed for the counter. "Susie saves him the leftovers."

Confused, Jenna removed her hat and followed him. "How does he know it's Wednesday?"

"Well, we dropped by here yesterday for lunch and I had the pork. He'd know the leftovers would be available today, I guess." Kane shrugged. "He's a smart dog." He gave Susie his order.

Jenna ordered a bagel with cream cheese and then relented and asked for a slice of apple pie. She turned to Kane. "This will have to be lunch as well. We can't waste any more time eating today."

"Okay." Kane turned back to Susie. "I'll have a pie to go as well, thanks." He looked at her and shrugged. "I can work and eat at my desk and the guys would appreciate a slice of pie too." He led the way to their table.

Jenna sat down and brought him up to speed on what she'd discovered. "So not much more than we already know and nothing at all about Christy. What about you?"

She listened with interest and then took his notebook and copied to her files the names he'd discovered. She emailed Rio and told him to add the names to the list of men they were already hunting down. She wanted to know everything about them and where they could find them this afternoon if possible. "I'm getting so used to finding dead ends when we hunt down suspects. This information is gold."

"Maybe it's too good to be true. I'm surprised he didn't clam up when I started to push him for information." Kane leaned back in his chair as one of the servers arrived with the food. "He mentioned he was an MP, which could be true. I guess we can find out, but his interest in the death of Willow Smith was a double-edged sword to me. There are so many psychopathic killers who get gratification out of being involved in the investigation of one of their kills."

Sipping her coffee and enjoying the rich taste spilling over her tongue, Jenna nodded. "You can read people. What impression did you get from him?"

"He comes across as a nice guy." Kane shrugged and bit into a thick steak burger and chewed slowly.

Trying not to allow the cold creeping up her spine in a warning to spoil her meal, Jenna stared at him. "A nice guy and someone who wants to be involved in the investigation and is suggesting others to maybe throw the scent off him? So, we put him on the list of suspects and check out his movements around the times of the homicides."

"Oh, yeah." Kane nodded. "He's at the top of my list."

Jenna swallowed a bite of bagel. "I think our priority is hunting down Evelyn Brown. We can only assume she married

William, as Thompson suggested, and they now live in town. If the killer is hunting down the wives of the men on the same team, she could be next."

"Then if he's our killer, why would Thompson give us her name, unless there's another woman he's keeping to himself." Kane dug into his wedge of apple pie. "While we're chasing down Evelyn, he's free to murder the one we don't know about."

TWENTY-FIVE

Finding a murdered young woman with no one on this earth left to care if she lived or died was sad. After the DNA collected at Christy Miller's house matched the body they'd found at the bottom of Death Drop Gully, Wolfe requested the X-rays from the local dentist and found a second match. With her identity confirmed, he spent the morning hunting down everything he could about Christy Miller. As a medical examiner, he spoke for the dead, as there was no one else to tell what happened to them. Discovering everything he could about a victim could often be crucial when making a determination, especially when it came to suicide. As an ME, people often gave him information when he requested it and he found the local art group only too happy to supply him with the contact details of the members. He called each one of them and found them all to have nothing but nice things to say about Christy. He'd sent Webber to hunt down the lawyer who'd handled the sale of the house she'd restored. He'd scratched his head when he read the name James Stone on the copies of the documents. That particular lawyer had died in a shootout with Jenna some years previously. From lawyer to one of the worst psychopathic killers in the state, seeing his name brought back memories he'd rather forget. Stone's clients had been taken over by Samuel J. Cross and one phone call had confirmed that Christy Miller had no living relatives. Her estate would go to the War Widows' Association. This wasn't common knowledge, so the motive for her death wasn't from anyone benefiting from her considerable fortune. It was an important find and he'd pass on all the information he'd gathered to Jenna.

He'd conducted a preliminary examination the night before and stared at the X-rays on the screen array. There was so much damage he didn't know where to start. The head injury would have killed her. The back of the skull had disintegrated on impact but he'd conduct a full autopsy and had already taken blood to scan for drugs in her system. He walked back to the covered body on a stainless-steel gurney and examined her hands again. The plant residue matched the samples he'd taken from the bushes at the top of the gully. The long ride to the top with Blackhawk had been essential. He needed to see the stripped bushes firsthand and examine the area where the victim fell. The scraping on the rockface and the stripped plants gave him a clear indication Christy Miller fell or was pushed from the plateau. The flashlight was a significant clue as it was still in the on position. She didn't stumble over the edge in the dark, and from the debris left behind by an unknown person, he concluded she was pushed. Now all he had to do was prove it.

He covered the body and removed his mask and gloves before heading back to his office. He needed to call the team and give them the information he'd discovered. He'd be starting the autopsy at two, by that time he should have identified a few of the specific drug markers from the samples he'd tested. He punched in Jenna's number. "Hey, Jenna."

He brought her up to date and listened as she gave him what they had so far. "I can go ahead with Webber and shoot the findings over I'm done. Or drop by at two and watch, but it's not going to be pretty. I'll need to discover the extent of the brain injuries."

"Have you estimated a time of death?" A powerful engine roared in the background and Jenna raised her voice. *"I figure as she left the lights on, she must have left at dusk."*

Wolfe had taken the body and air temperature at the scene and considered the state of rigor and made his estimation. "I'd say less than twelve hours before you found her. The temperature drops very low in the gully at night, but I took everything into account and six to twelve hours would be a reasonable time, but closer to twelve."

"Hi, Shane." Kane's voice came through the speaker. *"If Christy was getting calls at midnight the same as Willow, it makes sense that she'd have gone out to meet her husband a little after midnight. I figure the killer lured her to her death and if he risked walking up to the plateau at night, he knows the area."*

Wolfe had thought through many scenarios. "As so many First Nations people died in the gully, have y'all considered it might be one of them seeking revenge? You said the killer knows the forest."

"If Blackhawk refuses to go near that part of the gully because of the angry spirits, then I would imagine it would be a widespread belief and they'd all keep away." Kane cleared his throat. *"I can't imagine any of them would be out for revenge for something that happened a century or more ago, but your idea might be worth a phone call at least. I know a high proportion of Native Americans join the military but we'd have to speak to Blackhawk to discover if any of his people were involved in the conflict seven years ago. If so, they might give us the names of people they served with who live in town."*

Concerned about the possibilities of more deaths, Wolfe stared at the images of the victims on his screen. "With two murders so close together, he'll strike again soon. Have you discovered the location of the woman Thompson mentioned?"

"We're going on his recollections and only have her first name. She might not have married the serviceman she met in Helena." Kane sighed. *"How are you going to handle this, Jenna?"*

"Right now, locating the woman Thompson mentioned is a priority." Jenna took a deep breath. *"She could be next on the list. Until we discover otherwise, we'll assume she married Will Brown. We'll need a first and last name to run through the databases. We'll head back to the office and see if we can hunt her down."*

Wolfe stood. "Okay, if you're busy all day, Webber will stand in for you and I'll start the autopsy now. I'll send over the report and call with the cause of death." He looked at the files on his screen and sighed. "Before you go, the DNA we found on the cigarette butts are not in any database we have, so they didn't come from anyone in the military. I found nothing on the candy wrapper, no prints, nothing. One more thing. I have the autopsy reports for the apparent suicides of the women from other counties related to the military."

"At last. Did they find anything suspicious?" Jenna blew out a sigh.

Wolfe ran a hand down his face. "The findings were inconclusive but ruled as probable suicide. The cases are still open, so they have all the evidence on hand. I've requested it be sent to me. I've looked over the findings and there's nothing conclusive. I'll need a court order to have the bodies exhumed. The relatives will likely fight it, so it might be weeks before we get an answer. I figure we see how this case plays out. If we catch this guy, Kane might get a confession out of him, or we'll find evidence of his involvement." He sighed. "Waiting might save families a lot of pain."

"I'm not so sure." Jenna cleared her throat. *"Taking your own life is way different from being murdered. If I was related to*

one of these women, I'd want the truth. If we don't get a confession, will you get that court order?"

Wolfe pushed a hand through his hair. "That's a given, Jenna. I want the truth to come out for these women."

"Okay, I'll talk to you soon." Jenna disconnected.

Wolfe dropped his phone onto the desk as his door opened and his daughter Emily smiled at him. He smiled back. "No classes today?"

"Yeah, early this morning we observed a resection of the bowel operation." Emily shrugged. "It was interesting. Everything I study in the field of medicine is fascinating, even the drugs side of things and how they work."

Wolfe moved from behind the desk. "Are you thinking of becoming an MD now?"

"Well, I am expected to intern at Black Rock Falls General for a time, but I figure I'll come back to my first love of being an ME. It would be a waste of my time studying forensic science if I didn't follow my heart." She followed him into the hall. "Anything interesting on the schedule today?"

Nodding, Wolfe directed her to the alcove where they kept the scrubs, gloves, and face masks. "Yeah, a woman, mid-thirties, fell or was pushed from the top of a gully, multiple impact injuries. We need to find out what happened to her."

"Cool." Emily removed her jacket and hung it on a peg. "Let's get at it."

TWENTY-SIX

After a long sleepless night, Evelyn Brown headed downstairs and, Glock in hand, moved with care around the house. The disturbances had stopped around two but she'd stayed awake, too pumped with adrenalin to sleep. Her head ached but she checked the doors and windows and found no sign of a break-in. She methodically checked every room. Confused and feeling like she'd stepped out of a nightmare, she put on a pot of coffee. She called the phone company and they checked the line. Everything tested fine and the number they had on record for the calls was untraceable. They said it was probably a prank caller or kids playing tricks over Halloween. Unconvinced, she drummed her fingers on the kitchen table. She enjoyed her solitude and living with her memories, but now being alone was frightening. The room had always been a favorite of hers. The kitchen led to a sunroom that opened up to the backyard with views of Stanton Forest and the mountains. The lawn sloped down, hiding the fence line and giving the impression that her property went on forever. Even in the moonlight, she often watched deer, elk, or even a brown bear wander by. The unique wilderness on the other side of her property line was beautiful in all seasons. Now all she could see in the forest were men watching her and it made her skin crawl.

The terrifying realization that someone was stalking her had frightened her, but in the light of day the rush of terror had dissipated with the mist. She'd always been a realistic person, a straight shooter, and was now doubting herself. Had she seen a man in the woods or imagined him? Yet the calls were real enough and someone was intent on frightening her. Kids playing pranks aside, she decided to take action. The first thing she needed to do was to close the shutters. She went from room to room securing them and sliding the bolt across each one. It made the rooms oppressive and claustrophobic, so she closed the blinds and switched on the lights. She'd leave the upstairs shutters open so she could watch all around from above, but could do nothing to stop someone peering at her through the sunroom window.

Evelyn went back to the kitchen, poured a cup of strong black coffee, and stared at the old phone on the wall. She'd liked the quirkiness of an old sixties phone, with a dial and a unique ring, but suddenly she hated it. Worried the man might call again, or break in and murder her in her sleep, she decided to contact the sheriff's office for advice. The sheriff was very approachable and would listen to her concerns without making her feel like an idiot. "Hello, my name is Evelyn Brown." She gave her details. "I'd like to speak to Sheriff Alton."

"The sheriff is out on a call right now, but she'll be back later. Do you have an emergency?"

Evelyn's attention moved back to the phone, looking so innocent on the wall. "No, it's not an emergency, but I need to speak with her."

"I have deputies here. If one of them can help or if it's of a more personal nature, I might be able to help you. My name is Magnolia Brewster. I've worked with the sheriff since she started here. If you need help, we can protect you."

Not wanting to leave her concerns another night, Evelyn shook her head. "That's very kind of you, but I need to speak to Sheriff Alton. I'll drive into town and wait until she gets back. It can't wait. I need to see her today."

"Sure. Just come straight up to the front counter and speak to me."

Evelyn stood. "I will, thanks." She leaned back in her chair and drained her cup of coffee.

For now, no one could get to her, she had her Glock and the house was locked up tight. How someone had got inside and up into the loft puzzled her. Should she pull down the steps and look? She stared at the ceiling for a long time and then shook her head. The noise the steps made dropping down would have alerted her. Did she imagine the footsteps? She ran her palm over the scrubbed wooden table and sighed. When she and Will purchased the house, before he'd left for the last time, they'd made so many plans sitting at this very table. He'd promised to come back to her, but none of his team had made it out of the desert that Halloween night. She swallowed the grief that never went away. She'd buried an empty coffin; taken the folded flag and Purple Heart they'd given her and returned to their house of dreams. One good thing about being a military wife was she'd worked on base and moved around with Will all over the world. He taught her how to shoot and be confident with firearms. They'd settled into the house in Black Rock Falls three months before his last deployment. She'd understood she'd be living far away from his base during his time overseas, but the time had passed quickly as she converted the house into a home. A home he'd never see again.

She couldn't stay here alone another night and ran upstairs and packed a bag. She pulled on her coat and gathered her things. Fall had come with a promise of winter, high winds, and crisp mornings with the smell of snow not far away. After making sure the deadbolt was secure on the front door for the tenth time, she hurried through the kitchen and out the door to the garage. No one could see her leaving the house, and if anyone tried to stop her driving out, she'd run them down. She climbed into her Jeep, used the clicker in the vehicle to open the overhead garage door, and backed out. As she did a Y-turn her gaze moved along the tree line and her heart missed a beat. In the shadows of the trees something moved and she caught the flash of a reflection, like sunlight on glass. She stared long and hard, convinced a man wearing camouflage was peering at her through field glasses. Panic gripped her and she headed down the driveway, tore along Creeping Vine Trail, and hit the onramp to Stanton doing sixty. Taking deep breaths and forcing herself to calm down, she slowed the Jeep and arrived in town to find herself surrounded by Halloween bunting. It wasn't a time she enjoyed. In fact, she'd taken her annual leave from the office so she wouldn't be reminded of the time her husband died. She pulled to the curb opposite the sheriff's department, climbed out, and walked up the steps, through the glass doors, and straight to the front counter. "I'm Evelyn Brown. I'm here to see Sheriff Alton."

TWENTY-SEVEN

After returning to the office, Jenna stopped at the counter to speak to Maggie. "Handle my calls, unless it's Wolfe or an emergency. We have a few leads we need to chase down."

"There is one—" Maggie's mouth closed with a snap.

"Wait." Jenna held up her hand. "Give me fifteen minutes, is all."

She called Rio and Rowley to her office. She gave them the task of hunting down the next potential victim to check on their well-being. She gathered the information her deputies had found on Riley Sutton out of Gallows Hill, Mark Pittman out of Damien's Hollow, and Marco Myers out of The Devil's Crossroads. She looked up at them from behind her desk. "Great work. The safety of the woman is our priority right now, so get at it."

"I need to speak to you about the kid who tried to steal Kane's truck." Rio opened his notebook.

With so much to do, Jenna needed her deputies concentrating on the case at hand, but Rio had the ability to concentrate on a ton of things at once. She looked at him. "What do you have for me?"

"While I was hunting down information on the list of possible suspects, I asked Kalo if he could chase down info on Judith Ann Gates from Idaho and her kids Jimmy and Peter Gates." Rio sighed and shook his head. "The removal of her kids came through the Idaho social services but was a temporary action. The school contacted the department as the kids had gone missing and they couldn't contact their mother. Mrs. Gates' vehicle was stolen and found burned out. Without it, she couldn't get her kids to school or get to work. The lack of money and being isolated snowballed, no phone, no way to get to town to buy food or call anyone for assistance. So, they took the kids."

Compassion filled Jenna. "The poor woman. So where is she?"

"She was charged with neglect and served three-months' jail time." Rio raised both eyebrows. "She's working in a diner and living with a bunch of women. It's not a place she'd be allowed to have her kids."

"Is she on probation?" Kane spun around in his chair.

"Nope." Rio straightened. "The younger brother, Peter, is in foster care in Louan. He seems to be doing okay. I called the Louan social services and they arranged the placement because they were informed Jimmy was living in Blackwater. How he got there is sketchy."

Jenna thought for a beat. "Okay. Father Derry has been dealing with these people for years and knows the best procedure. He'll be able to have the boys transferred to Her Broken Wings. For us, the first thing is to get the mother to Her Broken Wings. The court will want some assurance that she is fit to care for her children and she'll be supervised while living there. The foundation will get her back on her feet, find her a job and a place to live. With Father Derry's recommendation, and everything set in place, she'll be able to petition the court to have the children placed back in her care." She smiled. "Ask Maggie to call her and explain things. We'll fly her here when she's ready to leave. It won't cost her a cent. Tell Maggie to make that clear."

"Okay, so who is paying for the flights and transport?" Rio looked dubious. "We can't just dump all that on the foundation."

"I'll pay for it." Kane shrugged. "Maggie will tell me what she needs and I'll make the arrangements. In cases like these, where the reasons behind problems are unknown, we don't send cash. I'll have travel vouchers drawn up for her. Father Derry is more than capable of assessing the situation when she arrives."

"Okay." Rio nodded and had his far-away look, as if the cogs inside his head were spinning. "I'll set that in motion and then get back to locating the next potential victim."

"I'll probably have that information before you're done." Rowley headed for the door, turned, and smiled at Jenna. "This is a good thing you're doing, Jenna. That woman deserves a break." He touched the brim of his hat and walked out the door.

Jenna waved Rio away. "Get it done ASAP and find Evelyn Brown. That's our priority right now."

"Sure." Rio folded his notebook and hurried out the door.

Jenna watched him go, closing the door behind him. She scanned the information they'd found on the possible suspects and looked over at Kane. "I want to move on these possible suspects today. Who looks a potential to you?"

"On paper, none of them." Kane pushed a hand through his hair, smoothing it, and looked up from his laptop. "None of them are hiding off the grid. One was injured and collects a military pension. Both the others work day jobs. I guess we go and see the one who is likely to be at home. The others, we'll drop by their homes after they finish work. We have zip on these guys, apart from possible association at one time, so there's no need to cause a problem by showing at their place of employment."

Jenna nodded and glanced at her watch. "Okay, which one was injured?"

"Not wounded. It says here Myers suffers from PTSD." Kane shook his head. "How did Rio get this information? It's not something we should know about. It's not what the military discloses."

"I guess he got the information from Bobby Kalo." Jenna stood and reached for her jacket. "He knows to use any information source available, and Kalo seems to be able to get into medical files. I figure we don't mention it to Myers when we speak to him."

Jenna's phone rang. It was Wolfe and she put the phone on speaker. "Hi, Shane, that was fast. What have you got for me?"

"I haven't completed cataloging all the injuries but the cause of death in the Christy Miller case was a brain stem injury. When we found her, she had massive blunt force trauma to the back of the head. During my examination, I checked for any signs of a gunshot injury, mainly to rule that out. If she'd been shot, it might have been the reason she fell. I found nothing to suggest that theory. The specific drugs I tested for came back negative and a full tox screen is on the way. Taking into account the evidence at hand—the flashlight, the signs someone else was on the mountain, the fact she left the lights on, and the garden bed—I can't find any reason to suggest this woman decided to walk up a mountain in the dead of night and throw herself off the top of a gully. The fact she evidently tried desperately to save herself, the Purple Heart pinned to her shirt, all point to a homicide. I'll complete the full autopsy, but it will be a time before you get my full report, but my findings will be the same."

Blowing out a deep breath, Jenna stared at Kane and raised both eyebrows. "Thanks, Shane. We have a few potential suspects to interview, and Rio and Rowley are hunting down a potential next victim."

"I hope you find out who is doing this." Wolfe leaned back in

his creaky office chair and sighed. *"He's broken our code and needs to be taken down. Get at it but don't take any chances. Y'all know, if he's a Seal or black ops, he'll be as slippery as an eel."*

Considering the implications of dealing with a professional, Jenna pushed a hand through her hair. "Then he won't be expecting our team on his tail. Don't worry, we'll find him." She disconnected.

Before she could discuss the autopsy with Kane, her desk phone rang. It was Maggie. *"Before you head off again, I have a woman waiting to see you. She won't give me a reason but says she needs to speak to you today."*

Jenna wanted to roll her eyes, but if the woman was suffering spousal abuse and needed help, she'd come to the right place. "Okay, what's her name?"

"Evelyn Brown out of Creeping Vine Trail." Maggie gave the rest of the woman's details. *"I'll show her up."*

Jenna recognized the name and jumped to her feet. "No, I'll come down." She rounded the desk. "The potential next victim has just walked into the office."

TWENTY-EIGHT

Unable to believe her luck, Jenna stared at Kane. "It's Evelyn Brown. I'll go down and get her."

"What?" Kane shot to his feet. "I'll tell the guys." He picked up his desk phone.

The woman waiting in the foyer was slim, in her late thirties, with long shoulder-length fair hair hanging around her face. Dressed in a warm coat, blue jeans, and hiking boots, she stood when Jenna walked toward her. "I'm Jenna Alton. Maggie said you wanted to see me. Come up to my office. We can talk there in private." She waved the woman to the stairs.

Once inside, Jenna introduced her to Kane and, after settling her in a chair, offered her a cup of coffee, which Kane made and placed beside her. Opening her notebook to a fresh page, Jenna lifted her gaze to the woman. "How can I help you?" She noticed the woman glance in Kane's direction. "If it's of a personal nature, Deputy Kane will leave the room."

"No, that's fine." Evelyn nodded toward him. "I figure Deputy Kane would be interested in what I have to say."

Jenna listened with growing interest as Evelyn gave a brief outline of the incidents. "Okay, I'll need to know everything that happened in order, at what time, and what was said. I'll need a timeline, so give me as much detail as you can remember. I'm going to record the interview, so you won't have to keep on going over it with me. Is that okay?"

"Yes, that's fine." Evelyn sipped her coffee and sighed. "I was worried you'd figure I was losing my mind. It sounds like a ghost story or the ravings of a lunatic."

Intrigued, Jenna allowed her to tell her story without interruptions. When Evelyn finished and mentioned the person watching her from the forest this morning, she glanced at Kane. "We'll have to think outside of the box on this one."

"One thing's for sure, you can't remain at the house alone." Kane frowned at Evelyn. "We have a safe place in town you can stay until we catch this guy."

"I'd already planned to stay in town. I packed a bag. It's in my truck." Evelyn shivered. "I can't go through another night like that. I'm exhausted and could easily fall asleep. I'll stay at the Cattleman's Hotel tonight and first thing in the morning I'll go and stay with my parents."

"You can't drive anywhere alone right now." Kane gave her a serious look. "This person could be watching you."

"Okay." Evelyn swayed in her chair and then grasped the table to settle herself.

"Have you eaten anything today?" Kane's brow wrinkled into a frown.

"No, I just wanted to get away." Evelyn's expression had turned distraught. "Do you think he's watching me now?"

Concerned by the woman's trembling, Jenna shook her head. "We don't know for sure. I'll have Maggie order you something to eat. While we're working out how to catch this guy, I want you to get some rest. We have a nice comfy sofa in the conference room. It's just along the hall, so it's very safe and you won't be disturbed. I'll bring you a pillow and blankets. Eat and then try and get some shuteye. Later, I'll have one of my deputies take you out the back door and drive you to Her Broken Wings. No one will see you leave the building and you'll be very safe there, I promise."

"Thanks." Evelyn sipped her coffee and let out a huge sigh. "I'm so happy you believed me."

"Do you have any animals that need tending?" Kane looked at Evelyn.

"No, I'm allergic to cats and frightened of dogs." She shrugged. "I'm happy just to watch the wildlife."

Jenna picked up the phone and asked Maggie to order some takeout from Aunt Betty's, adding extra items for the office. She listened as Kane questioned Evelyn. He had a way to extract memories from people and right now she needed all the information he could pull from her.

"Do you mind if I ask you a few questions?" Kane's expression was understanding. "I know you've been through hell, but we need all the details you can give us while it's fresh in your mind."

"I'm okay." Evelyn picked at her fingernails. "What do you need to know."

"Your husband was serving in Afghanistan when he went MIA over Halloween seven years ago, is that correct?"

"Yes, the information I have is that he's MIA. The DOD isn't big on giving out details." Evelyn dropped her gaze to her cup and her shoulders drooped. "I believe from friends of friends that the entire team died in an explosion. I know a few of the wives of the others in the team and there wasn't an official explanation."

"Some of the wives were friends from college, I believe?" Kane opened his notebook but the page remained empty. "You met the Seals in Helena is that correct?"

"Four of us did. The guys were already in the team then and pretty wild. They were older than us and meeting them was a rush. We had them only for a short time." Evelyn frowned. "The other wives we met later at cookouts. The team spent time together between deployments. They were like brothers." She stared into space. "They all loved visiting Black Rock Falls. I figure more of them would have settled here when they retired. Four of the others wanted to remain for the twenty years to retire on the pension. I know Will and Oliver Miller planned to open a garage. One of those two-hour service places with the high-tech equipment." She sighed. "I was close to Christy and Willow, but we kind of drifted apart when Will died. It was a bad time for the wives, I heard that one of them took their own life."

Jenna leaned forward. The media hadn't been informed of any of the current deaths. "When was this?"

"Oh, ages ago." Evelyn sipped her coffee. "Christy heard something, but we couldn't find out who it was. She called me and asked me if I knew. That was years ago."

"Okay." Kane gave Jenna a meaningful glance. "The man on the phone. Did he sound like your husband?"

"He called me Evie. It was his pet name for me but it wasn't a secret. He used it all the time. He asked me to open the door so he could come inside the house." Evelyn's eyes flashed in panic. "He wanted me to believe it was Will, didn't he?" She dragged in a ragged breath. "Why would someone want to do something like that. The phone company said it was probably a Halloween prank."

Concerned, Jenna leaned forward. "I'm glad you came to see us. If someone is on your property peering at you through the windows, it's not a prank."

"What did the man in the garden look like? Was he my size or smaller?" Kane stood and walked to the other side of the office. "Can you make a comparison?"

"Not as big as you but he was about the same size as Will." Evelyn turned in her seat to look at him. "Six-one maybe one hundred and eighty pounds. Will wasn't small but broad like you in the shoulders. He always said he was too big for a Seal."

"What was he wearing?" Kane sat down. "You mentioned camouflage. Was he wearing headgear as well?"

"He had green eyes." Evelyn blinked and stared into space. "It shocked me."

"Okay, you're safe now, so close your eyes and look at him again." Kane's voice dropped to just above a whisper. "Look at his head."

"I see him, plain as day." Evelyn's hands closed around the cup. "He's wearing a helmet and goggles. The green lights must have been his night-vision goggles, right?" Her eyes flashed open. "My husband trained in that gear." She shook her head and then looked at Kane. "This morning in the forest he had stripes on his face, and I couldn't make out his features. It could have been Will. What if it's a ghost? They say they can come back at Halloween."

"No, it wasn't. Ghosts can't make phone calls, or everyone would be getting calls from their dearly departed." Kane's expression hardened. "That's what he wants you to think. Do you honestly believe that Will would frighten you like this? If by some miracle he was alive after seven years, the DOD would have notified you and he'd have called you the moment he was Stateside and been running to the door to see you, not hiding in the forest. Even if you believed in ghosts, this is a stretch of the imagination."

"No, I guess so." Evelyn rubbed both hands down her face and lifted tragic eyes to him. "I've never given up hope that he might be alive. MIA doesn't always mean dead, does it? I mean men were found years after they were captured in Vietnam. Why is this different?"

"It was a very different war, Evelyn." Kane let out a long sigh. "If he'd been captured, you'd know. MIA often means unable to identify, which often happens in explosions. They know the team was in that position but there's nothing left. Death is usually instantaneous." His eyes never left her face. "If I'd been in that situation and had the choice, I'd have taken the latter."

"You were there?" Evelyn's bottom lip quivered. "In Afghanistan."

"Yeah." He stretched out a hand and squeezed her arm. "I was one of the lucky ones. Now it's my job to make sure you're okay. Trust us to catch this guy."

"Okay." Evelyn nodded and straightened in her chair. "What are you going to do?"

"We'll work that out after we've made a few calls." Kane smiled at her. "Don't worry. Nothing can happen to you now."

Jenna opened the door to a knock. She took a box of takeout from Maggie and set it on the desk. "Grab what you want from the box and I'll pour you another coffee. While you're resting, we'll work through a plan. Do you mind if we take over your house for a day or so and use your vehicle?"

"No, do whatever you need to do." Evelyn peered into the box and selected egg salad sandwiches.

Jenna smiled. "Okay, we'll have someone pretending to be you, so can you write down what you do from the time you get home on a usual worknight? The more detail the better, things like, which bedroom you use, where the light switches are in the garage, and anything you believe we might need to know. We want whoever is watching to believe it's you inside the house." She slid a pen and paper across the desk to her.

"Sure." Evelyn picked up the pen and wrote a list with approximate times. She handed it to Jenna. "There, that's what I do most nights, unless I'm going out, which isn't often."

After scanning the document Jenna handed it to Kane. She poured the coffee and stood looking at Evelyn. "We'll need your jacket and hat. I'll give you an FBI jacket to wear. Come with me." She took the cup and a bottle of water and led the way to the conference room.

She set the coffee and water on the table and went to pull blankets and a pillow out of the closet. She placed them on the sofa and smiled at Evelyn. "Make yourself comfortable. Try and get some rest. I'll make arrangements for somewhere for you to stay and we'll go and catch the idiot playing tricks on you."

"I'd appreciate it." Evelyn placed her sandwiches on the table and dropped onto the sofa. "I knew I could count on you, Sheriff." She pulled keys out of her purse and handed them to Jenna. "Everything you need is on the keyring. The house and car keys and the clicker for the garage door."

Jenna took the keys. "Thanks." She hurried back to the office. "I'll have to go out for a time, but my deputies will drop you by Her Broken Wings in a couple of hours. Stay there until we can catch this guy."

TWENTY-NINE

After watching Jenna's mind working, Kane had an uneasy feeling she was planning on putting herself in danger. He filled two cups with coffee and stared at her when she returned to the office. "You know, I can just about read your mind. If you think you can go back to the house and act as a stand in for Evelyn, think again. If the killer was a Seal or anything close, he'll be trained in observation and you'll never pass for her. She's way taller than you for a start and you've different builds. You're curvy and she's straight up and down."

"Yeah, but who is trained and would pass as her?" Jenna pulled out a bagel and cream cheese and dropped into her chair. "Oh, Kane, the observant one... think about it. Don't give me a blank expression. Jo would pass as her at a distance. She's tall and in baggy clothes no one would notice her figure. Carter has improved her hand-to-hand combat skills and she can shoot straight. She's calm in a crisis. She'll be perfect."

Kane rubbed the back of his neck. "We can't send her in there alone and we can't patrol the perimeter. This guy could have placed trail cams and silent alarms all over and be holed up anywhere. We'd be made in seconds."

"Do you recall what she said?" Jenna sipped her coffee and eyed him over the rim. "She left from the kitchen through the garage, right? Her garage is attached to the house with an interconnecting door. If Jo can drive her vehicle inside with us hiding in the back, we'll get into the house without being seen. She said she closed the shutters and anyone in the backyard could only see her in the kitchen. So, we keep out of the kitchen, take positions upstairs and wait until he tries to come inside."

Allowing the plan to run through his mind, Kane nodded. "Okay but how do we get Jo here? Carter is off the grid and not picking up. I'll call him again, to see if he can go get her but I doubt he'll respond in time and we need her here now." He made the call and it went to voicemail. "The message said to call the Snakeskin Gully office. He's gone fishing."

"I'll call Jo and explain the situation." Jenna's eyebrows rose. "Unless they have an emergency, she might be able to use the search-and-rescue team's chopper. The FBI can do things we can't. Trust me, she'll get here." She reached for the phone. "I'll call her."

Kane held up one hand. "Just a minute." He frowned at Jenna. "We'll be inside the house without backup, and we don't know what this guy has planned. We need backup. You could place Rowley and Rio some ways away in an unmarked vehicle. Maybe we could use Maggie's husband's old pickup. That would blend in anywhere without being noticed."

"Well, get at it." Jenna gave him a dismissive gesture. "We don't have too much wiggle room and he'll smell a rat if Evelyn doesn't return home at the normal time. I figure he doesn't know she's on vacation, so he'll be expecting her to return home before six." She picked up the phone. "Rowley, drop what you're doing, grab Rio, and come up here."

Kane lifted his phone and explained the situation to Maggie. "We'll make sure nothing happens to the truck and fill it with gas before we return it. I'm guessing we'll need it around five, but it might be late when we return it."

"I'll call him now but I'm sure it will be just fine." Maggie chuckled. "He won't say no to a full tank of gas."

Smiling, Kane disconnected and turned to Jenna. "Okay, we're set with transport for tonight. What's the plan for the guys?" He bit into a ham and cheese roll.

"Wait up and I'll explain." Jenna waited for the deputies to come into the office. "We need eyes on the potential suspects. A drive-by identification—anything will do. I want to know where they are and what they're doing. Whoever is doing this could be waiting in the forest for Evelyn to return, so he'll be missing."

"Maybe not." Kane twirled a pen through his fingers. "Let's assume he knows her movements. He's not going to sit up there all day. It would be a waste of time and energy. He'll be smart and make sure he has an alibi, so he'll do whatever he usually does during the day. I figure he'd head off to work. He would be planning to call her tonight at midnight, just like the others. He's already shown us he has a pattern of behavior. Tipping our hand now might scare him off. By all means, check out the potential suspects but tread lightly and leave Myers to us." He looked at Rio and Rowley. "If we can convince him, whoever he is, we're not actively hunting him down, he'll carry on as usual. The only reason we're risking going anywhere near the potential suspects this close to a sting operation is to gauge the threat. Are we facing a combat-trained fit adversary or an ex-military guy with a death wish?"

"Okay, so play it low-key and conversational?" Rio blew out a long breath. "Watch body language and slip in pertinent questions—got it."

Kane turned to Jenna. "If Jo agrees to do this, we'll get the wheels in motion to get her here, but it's going to be three hours before she arrives and we'll have to sneak her into town. She'll need to dress in Evelyn's jacket, so make sure when you call her that she'll be wearing the same clothes as Evelyn. I'm sure she has hiking boots and blue jeans."

Pushing hair behind her ears, Jenna nodded. "Okay, so why are we handling Myers?"

"I'll use the same excuse as before. I'm looking to join the group of ex-servicemen in town." Kane dropped the pen into an Aunt Betty's Café souvenir cup on his desk. "He's free to move around, so right now he is on the top of the list of potential suspects. I'd like to see how he ticks. We're going into a situation blind, and we'll need all the information on these guys we can get."

Impressed, Jenna smiled. "Good thinking." She turned to Rio and Rowley. "I've got an excuse for you guys to visit the workplaces of the other two suspects without causing undue attention." She opened her drawer and pulled out a book of tickets and tossed them to Rio. "Her Broken Wings Foundation is running a raffle to be drawn at the Halloween Ball. First prize is fishing gear, donated by the Outdoors Store. Second prize is a visit to the beauty parlor valued at two hundred bucks. Go and sell some tickets, find the suspects, and ask questions but be subtle. You know the drill. Before you leave, Rowley, call Father Derry and explain the Evelyn Brown situation. Find out when he can arrange a room for her. When you get back, you'll find Evelyn in the conference room resting. Get her to drive around the block and then into the back parking lot. Follow her, so you know she's safe. When she's back, smuggle her into the shelter. No one can see her. Okay?"

"I'm on it." Rowley nodded and followed Rio out the door.

Kane waited for the deputies to leave and turned to Jenna. "I figure we should make a video call to Jo. It's a big ask and it's more personal than a phone call."

"Sure." Jenna tapped away on her keyboard. "Slide around my side of the desk. She'll want to speak to you as well." She made the call. "Hi, Jo, we have a problem." She brought Special Agent Jo Wells up to speed.

The shadow that moved over Jo's expression concerned Kane. "If there's a problem, we might be able to persuade Emily Wolfe to take Evelyn's place, but she doesn't have the training and it would be risky."

"It's not the mission. I'm in and I'm excited to be doing something useful." Jo pulled back her long hair and secured it with an elastic tie from around her wrist. *"It's not having Carter as backup. It's real strange not having him around. I've gotten used to him having my back."* She stared into the camera. *"I have no idea where he is, so I can't ask him to give me a ride to Black Rock Falls. I'll make some calls and get back to you. I'll leave the moment I can organize a ride. I'll drop by home and pack a bag. It won't be a problem with Jaime. She'll be fine with our nanny."* A voice echoed in the background and Jo nodded and then turned back to the screen. *"Bobby has some gadgets he's keen to try out. I'll bring him with me. Catch you later."* She disconnected.

"She can't bring Bobby Kalo into a dangerous situation. He doesn't have any training whatsoever." Jenna's mouth turned down. "He can't come into the house with us. Anything might happen."

Kane closed his laptop and stood. "Bobby can shoot straight but he's just a kid. I know Carter has been working with him. He might have more skills than you imagine." He pulled baseball caps from his drawer. "We'll wear these and our street gear. We might just pass as an ordinary couple."

"Good idea. I'll send Kalo with Rowley and Rio, but he'll be staying in the cruiser." Jenna pushed back from the desk and took the jacket Kane tossed her. "We'll use the earbuds to keep in contact with everyone. Let's hope he has something we can use to track this killer." She blew out a long breath. "Okay, let's go and see what Myers has to say for himself."

THIRTY

The Devil's Crossroads sat out in the middle of nowhere about two miles north of the Triple Z Roadhouse, heading east along a cracked blacktop covered road. The old wooden sign looked as if it had been there since the establishment of the town. It tipped slightly to one side and had four destinations in faded white paint on boards pointing toward the compass points. Jenna turned in her seat, peering in all directions. "So, this guy lives here, does he? There is no 'here.'"

"There's a ranch behind those trees." Kane was zooming in on the map on the GPS. "That has to be the place." He turned the Beast to the right and headed down a dirt road with grass growing on each side of the tire ruts. He looked at Jenna and smiled. "Isn't there a myth or something about summoning a demon at the devil's crossroads?"

Jenna grinned at him. "I think it's a bit late to make a deal with the devil, Dave. I figure he already knows which side we're on."

The old-style ranch was set behind a wooded area, probably to shield it from the wind that tore across the lowlands. Surrounded by outbuildings and fenced areas with cattle and horses, it appeared to be a working ranch. They drove through an open farm gate with the name Myers hanging from the top rung by wire and set at a jaunty angle. "Sound the horn. I don't want him coming at us with a weapon."

"The place isn't posted with a warning, so I figure we surprise him." Kane slid the truck to a halt out front of the house beside a dark blue Chevrolet truck. He climbed out and opened the backdoor for Duke. "We don't look like cops, not when we're not wearing our department jackets and the baseball caps. We'll look more casual with Duke. Who takes a dog to a gunfight?"

At the sound of dogs barking, Jenna spun around, one hand on the door. "Or maybe a dogfight."

Two mixed-breed dogs with huge heads, teeth flashing and spittle flying, put the image of hellhounds in Jenna's mind. "Now what?"

"Stay in the truck." Kane indicated with his hand for Duke to sit and stood his ground as the dogs hurtled toward him, one hand resting on the handle of his weapon.

Sure the massive dogs would attack, Jenna stared at Kane's unmoving silent figure. He was just staring at the dogs and then he made a hand gesture. The two monsters skidded to a halt barking, their mouths drawn back to display dripping canines. Another hand gesture and they dropped down. Jenna stared in disbelief and then caught sight of a man walking from the barn carrying an ax. The man was maybe six-two and strong. He could have been between thirty-five and forty-five. "Behind you." She slid from the truck.

"How did you get past my dogs?" The man stopped some ways away and stared at Kane.

"I know a military-trained K-9 when I see one." Kane shrugged. "Marco Myers?"

"Yeah, but not many know how to control one." Myers

stared at Duke. "Now that there is a hunting dog, and he didn't react. How did you do that?"

"He trusts me to protect him." Kane straightened. "We're a team. Those dogs aren't ex-military. Did you train them to attack people on sight?"

"Maybe, but they're easily called off." Myers frowned at Kane. "I know a Marine when I see one. K-9 maybe. You a handler?"

"Was." Kane shrugged nonchalantly. "It was some time ago. I never made the twenty years."

"Casualty?" Myers regarded Kane's nod and blew out a long breath. "Me too. So, what are you doing on my doorstep?" He tossed the ax onto the porch and stood hands on hips staring at him.

"I was drinking at the Triple Z and mentioned to the barman I was looking for a local vets' group. He mentioned your name and said there's a group that meets up from time to time." Kane smiled. "I'd like to meet the other guys in town and talk over old times."

Noticing how Myers completely ignored her existence, Jenna moved to Kane's side. "Do you run this place alone?" She cleared her throat when his dark eyes swung in her direction. "It's a ton of work raising cattle."

"Yeah, it's just me and the dogs. I like solitude and I don't need no help." Myers turned to Kane. "It's a small group, all ages. They meet at the Triple Z Bar sometimes. I don't get involved much these days. Like I said, I prefer to be alone." He scratched his cheek and shrugged. "Maybe talk to Luke Thompson out of Dead-End Road. He hangs out with the guys."

"Did I see you out at Creeping Vine Trail earlier?" Kane indicated with his chin to the Chevrolet. "I was in the forest with Duke. I've been looking for cabins in the local area. I noticed someone in cammies out there. It reminded me of old times."

"Did you now? I'm in the forest most days but I don't recall if I went that far." Myers shrugged. "I took the dogs to hunt down some critters." He smiled. "It keeps them sharp, all the blood and all."

Disgusted, Jenna shook her head. "Blooding working dogs isn't a good thing." She lifted her chin. "How can you expect them to know the difference between vermin and someone's pet?"

"I had a wife once." Myers looked at Kane and the corner of his mouth twitched up. "She had the sense not to interrupt a man when he was talking to his friends."

"You don't say." Kane flicked a meaningful glance at Jenna. "Go wait in the truck. I'll be right along."

Understanding Kane's move to get the man onside, Jenna climbed inside the Beast, but with the window open, she could clearly hear their conversation. Kane would never treat her in a dismissive way, and it would be interesting to see if by doing so, he could make the man drop his guard and open up.

"What happened to your wife?" Kane leaned causally against the Beast.

"She went missing." Myers shrugged. "In this town anything could have happened to her." He smiled. "If you don't know this town is Serial Killer Central, you will soon enough."

Suddenly glad they'd decided not to wear their sheriff's department jackets, and wear baseball caps, Jenna stared at Kane's back. Myers seemed as if living among serial killers was a good thing. It amused him.

"Oh, I've heard the stories." Kane bent to pluck a burr from behind one of Duke's ears and then straightened. "You think she was a victim? Did the sheriff find her body?"

"Nope, she's never been found." Myers rubbed the back of his neck. "I did the right thing, waited a month or so to see if she crawled back home and then filed a report, but the sheriff wasn't really interested, but at least he was a man. Can't fathom why the town voted a woman to be sheriff. This is why I stay out here away from people. I can get anything I need delivered along with the stock supplies. I'm not running afoul of some woman running around town as if she's all that."

"I see." Kane straightened. "I didn't notice a strong law enforcement presence in town. The townsfolk are fine." He cleared his throat. "So, you've been here for a time? Did you serve when that entire team went MIA over Halloween? It must have been about seven years ago."

"Is that the story?" Myers barked a laugh. "They went MIA? I heard a different story, about a slaughter, but they say no bodies were retrieved. I figure if there were any remains, they were left out there to rot. It was a cover-up, that's for darn sure."

"Yeah, I heard something similar." Kane scratched his chin. "Let's hope they don't come back to haunt the living every Halloween."

Jenna noticed the hunch of Myers' shoulders, and the look he gave Kane chilled her to the bone. She slid her hand under her jacket to her weapon and held her breath.

"Funny you should say that. My wife went missing at Halloween. Must be six years ago by now." Myers gave himself a shake, as if he'd given out too much information. "I gotta go. There's always work to do on a ranch and I don't have time to stand here jawing all day. Go and speak to Thompson. He'll put you right." He whistled to the dogs and headed back to the house.

Jenna waited for Kane to secure Duke in the back seat and get back inside the truck. She turned to him. "Won't he be surprised when he runs into me in town and discovers I'm the sheriff."

"He won't remember you at all." Kane started the engine

and swung the truck around. "If he's not the killer and his wife went missing over Halloween, she might have been the first victim and this murder spree goes back a long time." He glanced at her as he turned back onto the blacktop. "One thing's for sure, he has no respect for women and waiting a month to report his wife was missing is suspect. It's just long enough for any investigation to run cold. By then people have forgotten seeing her or hearing anything unusual and the old sheriff was useless. I'd bet my last dollar he didn't follow up on the missing person's report."

Jenna scanned the missing person's reports on her phone. The files had been updated over time and all the old files were updated and added. "There's not even a missing person's report under the name of Myers, nothing at all interesting from six years ago. It must have been very quiet in town or the sheriff sat in his office twiddling his thumbs all day." She sighed. "It's impossible working like this. We rarely get to the bottom of cold case files and Blackhawk insists there are graves in the forest. Murders must have been committed here for decades and nothing was done about them."

"Well, unless someone stumbles over a grave, we don't have a case to investigate." Kane let out a long breath. "Right now, we don't need to chase down cold cases. Maybe you should ask Jo and Carter to look into them. Maybe they can speak to Blackhawk. They're always complaining about being bored."

Jenna leaned back in her seat. "Myers is a definite suspect. He admitted to being in the forest near Creeping Vine Trail. He could have been watching Evelyn. With his attitude toward women, he could be our killer." She chewed on her bottom lip. "Head back to the office. I want to know if Rowley and Rio got anything on the other suspects."

THIRTY-ONE

Deputy Jake Rowley had started the same day as the sheriff in the Black Rock Falls Sheriff's Office, and apart from old Deputy Walters, he had been at the office longer than the other deputies, and yet after four years, the sheriff still considered him a rookie. When Kane arrived, a slick and knowledgeable profiler from the big city, he'd accepted him as deputy sheriff without a problem, and then along came Zac Rio. They were about the same age, but Zac had been a gold shield detective in LA and had the bonus of a superhuman memory. Rowley let out a long sigh. It seemed he'd be considered a rookie forever.

Moving Evelyn Brown had gone like clockwork. They'd asked her to drive around the block and then park behind the sheriff's office. The sheriff's parking lot had solid gates, and no one could gain entrance or overlook it. Evelyn was able to get into his truck and leave without anyone noticing. With three roads to use as an option after leaving and Rio trailing them to make sure they hadn't been followed, Rowley had driven her to meet Father Derry behind the library. It was safer for the father to take her to Her Broken Wings. The shelter's parking lot had a secure entrance with gates, and no one could see her entering the premises. She was safe and would remain there until the killer had been caught. The moment the word came back that she'd arrived safely, Rowley turned his cruiser into Main and headed for Guns and Ammo, where they hoped to find one of the suspects, Riley Sutton.

He'd run a background check on him and found nothing unusual. Sutton had completed seven years of active duty and seven years in the reserves before leaving the Marines. An outspoken survivalist with a shelter in his backyard, Sutton was convinced World War Three was just over the horizon. Rowley found images of him on survivalist webpages with his wife and two college-age sons gunned up and ready to roll at the first sign of trouble. He pulled to the curb outside Guns and Ammo and looked at Rio. "I hope you have a list of questions for this guy. How are we supposed to slip in questions about Afghanistan when we're selling raffle tickets?"

"He's a survivalist. Show some interest in buying an arsenal, and he'll open up." Rio smiled at him. "You really need to get out more or read something." He shrugged. "You're great at your job, but Jenna isn't going to give you the lead in a case unless you become more confident."

Rowley stared at him. "How did you know I was thinking that?" The question tumbled unrestrained from his mouth and he regretted it. "You reading minds now?"

"Nope but I can read expressions. You didn't appreciate Jenna giving me the lead in the interviews." Rio pulled the tickets from the glovebox and a cloth bag filled with money. "You can take the lead in this interview. Let your head guide you. You know what we need to open up this case, so go for it."

Rowley reached for the door handle. "Thanks, I appreciate it." He gave Rio a look out of the corner of his eye and wondered if he'd been given a problem Rio wasn't interested in solving.

He strolled into the store, smiling and nodding at the

customers. Recognizing Sutton adding a new rifle to the display, he walked up to the counter. "Now that would look good in my gun locker."

"Indeed." Sutton turned to him with a smile. "It's one of the new range we have available this year. As you know, demand outweighs supply and not many new models have been produced of late." He narrowed his gaze. "I'm sure you're not here to buy a rifle, Deputy. Is there a problem?"

Rowley cast his gaze along the line of rifles. "Nah, I'm just here with my partner to sell raffle tickets to raise money for the sheriff's foundation." He lifted his chin toward the display. "What do we have? I can look now and maybe drop by another time."

"Okay." Sutton took down a rifle, bronze in color, and displayed it. "This is a beauty. It's a Browning X-Bolt Mountain Pro. It's lighter than previous versions and has a carbon-fiber stock filled with a noise-dampening foam."

Rowley took the rifle and examined it. "Oh yeah, I like this. It feels good to hold and the color is like camouflage—nice." He aimed the rifle at the ceiling and then laid it gently on the glass counter. "What about that one?" He pointed to another weapon. "I'd like that in my bunker."

"You have good taste. This will take down a grizzly. It's a Bushmaster 450 gas-driven carbine." Sutton held out the rifle for him to examine.

Rowley took the rifle and weighed it in his hands. "This I like." He acted nonchalantly. "There's nothing better than seeing a rack of rifles all set out, oiled, and ready for action. I love the smell of them, don't you?" He cleared his throat. "With all these weapons to tempt you, are you a collector?"

"Oh yeah." Sutton laughed. "It's an expensive hobby but mine is more like an addiction. I buy army surplus as well. Do you indulge?"

Rowley nodded. "It's the best store in town. Next to this one."

"You mentioned a bunker." Sutton met his gaze. "I'm a survivalist and after what I saw in Afghanistan, I want my family to be safe if anything happens in the future. I figure you're the same?"

Trying to keep his enthusiasm in check, Rowley nodded slowly, his attention fixed on the rifle but his mind focused on Sutton. "Yeah, I have twins and I want them to be safe. How long since you left the service?"

"Seven years." Sutton frowned. "I was only active for seven. There was some bad shit going down in Afghanistan. Don't get me wrong. I'll stand up and fight for Uncle Sam anytime, but that place broke stronger men than me." He gave his head a shake as if trying to dislodge a memory.

Rowley cleared his throat. "Yeah, I heard tell of a team that went MIA and they never found a trace to bring home. It must have been brutal."

"Yeah, that impacted on the teams, but we did our job and came home." Sutton narrowed his gaze. "How do you know about that? You're way too young to have been there at that time."

Shrugging, Rowley stared him in the eyes. "I guess I shouldn't have mentioned it, but someone I know was in that team." He glanced at Rio, who was moving through customers selling tickets and then back at Sutton. "I sure want the Browning. It's a fine rifle. I'm using a Winchester 70. What's your favorite hunting area? I like Death Drop Gully. It's remote and not many go up there in elk season."

"I know that area. The check station is a long way from there." Sutton looked suspicious. "I hope you're following the hunting regulations."

Rowley laughed. "I sure do. So, you know Death Drop Gully. I hear it's haunted. That's why I went up there." He rubbed his chin. "I never bagged one elk. Truth is, those twisted trees spooked me some. Have they always been there?"

"Yeah, as far as I'm aware. I like them, it gives the place character." Sutton looked over to the customer staring at the rifles. "I'll be right there." He turned back to Rowley. "Nice chatting. Happy hunting." He turned away to speak to the next in line.

At random, Rowley stopped to speak to four customers on the way to where Rio was circulating. He asked them if they'd ever been to Death Drop Gully and if they knew where it was located. All replied in the negative. He walked to Rio's side. "Did you sell a ton of tickets?"

"Well, yeah. I managed to sell tickets and get donations as well." Rio waved a handful of bills. "I used a persuasive argument, and they responded really well. I figure I could sell that rickety old bridge over Twisted Snake River, no problem at all." He grinned at Rowley. "Did you get any info?"

Rowley headed for the door. "Oh, yeah. Enough to keep Sutton on our list of possible suspects."

"Great." Rio pushed the bills and tickets into the cloth bag and pulled the tie string. "Now you can watch me work my magic on Mark Pittman. If he's a computer geek, we'll get along just fine."

Rowley opened the cruiser door and looked at him. "You speak geek, do you?" He chuckled. "Ah, yeah, I guess you do. With your super brain, you'd fit right in."

Rowley swung the cruiser around and they headed to the computer store. At this time of the afternoon, it was filled with school kids. The store had a selection of the new games available for the kids to try, so they all flocked there, speaking a language way over his head. He'd never been a gamer or had the time to spend hours in front of a screen. He was more the athletic type, preferring football and martial arts. He glanced at Rio, who went straight to the counter. Rowley noticed their presence in the store hardly raised a look from the kids. All of them were so engrossed he figured they could have tossed in a flash-bang and it wouldn't have made a difference.

The man behind the counter had just served one of the kids and frowned at the sight of them. Rowley identified him as Mark Pittman out of Damien's Hollow. Pittman wiped a hand over his mouth and glanced at the kids. Rowley hung back, feigning interest in the latest smartphones on display as Rio made his way to the counter.

"Hi there." Rio dropped the cloth bag on the counter. "We're selling raffle tickets for the Her Broken Wings Foundation." He rattled off the list of prizes, the price, and his five-for-the-price-of-four deal. "Would you or any of the people working out back be interested in purchasing one for the cause?"

"Okay sure. I figured you were here about the kids. I know some of them play hooky from school, but if they drop by during school hours, I send them right along." Pittman moved his attention over the kids and then back to Rio. He took out his wallet. "It's a good cause. I'll take the deal."

"Great, what name is it?" Rio pulled out a book of tickets and a pen. "And just a phone number."

"Mark Pittman." Pittman gave his details.

"Great." Rio added Pittman's name to the tickets. "Have you lived here long?"

"Nope, I'm originally from Colorado, but I met some guys in the service and we came here on a hunting vacation. I met a girl and when I left the service I moved here. I've been here maybe seven years." Pittman shot him a glance. "Why? Is there a problem?"

"Nah." Rio smiled. "I've been asking around about Death Drop Gully. I read an article in an old paper that said it was haunted. I've been trying to find out more information. There's zip in the library." He tapped his head. "My brain never stops working and it loves mysteries." He shrugged. "So have you heard about the place?"

"Yeah, it rings a bell." Pittman frowned. "Maybe you should be heading out to the res. I figure it's their history, not ours so much."

"Ah, I see." Rio waved a hand toward the kids. "Now this is more my environment. I figure finding a woman who likes gamers would be the charm. You married?"

"I was." Pittman blew out a long breath. "She died."

"Oh, I'm sorry for your loss." Rio frowned. "Kids?"

"Nope." Pittman leaned back against the bench and folded his arms across his chest. "It was a long time ago. I was in Afghanistan. I came to live here because some of the guys still come here for vacations, those that made it out anyways. A couple of them live right here in town."

"That's good. It's great to have friends close by." Rio straightened. "Ah, well. It's been nice talking but we have to keep selling tickets. Thanks for your time." He headed out the door.

Rowley hurried after him. "You didn't need gamer talk. I could have handled him just fine."

"It's all good." Rio shrugged. "We have two potential suspects. Bobby Kalo's initial research paid out in silver dollars."

THIRTY-TWO

Jenna glanced up from her desk, surprised to see Wolfe ushering Jo into the office. "Well, you got here in record time, Jo."

"Yeah, the chopper had to put down on the highway just outside town and I called Shane to give me a ride. Carter has the FBI chopper taking up the space on the helipad on top of the ME's office. Where is he? Wolfe hasn't seen him. Has he shown his face around here?"

Jenna nodded in greeting to Wolfe. "No, we haven't seen Carter."

"Oh, and this is..." Jo turned around, shook her head, and peered out the door into the hallway. "You don't have to wait outside, Bobby. You're part of the team. Come and meet Jenna and Kane."

Jenna smiled as a thin young man, close to six feet, wearing scruffy sneakers and faded jeans, a puffy jacket, and a ballcap turned backward edged into the room. His dark eyes flicked from Jenna to Kane and his mouth twitched into a tentative smile. He wasn't what Jenna had expected. Thick curly hair tumbled down his back, caught in an elastic band. If she didn't know better, she'd have placed him at about sixteen years old. "Hey, Bobby, it's great to meet you at last."

"Did the leads I sent work out?" Bobby flicked his gaze to Kane.

"Yeah, we have someone checking them out now." Kane stood and held out his hand. "Dave Kane."

"You're as big as Carter said. I figured he was joshing." Kalo shook Kane's hand and then pulled it away and flexed his fingers. "Hey, go careful, man. These fingers are worth their weight in gold and then some."

"We appreciate the assistance you give us." Kane smiled. "It saves us all the grunt work and we're able to spend our time hunting down killers."

"If you didn't send me work, I'd go crazy." Kalo glanced at Jo. "Snakeskin Gully is like living in a graveyard, isn't it, Jo? All the fun stuff is here."

Jenna frowned. "I don't consider murder fun stuff, but I do understand a mind like yours needs to be kept busy."

"It sure does." Jo sat down in a seat Kane pushed toward her. "Okay, what have we got?"

Jenna brought her up to date with the murders and outlined her plan. Looking at Wolfe leaning against the wall, she raised one eyebrow. It was unusual for Wolfe to come by unless he had new information. "We'll have more information as soon as my deputies have reported back from interviewing two potential suspects. They should be here soon. Shane, do you have an update?"

"Not really, Emily is typing up my report. It's long and will take some time. My findings stand in both cases. I figured if you planned on sending Jo in undercover, you'd need an expert in maneuvers directing traffic and feeding you the information. I can do that. You mentioned wanting Kane on the inside with you and Jo? To avoid being spotted your deputies are going to be a mile away—right? If all hell breaks loose, you don't have anyone on the outside to watch your back."

Smothering a smile, Jenna looked at Wolfe. "We'll have Dave. He's not going to allow anyone to come through the door."

"The killer must attempt to attack me, or we won't have probable cause to arrest him for more than trespassing." Jo pushed a hand through her hair. "If I'm bait, well that's fine. This guy isn't going to change his MO. For reasons unknown, he wants people to assume the victims have taken their own lives, right? So why would he come in guns blazing? It would ruin his fantasy. We must catch him in the act and if he notices Kane inside the house, he'll abort his mission. If we dress the same, he won't notice there's two of us. You'll be my backup, Jenna. I can deal with a psychopath, and if he comes at me, I'll trust you to take him down."

"Exactly." Wolfe pushed off from the wall and pressed both hands on the table. "If this guy is special forces, he'll be watching and listening. We don't know if he's planted listening devices all through by now. I've worked with these guys, and I know how they think. Trust me, Jo, you won't stand a chance against him. You must have someone outside with the same skill set to take him down if he attacks." He lifted his chin. "I don't mean me. Carter would have been a choice if he'd answer his darn phone, but you'll need Kane on the outside. He can move like a ghost."

"I figure he's using trail cams to monitor the forest." Kane leaned back in his chair. "There are two reasons we can't use a signal disruptor: we won't be able to use our coms and the moment the feed goes down he'll smell a rat. We'll have to work around them."

"Leave that to me." Kalo dropped into a chair and grinned. "I can control trail cams, no problem. I won't blank them out. I'll just send them a loop of video footage. Just give me the coordinates of the area and I'll hunt them down." He pulled a laptop out of his backpack. "I'll be able to find any video feeds in the house as well."

"My guess is he'd set up a perimeter around the house." Kane glanced at Wolfe. "He's alone, so if he's one of the people we interviewed, he'll be watching his back. Cameras inside would be too much information for him to juggle at one time." He swung his attention to Kalo. "You'll need to keep me away from his trail cams."

"Not a problem." Kalo looked at Jenna. "I'll be fine working here. I use satellite feeds, so distance isn't an issue. In fact, it would be easier if Wolfe remained with me. I can give him info and he can relay it to whoever needs it using the satellite coms."

"I'm familiar with working that way, but I might be needed on scene as backup and medical." Wolfe stared at Jenna. "It's your call, but we could work from the back of my van. There must be a suitable place I can park, where it won't look suspicious."

"The white ME's van might as well be a white flag." Kane frowned. "Think again."

"I'll scan the area and see if I can find anywhere suitable to set up." Kalo smiled. "There are cabins all over that area of forest."

The plan seemed to be coming together. All Jenna needed was Rio and Rowley's reports to get closer to the suspect. Jenna nodded. "Okay, get at it. My main concern is that we don't have a solid profile on the suspect."

"Oh, we do." Kane smiled at her. "Like Wolfe said, we're dealing with a special op. He's somehow involved with the team that went MIA. We have to assume that, as we don't have any access to the files to prove it. We know the victims' husbands all went MIA."

Thinking over the evidence, Jenna nodded. "Yeah, from the lack of evidence on scene and the information from the victims' friends, about them seeing ghosts in military gear and then receiving calls with information only their husbands would know, it has to be special ops."

"It would take someone with skill to move through the forest close by without me knowing." Kane glanced at Jo. "I can't say for a fact anyone was in the forest, but my gut tells me someone was watching us."

"Me too." Jenna blew out a long breath. "I know someone was there. I could feel his eyes on me." She turned back to Kane. "What else have you got on a profile? When Rowley and Rio get back, we'll need to narrow down the suspects."

"If we have four ex-military it's going to be difficult." Kane shrugged. "As Jo said, he's living out a fantasy, so maybe he's one of the men's brothers or was part of a team on the ground at the time. There's no way of getting that information. For some reason, he wants the women dead by their own hands. Something triggered him recently." He looked at Jo. "Help me out here. What would trigger him?"

"Halloween is an obvious factor." Jo shrugged. "Opportunity, maybe. Perhaps he's been hunting down the wives of his targets for a time and recently found them. Something could have happened in his personal circle to cause a trigger. Meeting with someone from his time in Afghanistan, watching a movie, so many things can trigger an episode."

Jenna glanced at the door as Rio and Rowley came inside. "Grab a chair and sit down. I'll bring you up to speed." She quickly outlined the plan. "We'll hear your information and try to narrow down the list of potential suspects." She looked at Wolfe rather than direct her questions to Kane. It was safer that way. It was common knowledge Wolfe was an ex-Marine medic. "How many men are we talking about? We've tracked down four locals and have no idea if the killer is a drifter."

"A platoon is sixteen. Teams can be eight men or four, usually depending on the mission." Wolfe's gaze was steady.

"Sometimes one or two on the ground, more in the air. As in the case of a sniper, for instance."

"Do you have any reason to believe these potential suspects were in the same platoon?" Jo narrowed her gaze. "It would be highly unlikely the men came from the same state, let alone the same county."

Jenna nodded. "Yeah, we came to the same conclusion until we spoke to the victim's friends. A group of Seals just happened to be on a hunting trip in Montana and met a bunch of girls from Montana State. We know at least three of them married, left with their husbands, and after they went MIA moved back home. Dave spoke to Luke Thompson, and he gave information on the others, and we went on to interview Marco Myers, who suffers from PTSD. All the men interviewed were in Afghanistan seven years ago, all are possible. They might have been in the same or different platoons and they're not confirming or denying that information."

"PTSD has so many variables." Jo frowned. "If he's getting violent flashbacks, it could trigger episodes. I'd move him up the list." She looked at Kane. "What did you get from him?"

"He's someone we need to be concerned about, if not for this crime. He needs watching." Kane stretched his legs out in front of him. "He exhibited a hostility that centers on women. He's trained his dogs to kill. That's a bad combination." Rubbing his chin, he looked at Jenna. "He said he *had* a wife, so what happened to her? Maybe we should look into him more closely."

Trying to juggle all the information, Jenna nodded. "Yeah, we will, but not right now." She glanced at her watch. "We're running out of time. If this guy is going to strike, it could be tonight. We have to have Jo and me arriving at the house by six, or the killer is going to figure something is wrong."

THIRTY-THREE

Jenna stood and went to the whiteboard. She'd filled it with extensive notes and added a few extra to the suspects lists. She turned to Rio. "Okay, give me the rundown on Mark Pittman." She underlined his name and flicked a glance over the others. "He works at the computer store in town."

"I spoke to him." Rio leaned forward in his chair. "He must have been friends with the group that came here on vacation. He's out of Colorado, been here seven years or so, married a girl he met here on vacation. She apparently died. I asked him about Death Drop Gully and he advised me to go to the res to get more info. So, he fits the profile."

"Okay." Jenna frowned. "Did he act evasive?"

"A little hesitant when I started pushing him for details, so I pulled back real fast." Rio indicated with his chin to Rowley. "He handled Sutton."

"Hesitant like he was hiding something or didn't want to discuss things with a cop?" Jo looked at him with one eyebrow raised.

"Like he wanted us out of the store." Rio shrugged. "Maybe

he didn't like discussing things with strangers, but in my experience, guys like to chat socially, but maybe not with a deputy."

Jenna paused, pen in hand, and looked at Rowley. "Okay, anything in your interview to say Sutton is our man?"

"He knows his weapons, that's for sure." Rowley rolled up the edges of his Stetson resting on his knees. "The interesting thing was he knows Death Drop Gully and likes the twisted trees. I asked him about the military and he clammed up. Well, he didn't want to discuss it. His attitude was smooth, not hurried. Maybe too smooth. He's more than a possibility."

"Hmm, he does sound interesting." Jo's mouth flattened into a thin line. "There's something you haven't considered. At least two of them could have been in the same platoon. Wolfe said sixteen men to a platoon, so we have ten possible who didn't go MIA. What if we have Sutton and Myers working together? Myers is unstable and Sutton sounds like a leader." She looked at Kane. "Two could outflank you, or one keep you busy while the other breaks into the house." Before Kane could reply, she picked up her phone. "Where the heck is Carter when we need him?" She thumbed in numbers and waited. "911, Carter. Call me now. That's an order." She looked at Jenna. "He's not picking up, and every time I call it goes to voicemail. He's taken himself off the grid."

"Calm down, Jo." Kane stared at Jo. "I'll be fine. I trust the team and Kalo will be watching my back. Wolfe will be close by. It's you and Jenna who need to be alert. We don't know what he has planned." He swung his gaze to Kalo. "I'll need the layout of Evelyn's house and the surrounds. Have you found somewhere as a command center?"

"One thing at a time." Kalo was on his laptop. "There's a hunting cabin not far from Evelyn's house. We could head there and make like we're there to hunt. It's in the area designated for elk hunting."

"Okay, we'll take Emily's Silverado and set up in the cabin.

He won't see us as a threat." Wolfe smiled. "Carrying weapons into the cabin will be normal behavior and no one will figure out Kalo is FBI, that's for darn sure."

"That's a great plan unless someone is living there." Jenna went back to her seat behind the desk.

"I'll send out the drone." Rio stood. "I'll grab it and head for the roof."

"I'll come with you." Kalo turned to Kane. "The blueprint of the house is printing now and images of the house surrounds and forest. I'll send the feed through to our laptop." He looked at Jenna. "I'll record the feed so we can go over it again if necessary, but the drone will give us a good layout of the area. When I get back, I'll find the feed from the trail cams and we'll have a better idea of his setup. With that information, Kane will be ahead of the game."

"Thanks." Kane stood and went to the printer with Wolfe at his side. "We need an exit strategy for Jenna and Jo. The killer has different MOs. He might decide to torch the house." He went to the whiteboard and attached the images. He ran his index finger along the driveway to Evelyn's house. "If there are no trail cams here, I'll drop out of the truck when it passes close by this crop of trees on the bend. If he's watching, he'll expect the truck to slow to make the corner. It's dense vegetation, so I'll roll out of sight and wait for orders." He turned to Jenna. "Jo will have to follow Evelyn's normal routine but come midnight you must remain on the ground floor. You have three clear exits: front door, back door from the utility room, and the sunroom into the backyard. The windows, if necessary, are an easy drop."

"Got it." Jenna looked at her team. "We have three hours to finalize the plan before we leave. If the killer is going to strike, I figure it's going to be around midnight. Call who you must to let them know you'll be working tonight. Grab your gear and we'll make this happen. Dave, you'll need to drop by home and feed the animals. Duke will be safer at home. Let's get at it."

One hour later, Jenna stood and stretched. Everyone had returned to the office and the plan was firmly set in place. "Okay, one more time. Rio and Rowley will be driving Maggie's husband's truck and be on the fire road half a mile west of Evelyn's house." She pointed to the map. "Wolfe and Kalo, you'll be set up inside the hunting cabin—here. You'll be all leaving ahead of us. Is fifteen minutes enough time for you, Kalo?"

"I'll be set up before I leave. We're taking a portable power source, so all I'll need is my laptop." Kalo's hand trembled in excitement. "There are eight trail cams, and when Kane moves, I'll feed a prerecorded video loop into them. The perp will have access via his phone, so he'll see what I want him to see. I picked up footage of a deer earlier and we can use that if Kane makes a noise."

"I won't make a noise." Kane stared at him and then looked at Jenna and Jo. "Just make sure you don't mistake me for the killer if all hell breaks loose. I'll be wearing cammies, face paint, and a helmet. I might be wearing liquid Kevlar, but knowing Carter as I do, he's trained Jo to make headshots—right?"

"Yeah, but I'm sure I'll recognize you. You're one of a kind, Dave." Jo took her phone out and checked it again and then thumbed in a number. She winced and stared at Jenna. "Voice-mail again. I just hope Carter isn't lying in a ditch somewhere. If we don't hear from him soon, we might have to trace his phone."

"That won't work." Kalo glanced up from his laptop. "You wanted your phones to be secure, which means they can't be tracked."

Jenna stood. "Forget Carter. He can look after himself." She glanced at her watch. "Okay, Maggie can handle the office until closing. Get changed into civvies and go for a meal. I want you back here no later than five." She waved them away and looked at Kane. "Do you have everything you need here?"

"Yeah, I needed cammies and grabbed them from the army surplus store. Everything is in the Beast. I'll drive it around back and bring inside what we need." Kane headed for the door. "If I park out front when we come back from dinner and we leave the lights on upstairs, people will figure we're working late."

Calm and in control—the usual adrenalin rush when heading out on the hunt for a killer hadn't arrived—Jenna nodded. "Good idea. Now, let's get at it. This killer's reign of terror ends tonight."

THIRTY-FOUR

As time ticked by and the team returned to the office for final instructions, the anticipation of facing a serial killer gripped Jenna. Not fear or panic but butterflies in her stomach and the weight on her shoulders she carried whenever placing people at risk. Jo would be a target and none of them had a clear picture of what might happen, other than if he followed his MO, he'd strike at midnight. How would the killer come at Jo? Would he try and lure her to her death or enter the house and shoot her? The possibilities were endless, and although they'd talked through a ton of scenarios, it was all guesswork, and before they arrested the killer the entire team would be flying by the seat of their pants. Anything might happen and he might not even show. She would be locked inside the house with Jo, but over the six long hours before midnight, Kane would be outside and vulnerable. The idea of him being out there all alone made her stomach clench.

She'd dressed in the same clothes as Jo, with her hair pushed into a black woolen cap drawn down over her ears. If she was spotted in the house, she could be mistaken for Jo at a distance. When Kane walked into the office, Jenna looked up from checking her weapons. The sight of him, wearing cammies, a helmet, night-vision goggles, gunned up with his sniper rifle in one hand, and war paint smeared over his face startled her. In front of her stood the man she'd seen only glimpses of before—the sniper, the assassin. Apart from his size, she recognized only his blue eyes peering out from between the stripes of green and brown face paint.

"Are you concerned or did I scare you?" Kane slid one arm around her shoulder and pulled her against him. "The color drained from your face when you looked at me." He rubbed her back. "You're not feeling sick again, are you?"

Shaking her head, Jenna looked up at him. "I'm okay. I was just imagining how the victims would have felt if they saw you right now, dressed like this. I mean, I couldn't recognize you close up. No wonder they believed the killer was their husband... or his ghost outside in the shadows." She forced a smile. "I guess that's the idea, right? You all blend into the background."

"Yeah, and we all dress the same so the enemy doesn't target the team leader." Kane held her close. "If he's out there, and dressed like me, you won't recognize him until we remove his helmet and goggles, but he'll be the one coming at you. I'll call out if it's me, Jenna."

Pressing her face against his vest, she sucked in a deep breath. "It will still be light until eight. That's a dangerous time for you. We don't know what this person is capable of, Dave."

"He doesn't know what I'm capable of, Jenna." Kane held her away from him and looked at her. "I'm probably younger and fitter than he is. I can wait for hours without a problem in any conditions. I'll have Kalo and Wolfe watching my back. I figure I already have an advantage. From what we know about this guy, he hides in shadows and frightens women. Don't think about me. Concentrate on what's happening inside the house."

Checking her watch, Jenna nodded and looked at Jo. "I

figure we shouldn't speak to each other either. If he has bugged the house, he'll know I'm there."

"Okay, we'll use the coms." Jo pulled on a pair of gloves. "They pick up a whisper. I'd consider turning on the TV, well, at least until, say, eleven to cover our conversations. I guess then I'll have to make it look like I'm heading for bed."

"If you're doing that, that's fine, but when you turn off the bedroom light go back downstairs." Kane looked from one to the other. "Stay together and out of sight. I'll be feeding you information. If I see anything, you'll be the first to know."

Mouth suddenly dry, Jenna nodded. "He might wait until Halloween. Even you can't hole up outside that long."

"I don't think so." Jo slid in her earpiece and then pulled on her cap. "He's following a pattern. It's going to be tonight." She squeezed Jenna's arm. "Ready?"

Jenna tossed her Evelyn's keys. "Yeah, let's go."

Outside in the parking lot, Jenna sat in the seat well in the front and Kane curled his long body low down in the back seat and rested his rifle on the floor. She looked at him and pulled a face. "I'm going to have a stiff neck sitting hunched up like this."

"If no one is on the highway, we'll be able to sit up, but once we get close to the turn to Evelyn's house, we'll need to hide." Kane closed his eyes. "Okay, Jo, hit the gas."

Wondering how Kane could be so relaxed when facing a dangerous situation, she sighed. The silence in the vehicle was unnerving. Each person having their own thoughts about the future. She wanted to lift the mood. "Lighten up, guys. We're not going to a funeral."

"I hope not." Jo kept her eyes on the blacktop.

The journey to Creeping Vine Trail was cramped and uncomfortable for Jenna. With vehicles traveling in both directions along Stanton, it was impossible to climb back into the seat. She rested her head against her arms and tried to relax. Her attention moved over Kane. He hadn't stirred since they'd left and seemed to be asleep, but Jo had kept up a stream of conversation about Carter since she'd complained about the silence. "If you want my opinion"—Jenna glanced up at her—"just leave him be. He obviously needs some alone time."

"Ha. I thought you knew, Carter." Kane opened his eyes and looked at her. "It's probably a woman. He's been back and forth for a week or so and then he dumps the chopper and vanishes. He's found himself a girlfriend and it's serious or he'd be crowing about it."

"Really?" Jo slowed as the GPS gave instructions. "Sharp turn ahead, we're heading to Creeping Vine Trail now. Get ready to jump out soon, Dave."

"I'll be ready. Drive into the long grass if possible and make it nice and slow, I don't want to damage my rifle." Kane stretched and picked up his rifle. He handed Jenna a length of string attached to the door. "Make sure I'm clear before you pull the door closed." He opened the door a crack and wind whistled through.

The Jeep slowed and the sound of long dry grass brushing against the doors filled the cabin. Before Jenna could take a breath, the door opened and Kane dived out the door and rolled into the dry golden wheatgrass. She tugged on the string and the door swung shut but didn't close. At every bump in the driveway, it threatened to blow wide open. "Can you see Dave?"

"No, and I was watching. We were waist high in dead grass, and the shadows from the trees covered him as well." Jo kept her eyes on the dirt road.

Fingers cramping from holding the string, Jenna ground her back teeth. "How much farther?"

"Not far. I can see the house." Jo fumbled in the console for the clicker for the garage door. "Heading into the garage now."

Plunged into darkness as the garage door closed behind them, Jenna dropped the string and rubbed her hands together. Jo was out of the vehicle and heading for the light switch. When the garage flooded with light, Jenna unfolded herself from the Jeep and shook out her arms and legs. She waved at Jo to open the door to the kitchen and scooted around the back of the vehicle to push the back door shut. The only light came from the kitchen, the interior of the house dim but not too dark. From her position, she could see the backyard and partially into the sunroom, which meant anyone outside could see her. She waved Jo to go ahead. The first thing that Evelyn did when she returned from work was to set up the coffee maker and go about making supper.

As Jo played her part, Jenna dropped to the floor and slipped into the hallway. She waited as Jo filled the coffee maker. The plan was for them to clear the house. She pressed her com and kept her voice to just above a whisper. "Dave, we're inside."

"Copy."

As Jo walked from the kitchen, Jenna led the way through the ground floor. She used a scanner Kalo had provided to check for bugs as they cleared each room. With the shutters closed the rooms were dark but secure from anyone seeing them inside. The family room, alongside the kitchen, was once the dining room by its size. Two other larger rooms were sparsely furnished but this one had a comfy sofa set beside the fireplace and a coffee table with a romance novel left face-down at the last page Evelyn had read. Jenna pointed to a flatscreen TV and they searched around for a remote control. Once the TV burst into life, she moved closer to Jo. "We'll clear upstairs and then make this room our base. I haven't found any bugs."

"What about the cellar?" Jo opened a door and peered into darkness. "We should check it. Just in case."

Swallowing the apprehension Jenna always had about walking into dark cellars, she nodded. If they overlooked a possible entry point, it could cost them their lives. "You stay here and watch my back. I don't want that door shutting on us and trapping us down here."

Searching the wall for a switch, she sighed with relief when a dull light came on at the bottom of the stairs. Moving slowly one step at a time, she'd made it halfway down the flight when a noise came from below. She froze and slid her weapon from the holster. Unable to call out a warning and ruin the stakeout, she moved down the steps, scanning the dark room, which seemed to cover the entire footprint of the house. So many dark corners, boxes piled high, and dusty furniture stacked all over. Heart thundering, she reached the bottom step and the light flickered and plunged her into total darkness. A noise close by made her step back, trip on the steps, and fall hard on her hip. She bit down the cry threatening to break from her lips and, still gripping her weapon, crawled onto her knees. The noise came again and something ran over her legs. Not one but a stampede of warm bodies. *Rats!* Pain shot through her hip as she scrabbled for the stairs, making it out the door to see Jo's startled expression. Breathing heavily, she slammed the cellar door shut and leaned closer to Jo. "The cellar is full of rats. I hate rats." She limped toward the stairs. "We need to clear the floor above."

"You're hurt." Jo tried to lead her back into the family room. "You need to sit down."

Shaking her head, Jenna pointed upstairs and kept her voice low. "When we know we're safe."

They moved cautiously through the next floor. Jenna checked the readings on the scanner and found nothing. Three bedrooms, two furnished and the other used for storage. It was lighter upstairs, the shutters flung open, but the drapes tightly shut. Jenna peered cautiously around the edge of the drapes to the garden surrounding the house. Only a small area had been cleared before it met the tree line. The forest seemed alive, moving with each gust of wind. The dry golden grass covering the backyard shimmered as the wind kissed the seed-filled tops.

Wind buffeted the house and tree branches scratched at the windows as if someone with long nails were trying to get inside.

The skin on Jenna's arms prickled and she pushed down the creepy feeling threatening to engulf her. She couldn't imagine living here alone. Moving to the next room and finding a bathroom empty, she moved slowly along the hallway checking closet doors, stopping when she found a flight of stairs inside and a light switch. She turned slowly and looked at Jo. "I guess this is the way to the loft."

"I'll go." Jo pulled her weapon and walked up the narrow staircase.

At the top of the stairs was a solid door with the white paint cracked and peeling. It had a keyhole on one side and no key, but Jenna spotted a hook where a key might have hung at one time. She shivered at the idea of being locked inside and held her breath as Jo turned the doorknob. The handle creaked but the door remained closed.

"It's locked." Jo turned and came back down the steps. "If I owned this place and lived here alone, I'd keep the doors to the loft and cellar locked." She looked at Jenna. "We'll make sure she has the exterminator out here before she comes back and that light replaced in the cellar. She must have to go down there from time to time to check the furnace."

Shuddering at the thought of rats running over her, Jenna pushed the closet door shut. The peeling ring of the landline rang out and she looked at Jo. "Evelyn says she doesn't use the landline. This might be our killer." She glanced at her watch and they headed for the stairs. "It's a quarter after seven. He's early."

They'd gotten halfway down the steps when the phone stopped ringing. Jenna pressed her com. "Dave, the phone just rang and then stopped. Can you see anyone?"

"*Negative.*"

Jenna pressed her com again. "House clear. No bugs. Heading downstairs now."

"Copy."

She followed Jo downstairs and through the house, but before they reached the kitchen, the phone peeled again. Ahead of her Jo stiffened and pressed her com. "I'll answer the phone. Leaving my com open."

Jenna pressed her back against the wall in the hallway and slid down to sit on the floor. In this position she couldn't be seen from the kitchen or sunroom windows. The cold floor seeped through her clothes and her hip throbbed as she made contact with the hard polished floor. She held her breath as Jo picked up the phone.

"Hello." Jo pressed the receiver to her ear.

Through Jenna's com, she could hear a low whistle.

"Man, you get more good-looking every year." It was a man's voice, the accent familiar. *"Are you going to open the door and let me inside tonight? I'll be by real soon. You miss me don't you, Evie?"*

"Who is this?" Jo had listened with interest to Evelyn's interview and knew the tone to use with the unwelcome caller.

"You know who it is. I'm coming, Evie. Wear something nice." The line went dead and Jo hung up the phone. She pressed her com. "Kalo, did you trace that?"

"No, sorry. It wasn't long enough. If he calls again, keep him on the line." Kalo sounded apologetic. *"No one has showed on the trail cams. You're good for now."*

"Copy." Jo leaned over the kitchen sink and closed the blinds. She took two cups out of the cabinet and poured the freshly brewed coffee, added fixings, and handed one to Jenna. "If he is outside, he can't see what I'm doing now, so long as I keep down this end of the kitchen. Let's head back to the family room and get comfortable. He's started his fantasy."

Limping back to the family room, Jenna sat down on the soft sofa and sighed. "What do you mean?"

"From what we know about the contact he's made with the other victims, he calls them. Frightening them is part of his fantasy. The phone calls, the shadowy figure in the garden, it's all part of his plan." Jo sipped her coffee.

Intrigued by Jo's profiling skills, Jenna wanted more details. "How does he know so much about the victims? I mean, he seems to know almost intimate details: pet names, where they met. It seems incredible."

"This is where Carter is a great source of information. I wish he'd been here to help but we've often discussed the closeness of a combat team. They discuss their families, show off their photographs. They are close, like brothers, and this is what makes me believe our killer was once part of the team that died on Halloween. Maybe he was in the team for a time and then was moved on or discharged, but I'm convinced he knew them all."

Jenna nodded. "So, he gains their confidence by feeding them information that they believe only their husbands would know?"

"Exactly, but I figure he plans everything. Just look at his MO, they're all different and yet have the same conclusion—apparent suicide." Jo's eyes flashed with excitement. "First, he made it inside the house and overdosed the victim. The next, he lured her to her death. It's all about control. He is trying to make the outcome favorable. When he called Evelyn, he asked to come inside, right? She got angry. So his first contact tonight is a compliment. There was no malice in his call, no threats. He truly wants his victims to believe he is their dead husbands, back from the grave for one last goodbye."

Jenna rubbed her hip and nodded. "Good luck with that angle tonight. How far can you push him before he gets frustrated enough to break into the house and strangle you?"

"Unknown but midnight is special to him, so we must expect an escalation of hauntings." Jo stared at Jenna as if appraising her. "Do you believe in ghosts?"

Heat crept into her cheeks but Jenna nodded. "Yeah, seems that I do."

"Well, don't believe everything you see and only aim for flesh and blood." Jo looked at her over her cup. "It's going to be a long night. I'll keep the coffee coming. We can't risk getting sleepy."

A cold shiver tumbled down Jenna's back. "Trust me, when it comes to psychopaths, I'm always on full alert."

THIRTY-FIVE

Eleven-thirty ticked by without another phone call. This had to be the longest Wednesday Jenna had ever experienced. She'd been on the job for almost sixteen hours, exhaustion was making her mind play tricks on her and now, without the TV to block the sounds of the night, the house was creeping her out. Wind rattled the shutters and tree branches clawed at the walls and windows like shrieks of banshees. She contacted Kane, concerned he was outside in the elements and just wanting to hear his voice. The temperature had dropped considerably and the plate in his head would be throbbing. Everyone in the team could hear the com transmissions, so she kept it short. "Apart from the house trying to insist it's haunted, it's quiet here."

"If he's out here with me, he's a ghost."

Jenna's attention fixed on the clock on the mantel as the minute hand clicked to midnight. She sucked in breath as footsteps, slow and distinct, came from above. The hairs on the back of her neck stood to attention. She stared at Jo. "Did you hear that?"

"What is it, Jenna?" Kane's voice came into her ear.

Unable to control a rush of fear, Jenna pointed upward and

Jo nodded. "Dave, we hear something moving about upstairs. The house was cleared. We checked every room. The door to the loft was locked. No one has gotten inside. We'd have heard them."

"*I'm close by. You know old houses make strange noises. Stay focused. Kalo is using the trail cams to watch all paths to the house.*" Kane's voice seemed to brush her ear in a whisper. "*I'm moving around the perimeter. There's nobody here yet, Jenna. I'll do another sweep. It's probably the wind. It's blowing strong gusts out here.*"

The footsteps came again, slow, deliberate, and with each step the floorboards above them creaked. *That's footsteps. I'm darn well not freaking out.* Alarmed, Jenna pulled her weapon from her shoulder holster and ground her teeth. "Copy."

Indicating to Jo to spread out each taking one side of the family room door, she poked her head outside and listened. The sound stopped for a few seconds and then started again. Every hair on Jenna's body rose as the footsteps moved across the floor toward the staircase and stopped. She turned at Jo's low hiss, and Jo pointed to herself and made walking motions with her fingers. Jo wanted to draw out the killer. Jenna trusted her judgement and nodded. Without hesitation, Jo sucked in a deep breath and, holding her pistol down along her thigh, headed for the stairs. As Jo climbed the stairs, Jenna took aim. If anyone came along the hallway, she'd have them in her sights.

Holding her aim true, Jenna pressed her back to the wall and, keeping in the shadows, eased out of the family room. The silence shattered as an old-fashioned peeling echoed through the house as the phone in the kitchen rang. Startled, Jenna kept her gun aimed at the top of the stairs, but Jo spun around and hurled back down the steps and ran to the kitchen. She grabbed the phone. "Hello."

Jenna followed, stopping at the kitchen door and peering all around. Footsteps came again, stronger now, and she turned to see Jo's strained expression. She'd dropped the phone leaving it swinging from its cord. "What did he say?"

"He's in the house." Jo came up beside her and whispered in her ear. "He said he has his Purple Heart and wants me to wear it. He wants me to go upstairs to be with him. He wants us to die together." She squeezed Jenna's arm. "I can do this. Give me the chance to talk to him. When he knows I'm not Evelyn, he might back down."

Pulse thumping in her ears, Jenna pressed her com. "Dave, he says he's in the house."

"Copy."

Holding her weapon with both hands, Jenna stared at Jo walking with her back straight, toward the staircase. She followed at a distance and, keeping out of sight, she peered to the top of the stairs. Out of the darkness a shadow appeared. The light from the kitchen offered a distorted view of a ghostly apparition of a man over six feet dressed the same as Kane. She pressed her com. "I see him. Top of stairs. He's in full combat gear, vest, helmet, and face paint. Jo is going to talk him down."

"She can't. Don't hesitate. Aim for the shoulder or thighs. His vest will catch a bullet. Your only chance is to slow him down. I'm on my way."

"Please stop." Jo lifted one hand like a cop stopping traffic. "I'm not Evelyn, or Evie. My name is Special Agent Jo Wells and I'm not afraid of you." She moved into a shaft of light spilling from the family room doorway.

"Well, you should be." The accent sounded familiar but the tone was as hard as nails. "I don't take prisoners, don't you know?"

"I'm interested in why you're killing wives of MIA Seal teams." Jo stared up the stairs. "Do you have a reason or is this just a Halloween thrill to you?"

"You should know, honey." He snorted. "You're the expert on serial killers." He moved closer to the top of the stairs.

How could he know that? A trickle of sweat ran down Jenna's back. Jo wasn't handling the situation at all. This guy was all over her and not giving an inch. A wave of terror gripped her as the glint of a knife in the man's hand caught the light. It was a split-second decision. Jenna squeezed the trigger. The man had moved so fast her bullet slammed into him just as the knife took flight. The blade thudded into the wall inches from Jo's head as the soldier fell forward and tumbled down the stairs, sprawling at her feet. Glass smashed as someone hurled through the sunroom door. She heard Jo make a cry of distress and turned to her. "Are you hit?"

"Oh my God, it's Carter." Jo fell to her knees beside the inert body.

THIRTY-SIX

Disregarding the shards of glass, Kane charged through the sunroom door. With splinters crunching under his boots, he ran through the sunroom and into the kitchen, only stopping to peek around the kitchen door. In the hallway at the bottom of the stairs, Jenna was holstering her weapon and Jo kneeled on the floor. A pool of blood was surrounding a man lying face down at the bottom of the stairs. He wore a helmet and blond hair poked out over his collar. Alarm bells sounded in his head. "Get away from him—now."

It was as if time slowed. He'd never get there in time. The twitch of the man's hand was the only warning as he struck like a snake and grasped Jenna's ankle. One vicious tug had her falling backward and hitting the wall hard. As the man rose up on his knees and grasped Jo around the neck, Kane dashed forward and aimed a kick between his legs. The attacker howled and fell on one side, knees drawn up and gasping for air, but he wasn't down yet. His head turned toward Kane and he aimed a punch to his thigh. Seeing it coming, Kane moved, and the fist brushed over his leg. Hampered by the small space, Kane spun on one foot and smashed a heel into the intruder's kidney. The force would have disabled most men, but it wasn't over. Before him was a trained and fit fighting machine and the man was reaching for a weapon.

Grabbing the intruder's wrist as he aimed the weapon at Jenna, laying sprawled and dizzy on the floor, Kane noticed a flash of triumph in the man's eyes. He forced the pistol upward as three shots rang out. Debris fell from the ceiling, peppering his back. Close by, Jo was gasping on the floor. "Get out of the way, Jo."

"I'll kill them and then you." The man's face split into a grin, his teeth white against the forest face paint. "You can't stop me."

They rolled into the hallway face-to-face. Kane smashed the intruder's hand on the tiled floor until the fingers opened and the gun slipped from his grasp. As he jerked his head back in time to avoid a headbutt, a hand clamped on his throat. Strong fingers dug into his carotid artery and his vision blurred. He had seconds before blackout, and with all the force he could muster, he slammed a punch into the man's armpit. The grip on his throat dropped away and, gasping, Kane rolled onto his knees, tossed the man facedown, and cuffed him. After hog-tying him with zip ties, he frisked him and relieved the intruder of his sidearm and the backup weapon attached to one ankle. Needing to know his identity, Kane removed the prisoner's helmet and then dragged him into the kitchen. He glared at him. "Don't as much as twitch."

The look his prisoner gave him was filled with malice. This guy wasn't used to being beaten and the first chance he got he'd strike without mercy. This was a new definition of a serial killer —trained to kill by peacemakers to protect his country, a deadly and vicious traitor to everything Kane believed in.

Kane turned to check on the condition of Jenna and Jo. He grabbed Jenna's arm as she staggered to her feet. A nasty bruise was forming on one cheek from where she'd struck the wall. Jo was bent over, coughing. He touched her arm. "You, okay?"

"Yeah." Jo's eyes streamed. "I was sure that was Carter, although the face paint made it difficult. That looks like his hair."

Kane stood over his prisoner. The man might be injured and secured, but he'd never give up. He could see it in his eyes. Not wanting to take his attention off him for a second, he reached back to take Jenna's hand and squeezed it before reluctantly letting it slip from his grasp. "Jenna, are you hurt?"

"I'll live." Jenna leaned against the wall. "How did you know that wasn't Carter?"

"This guy"—Kane switched on more lights to get a better look at him—"has a tattoo on his neck, but from a distance the hair might have fooled me too. He's the same size, but Carter's green eyes are hard to miss."

"I'm sure glad it's not Carter." Jenna kept her distance, but her weapon was aimed at the prisoner's head.

It was difficult to ID the man with face paint smeared over his face. Kane tried his military tone with him. "What's your name, soldier?"

The man just glared at him.

Kane pressed his com and contacted Wolfe. "Shane, we have a man down. Gunshot wound to the shoulder. A through and through."

"Copy, we're on our way."

"Rio." Jenna pressed her com. "We have a prisoner in custody. Go home and get some rest. I'll need you here first thing to process the scene."

"Copy." Rio sounded relieved. *"Who is it?"*

"I'm not sure." Jenna was staring at the prisoner. "Head off home. I'll need you both fresh in the morning."

"Copy."

"Jo, do you recognize him? Can you check the image files?"

She looked at Kane. "I'll come with you to transport him to the office, unless he needs surgery."

Kane ran a thumb over the bruise on her cheek, suddenly glad where he'd aimed his kick. "Keep your weapon on him and I'll scan his fingerprints." He stared at the man. "If you were ever in the military, we'll have your name in seconds." He pushed the man forward and, ignoring his grunt of pain, dragged off one glove and scanned his hand. He sent the file directly to Kalo and pressed his com. "Can you run the prints I sent you? The prisoner isn't talking. He'll be in the military files —Marines. That's for darn sure."

"There's only one man this can be." Jo was peering at her phone. "Mark Pittman out of Damien's Hollow." She gave the man a cursory glance. "He's the only blond-haired man on our suspects list and he meets the general description."

"The guy from the computer store?" Jenna shook her head. "That's the second time we've had a murderer holed up there. And they say lightning doesn't strike in the same place twice."

At that moment Kalo's voice came through the coms. "I have him. Mark Pittman, Navy Seal, listed as MIA seven years ago but was repatriated after being rescued from a militant camp a year later. It doesn't give details. He might have been in the Halloween bombing. There's nothing in the files."

Kane crouched down in front of Pittman and read him his rights. "What's the deal, Pittman? I've never met a Seal who's gone bad. You planning on staying silent, or do you have a story to tell?"

Nothing.

"Do you want a lawyer?" Jenna touched her cheek. "Just because you remain silent, we can still ask you questions."

Nothing.

"Okay, have it your own way." Jenna shook her head. "Dr. Wolfe will take a look at you. Don't try anything. Deputy Kane is itching to break both your legs. He's seen what you did to the women you've murdered, and as Dr. Wolfe did the autopsies, you don't have any friends here. If you have an excuse for murdering five women, it's best you have your say while we have Agent Jo Wells here. You seem to know her reputation. She is trying for a better understanding of why people like you have the urge to kill." She shrugged. "Talking to her could prevent you from receiving the death penalty. I know it's been a while since we executed anyone in Montana, but with the increase in serial killers of late, I figure the people in this state are losing patience with guys like you."

"I'm already dead." Pittman shook his head. "You can't kill me twice."

"Go on." Jenna had her weapon trained on his head. "Why did you murder innocent women? You must have a reason. Don't you think they suffered enough by losing their husbands?"

"That's the point, isn't it?" Pittman grinned at her. "They couldn't wait to join them. I was doing them a favor."

A horn sounded outside and Jo thrust her phone into Jenna's top pocket and then hurried to open the front door. Moments later, Wolfe came striding down the hallway with Kalo close behind. Kane stood and nodded to him. "Can you patch him up or does he need to go to the ER?"

"Let me take a look." Wolfe placed his bag on the floor. He looked at Jenna. "You can holster that weapon. He's not going to get the drop on Kane or me when he's hog-tied."

"Okay." Jenna holstered her weapon and slid out Jo's phone from her pocket. "You recorded everything?"

"Yeah." Jo took the phone and stopped the recording. "Right from when Kane had him cuffed. I wanted to make sure there was no doubt we'd read him his rights. I have everything." She looked at Pittman. "You know it's over for you now. Talk to me and I'll make sure the judge knows you cooperated."

"It's never over." Pittman didn't flinch when Wolfe sliced

off his shirt to examine his wounds. He stared at her, his expression guileless, almost friendly. "This just means I've extended my list, is all."

"I'll clean and dress the wound, but he'll need an X-ray. There could be bone fragments in there and they'll need to come out before it's sutured." Wolfe frowned at Jenna. "I'll call the paramedics."

"No!" Jo was watching Pittman closely. "We need to keep him under close guard. He'll kill anyone to get away. That wound won't slow him down and you darn well know it. I'm not letting him out of my sight. We'll be placing too many people in danger if he escapes from the hospital. With his skills it's not worth the risk. You'll have to take him to the morgue."

"That's not necessary. I have a portable X-ray unit in my van." Wolfe gave her a direct stare. "After we move him to the office and secure him, I'll go and get it."

"I'm innocent until proven guilty, right?" Pittman grinned at Jenna. "You're the sheriff and duty bound to treat me with due care. I demand to be taken to the ER."

"You're getting medical assistance right now." Jenna nodded to Jo. "Take some shots of Wolfe patching him up." She looked at Kalo. "You drive Emily's Cherokee and follow us to the office. It will leave Jo's hands free to shoot this asshole if he attempts an escape." She looked around at the blood-soaked hallway and shook her head. "This is a crime scene, so don't touch anything. Rowley and Rio will process it in the morning."

"I'm wearing gloves." Kalo smiled at her. "I like being on the job."

Kane flicked a glance at him. "You'll get yourself killed if you hang out with us. Maybe you should think that through some."

"I agree." Jo gingerly touched the red marks on her throat. "Can we get out of here now?"

Kane nodded. "Okay, but before we leave I want to know how he got into the house. He didn't get past me."

"Dammit, how can you be so darn stupid?" Pittman chuckled and shook his head. "I've been living in the loft. I left when Evelyn went to work, came back before she got home. I'd been hunting her down for months and then she walked into the computer store looking for a new phone. I helped her out." He smiled. "I came by to check the signal and installed a signal booster in the loft. It was easy to pocket the key and the lock on the sunroom door opens with a credit card." He looked straight at Kane. "Not that I needed a key. I can get inside most places."

"Dave." Jenna pulled him to one side out of earshot. "I know he's a psychopath and unpredictable like they all are, but just what level of dangerous are we talking about?"

Kane shrugged but his gaze never left his prisoner. "Hand-cuffed, he's still capable of breaking someone's neck. He'd use his legs. Get close and he'll try to headbutt you. There are many ways to get free, Jenna." He looked at her. "The handcuffs and zip ties wouldn't stop me even if you held a gun on me. Right now, he's got nothing to lose and will try anything to escape or cause an accident. We can't lock the truck doors to prevent him getting away. If he has skills like mine, he'll have a few tricks up his sleeve. For him, wrecking the truck would be worth the risk to get away."

"Okay." Jenna flicked her attention from him to Wolfe and back. "Transporting him without a cruiser will be dicey. We go to plan B." She gave him a small smile. "Get him on his feet. It's time to move out." She went to Wolfe's side. "Have you got something in your bag to slow him down for the trip back to town?"

"Yeah, but it's not necessary." Wolfe flicked a glance at Kane and then back to her. "If you drive, we can handle him."

"Can you?" Pittman chuckled. "It's the duty of every soldier to escape." He lifted his chin. "By any means possible. I haven't decided if I should kill you yet. It wouldn't be thrilling. You'd be collateral damage and I'll take you down in a second. You have my word on that."

Kane cut the zip ties around Pittman's ankles and dragged him to his feet. He dug his pistol into the man's ribs. "If I'd had a choice, you'd be dead by now. You're alive because the sheriff and the FBI find you interesting—I don't."

"Duty of care, Deputy." Pittman grinned at him. "Come on, Doc, how about some pain meds? This ape has made my shoulder bleed again."

"Are you sure, you want him sedated, Jenna?" Wolfe looked concerned. "You can't legally interview him if he's medicated."

"What if you give him just enough for us to get him to the office. I'll call someone in to watch him. How long before it's out of his system?" Jenna nodded as if making a decision.

"Twenty-four hours to be legal." Wolfe frowned. "It's not a good idea."

Kane shook his head. "I agree with Shane. If we sedate him, we'll have him at the office for twenty-four hours and that's too dangerous." He stared at Jenna. "If you're concerned about his pain, don't be. Wolfe can numb the area and then it won't affect him, but then he'll be more lethal. Right now, the pain is slowing him down."

"You think?" Pittman chuckled and glared at Kane. "I'm going to enjoy killing you and I'll take my time with the women."

Unimpressed, Kane holstered his weapon and grabbed Pittman by the arm. "Good luck with that."

"Okay, get him into the truck." She turned to Jo and Kalo. "Follow us back to the office. Jo, if you could wake up the DA for me and explain what's happened and the threat he is posing. I want Pittman in county jail once we've questioned him. I don't want him in town. Our jail won't hold him. The DA will make arrangements for armed guards to come by and collect him."

"I'm on it." Jo pulled out her phone and made the call.

Kane escorted Pittman to the truck, pushed him into the back seat, secured the seatbelt as tight as possible, and climbed in beside him. Wolfe took the front, turning in his seat, weapon aimed at Pittman. When Jenna slid behind the wheel and the garage door opened, Kane squeezed her shoulder. "Let's get this animal into a cage."

THIRTY-SEVEN

Mist swirled across the blacktop, making the way ahead like negotiating whitewater rapids at night. The beams of the headlights only emphasized the white diaphanous swirling mass oozing out from between the trees and spilling across the road. Driving an unfamiliar truck, with a psychopath directly behind her, didn't do much to calm Jenna's nerves. She swallowed her fear and aimed the truck along the tree line. Creeping Vine Trail had been well named; it snaked all the way back to the highway. Kane kept up a conversation with her, mundane things, she figured just to keep her awake. By the time they reached Stanton, the adrenalin rush had given way to a throbbing headache and the cut on the inside of her cheek stung. She let out a sigh of relief when the Halloween decorations and ghoulish displays came into sight on Main. At this time of night, with the swirling mist and dancing skeletons, anything or anyone could be hiding or watching. A shiver slid down her spine at the skeletons' black eye sockets turning as if to watch them drive by. Ahead, the lights from the sheriff's office spilled out onto the sidewalk, over the Beast out front as if it were standing sentry. It was a welcome sight after such a harrowing night and she pulled into a slot. Moments later Jo and Kalo parked beside her. When they all climbed out, she turned to Kane. "Take him straight into interview room one and then come to my office. Shane, do you mind watching the prisoner until we get organized?"

"Sure." Wolfe nodded. "We'll need a ton of coffee if you're planning on interviewing him now."

"Is he going to be secured?" Kalo stared at the prisoner and back to Jenna. "I'll watch him. I'm not tired."

"Yeah, leave the kid with me." Pittman chuckled. "Fresh meat."

Jenna turned to Kalo. "Yeah, you can watch from outside. The room is secure. Dave and Wolfe designed it." She turned to Pittman. "You won't kill again on my watch."

"You have to sleep sometime, Sheriff." Pittman's mouth turned up at the corners. "That's where we're different. I can stay awake for days, but you're dead on your feet."

"I'm not." Kane shoved him up the steps. "I'll outlast you, old man."

Jenna dashed up the front steps to unlock the door. She headed straight to the interview room, scanned her card, and entered. She switched on the camera and recording device and then waited at the door for Kane to bring in the prisoner. She drew her weapon and waited as Kane shackled him to the table and floor. Mark Pittman wasn't going anywhere. The wait for them to get organized wouldn't hurt him. She indicated to a chair opposite the one-way mirror on the outside of the interview room. "That's bulletproof glass and he's secured. Watch him, and if he makes like he's getting out of the cuffs, use your com to contact Kane. He'll get here in seconds. Don't wait and see—act. Okay?"

"Got it." Kalo filled a cup from the watercooler and sat down. "I'm good."

"Don't play games on your phone or you'll end up his next

victim." Jo stared at Kalo. "That man is more than capable of escaping. Do you understand?"

"No games, no phone, watch the dude until you come back." Kalo shrugged. "I could maybe arrange a place for us to stay for what's left of tonight."

Jenna smiled at him. "That's already taken care of. You'll be staying with us at the ranch." She pushed hair from her eyes. "Watch the prisoner. We won't be long." She followed the others up to her office.

As Wolfe set up the two coffee makers they used for meetings, Jenna removed her coat and dropped into her office chair. "Let's make this quick. He's as good as confessed already but I'd sure like to get more details, and if he confesses to the three women we believed he killed in other counties, it will tie up the case."

"We'll concentrate on our victims now and if Jo can lead him into the other confessions, well, that's good." Kane rubbed both hands down his face and looked at Jo. "What did the DA say?"

"He was very cooperative and will have an armored transport van here ASAP." Jo leaned back in her chair and sighed. "Do you want me to take the lead in the questioning?"

Having a behavioral analyst at hand, and a specialist in the field of psychopathic behavior, Jenna smiled at the offer. She always utilized the assets on hand by placing the most qualified person on her team to oversee each part of an investigation. Not allowing her position of sheriff to cloud her judgement by overindulging in self-importance had made her team stronger. She could take the lead but didn't need to prove her abilities to anyone. "Please do. He doesn't see you as a threat. It's worked with other psychopaths we've interviewed, and he's no different."

"He is to a degree because of his training." Jo took the coffee from Wolfe with a smile and sipped. "He's been trained to withstand interrogation. Add charm and high intelligence and he is more than capable of twisting me around his little finger." She looked at Kane. "You know about interrogation techniques, don't you? Well, some, I guess." She let out a long sigh. "I wish Carter were here. He's been there and trained with guys like him."

"I have too." Wolfe passed out cups of steaming brew. "Kane was in the Marines. We'll be able to break him down if necessary, but I figure it will take most of the night." He passed around energy bars. "Eat and finish that coffee, Jenna, before you fall on your face." He examined her cheek, pressing gently, before looking at Jo. "Those bruises are going to look great for Halloween." He sat down. "When this is over, Jo, I'll fly you back to Snakeskin Gully. You'll want Jaime here for Halloween, won't you?"

"Yes, my daughter is so excited about coming. We'll bring Clara, our nanny, as well. She'll care for Jaime if we're all going to the ball."

Jenna sighed and sipped her coffee. "If we can get this case tied up by Saturday, it will be a miracle."

"Oh, I figure if he confesses and we have a statement and a video of his interview, once Pittman is safe in county jail we can hand the case over to the DA. If we gather information on cases outside our jurisdiction, we'll hand it over to the sheriffs in those counties." Kane tore open an energy bar. "It's a quarter after two. Let's get at it."

"Your team is like an FBI taskforce. To apprehend this killer so fast is amazing." Jo walked down the stairs beside Jenna. "I don't know how you do it."

Jenna gripped the handrail. "It was a lucky break this time. If Evelyn Brown hadn't walked into my office asking for help, we would still be hunting down this guy. We had possible suspects but nothing apart from a vague connection to the team who went MIA in Afghanistan seven years ago. We might have been following this guy's victim trail for years."

Everyone apart from Wolfe locked their weapons in the gun safe outside the interview room. He would watch through the mirror with Kalo. They would be able to hear everything through the intercom. When Kalo walked up to her, she hung back to speak to him. "Anything happen?"

"Nope, he just sits there staring at his hands." Kalo cleared his throat. "I can type up a record of the interview as you go and have it ready for him to sign when you're done. It will save time." He smiled. "I write statements from interviews for Jo and Carter all the time."

Jenna stopped at the door to the interview room. "Yeah, that would be a great help, thanks."

She waved Kane ahead and he swiped his card and entered with Jo. After getting a drink from the watercooler, Jenna stepped inside and offered Pittman the water in a paper cup. She introduced everyone inside the room for the record with time and date. She sat down with Jo opposite Pittman, and Kane leaned against the door. "Mr. Pittman. Deputy Kane has read you your rights and you have declined representation. Is that correct?"

"For now, yeah, but I'll want someone to stand up for me in court." Pittman stared at Jenna. "I'm not representing myself. Is that clear?"

The way Pittman looked at her, his expression cordial and his stare almost seductive, made Jenna's skin crawl. She'd experienced a psychopath's charisma. It reminded her of the way a cobra fixes its unblinking eyes on its prey just before it strikes. "It's on the record. Agent Wells would like to ask you some questions but before she starts. Do you smoke?"

"Never have, nope." Pittman narrowed his gaze. "Why?"

"It's not important." Jo glanced at her notes. "Did you serve in Afghanistan seven years ago and were you in any way involved with the team that went missing over Halloween?"

"Yeah, I was there." Pittman shrugged. "It's classified but I guess now the truth will come out. Do you want the reason why I killed those first women? I killed them all for the same reason. The first ones were Joanne Nelson out of Helena and Alma Ritter and her daughter Tina from Louan. I found them first. The last two were harder to track down. I didn't know they'd moved to Black Rock Falls. It was a nice surprise. I didn't like having to travel but I knew from the guys in the team their intention was to settle around these parts when they'd retired."

"It took you seven years to hunt them down?" Jo narrowed her gaze on him. "You had their names. It's not that difficult to find people these days. What was the delay?"

"I was captured and held for four long years before they got me out." Pittman's eyes hadn't changed. "Before they allowed me back home I was interrogated by my own superiors to ensure I hadn't turned. As soon as they discovered I suffered PTSD episodes they dropped me like a hot potato. I went home to my wife in Colorado. She couldn't cope with my crazy times and took her own life. I figured then she did it to make me see things straight. This is why I'm telling you everything. I welcome death. Like I said before, inside I'm already dead."

Jenna glanced at Jo. She needed to know what had happened. It was significant to the case. "What happened that night in Afghanistan? I know there was an incident and everyone died, right? So how do you claim to have saved them?"

"There were a series of explosions. IEDs all over." Pittman clanked his chains, agitation shimmered through him. "There were no signs and we walked right into an ambush. The guys were all injured and the militants were closing in. We didn't stand a chance. So, I killed them all."

THIRTY-EIGHT

"You killed your team?" Kane straightened and swore under his breath.

"Yeah." Pittman gave him a direct stare but his eyes held nothing, no remorse, no pain—nothing. "The militants thought I'd changed sides but they didn't trust me."

Jenna exchanged a meaningful look with Kane and he gave her an imperceivable nod. She looked at Jo. "Go on."

"So, tell me about Willow Smith." Jo leaned forward in her chair. "Why did you terrorize her and then murder her?"

"She wanted to hear from Oliver, so I gave her that and then I killed her." Pittman shrugged. "Well, technically, she took her own life. I didn't force her to drink the hot chocolate, did I?"

"How did you know so much about these women?" Jo leaned forward. "After seven years, most people forget details."

"We talked, about families and our hopes and dreams." Pittman blew out a breath. "I was just waiting for a chance to take them out and I kept a few things: letters, photographs from each of them."

Jenna swallowed bile. "You mean like trophies of the men you planned to murder?"

"I guess." Pittman smiled so sweetly it was as if he'd relived a special memory. "I was never part of the team, the brotherhood. Having their things now makes me recall how it felt to pump bullets into them and watch them twitch before they died."

"Okay and Christy Miller?" Jo frowned. "How did you lure her to her death?"

"That one took a ton of time and patience." Pittman shrugged. "I have that in spades. I went with Hank a few times to Death Drop Gully to look at that old house. He had plans, big plans to renovate it years before he died. When Hank was on his last deployment, Christy moved there and started the renovations." He stared into space as if remembering. "I heard she refused to believe he'd died. That made my task easy. When she went to paint at the plateau, I'd appear dressed in combat gear in the forest giving her a glimpse now and then. It didn't take her long to believe I was a ghost."

"What interests me is how you got her to leave the house at midnight. It was midnight, wasn't it? The same time as the team died?" Jo leaned back in her chair. "How did you get her to leave the house? That must have taken skill."

Inside Jenna smiled. She admired the way Jo played to his ego to draw out information. She glanced at Kane but his attention was fixed on Pittman. Kane's mouth had formed a thin line and his hands hung loose at his sides, in his classic attack position. Did Pittman realize the man in the room was more lethal than he could ever imagine? She moved her attention to the smiling Pittman.

"It's nice to see someone who appreciates my skills." Pittman shrugged. "Yet you can't see why I killed them, can you?"

"We'll get to that, but the suspense is killing me. How did you make her jump into the gully?" Jo placed her notebook on the table. "Did you scare her out of the house?"

"Nope." Pittman towered his fingers. "She left the front door open, so I went into the cellar and left an old walkie-talkie down there and used it to contact her. She came looking when I started calling her name. They like that, being able to speak to their husbands one last time. I told her to meet me on the plateau and to wear the Purple Heart." He shrugged. "She came—they all come. They can't miss the chance to see if their husbands are still alive. When she got to the plateau, I had a target of a soldier and set it up in the bushes. She aimed her rifle at it and I came in from behind and took the weapon out of her hands. She stepped back and I tossed a rock at her. She did the rest herself." He swung a gaze to Jenna. "You almost had me, you know. You saw me in the forest. Well, maybe you felt me watching you and when the deputy left you on your lonesome, it took everything I had not to push you over the edge, but I needed to get back to the house and get my walkie-talkie before you discovered it was Christy splattered all over the gully."

Realizing just how close she'd come to dying, Jenna swallowed hard. "Was that you in the house when we came by? Did you brew the coffee?"

"Yeah, that was me." Pittman blew out a sigh. "She didn't need it, did she? You can't steal from a dead person, can you?" He looked at Jo. "I'm over talking about Christy. I didn't get to see the body. Can you show me a picture? Were her brains splattered all over? I planned to make Evelyn real messy and you spoiled everything by taking her place."

"Okay, just one more question?" Jo stared at him emotionless. "Why did you kill the team?"

"Hank thought he was better than me. He took it hard when I was promoted. I hung out with him to be one of the boys. I don't need friends. I took my chance to take him out when his foot was blown clean off in the explosion. When I aimed at his head, he begged me not to kill him. He told me he and all the married guys on the team wanted to see their wives again." Pittman lifted his chin. "I said, 'Sure, I can do that. It will be a pleasure to kill them all too,' and pulled the trigger. I didn't think about any of them after that—not until I found my wife in the bathtub bleeding out. We married straight out of high school before I joined the service, and she was the only person who really understood me."

"How so?" Jo's expression was unreadable.

"The wives." Pittman smiled. "They weren't my first kills. I used to bring girls home and she'd watch me strangle them. She like to watch." He stared into space and his hands clenched and unclenched. "We buried them under the floorboards when we lived in Blackwater. When people started asking questions, we moved to Colorado and, to be safe, I joined the Marines." He laughed. "There I got paid to kill."

Astonished, Jenna shook her head. "So, what made you take up a killing spree after seven years?"

"It wasn't seven years, like I said before. It took time to hunt them down." A slow smile crossed Pittman's face. "I figured it was time I made good on my promise and reunited the team with their wives." He shrugged. "If I were taken out before I finished, I'd meet up with my wife on the other side. This time the team would see me as a hero and we'd all be together up there in the clouds."

"Problem with that idea, Pittman"—Kane straightened and stared at him—"is that you're going straight to hell."

THIRTY-NINE

Halloween

The chatter over the kitchen table at dinner was all about costumes and the Halloween ball. Jaime, Jo's daughter, was ecstatic to be trick-or-treating along Main with Wolfe's youngest, Anna, and a group of the neighborhood kids. Jenna had her costume. She had decided on a slightly bruised and battered good witch. Although, she'd really wanted to be a fairy but the wings would have gotten in the way at the ball at the town hall. Jo was going as a vampire, figuring her bruised neck would make her look as if she'd just been inducted into the clan or whatever happened to people after they'd been bitten. Kane was in constant motion, moving around, making coffee, and serving dessert. He liked to cook and always made sure everyone was happy.

It had been a stressful time since catching Pittman. Jenna had the team working hard to make sure they'd collected every scrap of evidence against him to present to the DA. After

Pittman admitted to killing the other women, Kane had been able to extract details and with them Wolfe was able to avoid exhuming the poor women's bodies. Jenna had sent a team to clean and repair Evelyn's home but somehow she doubted the woman would ever return to Black Rock Falls to live.

The Pittman case was closed and handed to the DA, with all the evidence necessary to convict him in Black Rock Falls and other counties. An investigation into the bodies buried under the floorboards in Blackwater had been initiated by the local sheriff and no doubt more charges would be laid in the coming weeks. Pittman would never see the light of day, but it hadn't been the Pittman case causing sleepless nights. Jenna had been intent on getting Jimmy Gates, the kid who had tried to steal the Beast, and his family back together. She'd even dragged her nemesis, the lawyer Sam Cross, to assist them with the legal tangle. With the children, Jimmy and Peter, in different counties and their mother, Judith, in Idaho, locating everyone had been difficult and springing Peter from his foster home had taken a court order. These proceedings usually take weeks to achieve, but with a little intervention from the right people, Jenna had moved mountains and the family would all be together real soon. They'd be under the supervision of the Her Broken Wings Foundation for a time, but if all was well, as Jenna suspected, they would receive suitable housing and financial support for six months. Before the family left Her Broken Wings, Judith would have a secure job and the kids would be in school. The support for the family would always be there. Prior similar cases had proved to be very successful and when Jenna and Kane had created the Her Broken Wings Foundation for abused women and children, the town, with Father Derry's support, had now become a haven for anyone bullied or abused.

"You, okay? You're a little pale." Kane pressed a kiss to Jenna's head before sitting down beside her. "Not feeling sick?"

Jenna leaned into him. "No. I'm fine. I figure I was fighting off that bug that Sandy and her mother had earlier in the week."

"Ah... I see." Kane's eyes fell to his plate as he dug into a slice of cherry pie with cream.

Jenna stared at him and her heart sank. "Oh, did you think I might be pregnant?"

"The idea had crossed my mind." Kane slid a forkful of pie into his mouth and closed his eyes and then opened them and looked at her. "Are you?"

The room fell silent and heat filled Jenna's cheeks, but Kane's eyes held a hopeful expression. They both wanted a baby so much and it seemed to be taking forever. She shook her head. "Not yet."

"You'll tell me, right?" Kane pulled her close and hugged her. "Like the second you know?"

Laughing, Jenna hugged him back. "The second I know —promise."

The conversation had just started up again when the sound of a chopper hovered over the house and then got louder. "Someone is landing in the front yard." Jenna sprang to her feet and ran through the house to look out of the front door. "It's Carter."

"I can't wait to find out where he's been hiding." Kane walked up behind her and slid a hand around her waist. "It's just as well I made a ton of fried chicken tonight. He'll be starving."

"I figured y'all would be here." Carter waved his Doberman, Zorro, into the house. "Playtime, go see Duke." He removed his Stetson and dropped it onto a peg in the mudroom before removing his jacket. "I made it here in time for Halloween." He grinned and pointed to his bag. "I've brought a costume for the ball. We're going, right?"

Jenna grinned. "Wouldn't miss it."

"You missed a case." Jo folded her arms across her chest. "I've been leaving messages all over for days."

"Yeah, I found them before." Carter shrugged. "I needed some downtime and left my phone in the chopper. I figured you could manage without me for a time."

"I thought Jenna had killed you." Jo shook her head. "It's been a crazy few days."

"Killed me?" Carter stared at Jenna. "How?"

"That's a long story. I'll tell you later." Kane waved him to the kitchen. "We're still eating dinner. Hungry?"

"I sure am." Carter sniffed. "Do I smell fried chicken?"

Jenna laughed. "Sit down and tell us where you've been hiding."

"I was fishing and then Blackhawk came by, leading horses. I told him I needed some downtime and I was feeling kinda restless. He asked me if I wanted to spend some time on the res. You know, to chill out with the guys and forget about work for a time." Carter smiled. "I feel good now and I've made a ton of friends." He looked at Kane. "I'm going to the ball as Billy the Kid. You?"

"I have a few options but I'm thinking werewolf." Kane grinned and slid a plate of fried chicken toward him. "I like to howl at the moon with Duke."

"Good choice." Carter dug into his meal. "I sure hope we're going trick-or-treating with the kids first. That's the part of Halloween I like best."

Jenna stood and collected plates. "We're meeting Wolfe in town with his family at seven at the town hall." She looked at Jo. "We'd better start getting ready."

EPILOGUE

With the kids' buckets filled with candy, Jenna waited with Kane and Carter in the Beast for Jo to settle Jaime at Wolfe's house. The little girl wanted to stay with Anna for a sleepover and it had meant Clara, Jaime's nanny, had decided to remain in Snakeskin Gully. Jenna smiled at Kane and reached for his hand. "That was so much fun. The townsfolk went all out with the displays this year. That corpse outside Aunt Betty's Café was gruesome and the mist we all hate so much really added to the creepy atmosphere." She peered out of the window. "Oh, good, there's Jo. It's cold in here even with the heater on high. I hope the hall is well heated."

"Most times it's too hot." Kane smiled at her showing long fangs. "You'll be fine. I'll keep you warm."

It was a short drive into town and they had the benefit of a reserved parking space right outside. The all hurried inside the hall, decorated with ghosts and pumpkin lanterns with bright red eyes. After stopping to speak to the townsfolks, they found their table. The event was well under way and Kane took Jenna's hand and led her into the mass of swirling bodies. The live band was so loud it bounced the floorboards under their feet. She looked up at Kane and laughed at his pointed ears and wild hair. "I wonder what would happen if a werewolf bit a witch?"

"I'd say they'd make something magical together." Kane grinned, displaying fangs. "Wanna try?"

Jenna laughed. "It's a mighty tempting offer but not on the dancefloor."

As Kane swung her around, she noticed Jo, dressed as Annie Oakley, twirling by with Carter. "They make a nice couple."

"It will never happen." Kane indicated with his chin to Emily and Rio. "Now there's a match made in heaven, but I see another possibility just walking in. What a surprise."

Jenna went on her tiptoes to look at the door as Wolfe walked in with a very attractive woman on his arm. They'd both dressed as Vikings and looked incredible. "Is that the forensic anthropologist from Helena? Wow! She's beautiful."

"Yeah." Kane grinned. "She just joined Wolfe's team. That's Norrell Larson." He swung her into his arms as the band went into a slow tune and nuzzled her neck. "She is good looking but no one comes close to you."

Jenna grinned up at him. "Oh, I bet you say that to all the girls."

"Not a chance." Kane led her toward the door to the court-yard. He pulled her close. "Come outside with me. I feel like howling at the moon."

A LETTER FROM D.K. HOOD

Dear Reader,

Thank you so much for choosing my novel and coming with me on another of Kane and Alton's thrilling cases in *Chase Her Shadow*.

If you'd like to keep up to date with all my latest releases, just sign up at the website link below. You can unsubscribe at any time and your details will not be shared.

www.bookouture.com/dk-hood

I often sit for a time just staring into space as the stories filter into my head. I've heard this is called "the author's stare." It was nice to discover I wasn't the only person out there listening to my muse. I wish I could explain how the stories come into my head, but however they do, I'm eternally grateful to be able to share them with you.

If you enjoyed *Chase Her Shadow*, I would be very grateful if you could leave a review and recommend my book to your friends and family. I really enjoy hearing from readers, so feel free to ask me questions at any time. You can get in touch on my Facebook page, Twitter, or through my blog.

Thank you so much for your support.

D.K. Hood

KEEP IN TOUCH WITH D.K. HOOD

www.dkhood.com
dkhood-author.blogspot.com.au

 facebook.com/dkhoodauthor
twitter.com/DKHood_Author